Sarah Armstrong is an Associate Lecturer in Creative Writing with the Open University. Her stories have been published in magazines such as Mslexia and Litro and her poem, 'The Polesworth Pact', is part of the Polesworth Poets Trail. *The Insect Rosary* is her first novel and is inspired by seventeen years of summer holidays in Northern Ireland. She lives in Colchester with her husband and four children.

... the Open ... ... has ... ... been published ...
... ... and ... ...

The Insect Rosary

Sarah Armstrong

SANDSTONEPRESS
HIGHLAND | SCOTLAND

First published in Great Britain and the
United States of America 2015
Sandstone Press Ltd
Dochcarty Road
Dingwall
Ross-shire
IV15 9UG
Scotland.

www.sandstonepress.com

The publisher acknowledges subsidy from
Creative Scotlandtowards publication of this volume.

ISBN: 978-1-910124-32-1
ISBNe: 978-1-910124-33-8

Cover design by Antigone Konstantinidou, London
Typeset by Iolaire Typesetting, Newtonmore
Printed and bound by CPI Group (UK) Ltd, Croydon, CR0 4YY

Dedicated with love to Mark, Alfred, George, Henry and Mabel and with thanks to Mark Hardie and Lucy Yates

1

Then

I would have been asleep except for Nancy.

'Bern,' she whispered. 'Tell me.'

I said nothing. I was still cross that she wouldn't say sorry for getting me into trouble. Usually she would say something. Not sorry, but something that made me feel better. This time she just wanted to know what he'd said and I was not going to tell her. Not yet. I could still feel my fingers round the door handle to Cassie's room and Tommy's hand around my neck.

'Just what do you think you're doing?' he had said.

I turned. I couldn't see Nancy anywhere. He shifted his hand to the front of my neck. His eyes were narrowed and he smelled of apples.

'Do you not know what curiosity did to the cat, Bernadette?'

I nodded.

'Say nothing or I'll split your tongue. I know what you're up to all the time, and next time your hand is on this handle,' he bent down, his mouth against my ear, 'you'll find yourself on Skull Lane.' His hand released me and I ran.

Now it was really late, and still Nancy kept trying to make friends until we saw the car lights curve across and over the ceiling.

I could hear the door slam on his car and the crunch of his boots. It stopped. That meant he was on the doorstep and now Nancy was quiet too. Florence turned in her single bed by the window. She could ignore it. She didn't know what he would do.

'Bern,' Nancy whispered again.

This time I turned to her, my lips pressed together. I tried, but I could never say no to Nancy for long.

The front door closed, then the inner porch door and then the parlour door. I could hear Nancy breathing, or was it me, and my heart banging against my ribs and the way my breath whistled through my nose because I would not open my mouth, not with him in the house, because I knew what happened to tell-tale-tits. And so did Nancy. So what did she want me to say? Right now I hated her more than him. He was trouble but she could get me into trouble. She persuaded me to do all sorts just with a little look or a blink. The killer was, 'If you do this, Bern, I will never call you Bernadette again, cross my heart, hope to die.' She never kept her promises but I thought that one day she might really mean it, so if I didn't do it then, that very special one time, I'd miss the chance forever. Yes, my mum and dad would still beat out 'Bern-a-dette' but my big sister, the one whose voice I believed in, was the one who counted.

She raised herself up on one elbow and bent towards me. I shook my head, knowing the words without hearing them, closed my eyes and tried to see sheep, like the ones outside only smiling and clean and, most importantly, jumping one after the other over a freshly painted fence. If I could just go to sleep she couldn't make me. My eyes hurt from being squeezed so tight, my legs straight and stiff as a dead man. Still she whispered.

'If you don't come with me I'm going on my own.'

I couldn't keep my eyes closed. 'No, don't go.'

'I am.'

I couldn't let her get caught alone. Even Sister Agatha told us to stay away from him and she never said bad things about

2

people, she told us. She wasn't allowed or she'd be thrown out of the convent before she got in. So it must be true, or God would have struck her down, like she was always inviting him to.

Nothing was going to stop Nancy though, not God or Sister Agatha, or me. She was already out of bed and shrugging her dressing gown on. She wasn't looking at me or saying anything else, but she was doing it all very slowly, very carefully. She was giving me time to catch her up. I knew she didn't want to go on her own. And she knew that I wanted to be part of it, to listen and know and if she went on her own she would never tell me what happened and always, always call me Bernadette. She would let me explode with curiosity before she breathed a word. She knew how to be quiet, more than anyone.

I sat up and the bed springs twanged underneath me. I held my hands to my mouth, as if the noise had come from there, and listened for a step on the stairs. Nancy rolled her eyes, I expect. It was too dark for me to see her expression, now she was nearly at the door. I inched my lower legs off the bed until my feet settled on the floor and pushed myself upwards. About ten bed springs went at once.

'For God's sake, Bernadette!' she hissed.

I scowled at her, although I was facing the chimney breast, and then pulled my dressing gown on.

'Are you putting your slippers on?' I whispered.

She tutted at me, like Mum does. I looked at Florence asleep in her bed. Maybe I could poke her. She'd cry, someone would come and I could be back under the covers. Even Nancy wouldn't dare twice in one night.

Nancy caught my arm with one hand and gently turned the squeaking door handle with the other. The light from the landing seeped and then poured into the bedroom. I squinted against it, painful like a torch shone right in my eyes, and then we were out of the room and creeping along the carpet

3

to the top of the stairs. Her long blonde hair was matted at the back. I tried to keep my hair in a plait, hoping for curly hair like hers instead of wavy, but it had always fallen out by morning.

I could hear a blur of loud voices as I held onto the dark wood of the stair spindles. I couldn't get both hands to meet around the fattest part, but one hand could span the thinnest. Nancy had made it down to the lower landing, outside the bathroom. She hadn't made a single sound on the three steps down to it, but I didn't trust myself to copy this feat. I sat on the top of those steps and listened.

Someone was angry, but it wasn't Tommy. It was a woman shouting but one man, no two men, were laughing.

'What's she saying?' I whispered.

Nancy hissed, 'Shhh.'

I leaned my head against the banister and yawned. Crying always made me tired. The shouting turned to a short scream and the kitchen door opened and banged against the wall.

'Dirty traitor!' Tommy shouted. 'You're just a slut, Eithne!' The door slammed.

We scrambled for our bedroom, not caring about the noise for fear of being caught. I got to the door last, even though I'd been in front. Mum saw me, but was crying so hard she didn't even say anything. I wished she had.

We were back under the blankets before we said anything else. I didn't want to talk, I wanted to listen out for his footsteps, but I had to.

'Why did he call Mum a traitor?'

'I don't know.' I could hear a shake in Nancy's voice.

'Why does he come here? I hate him. I don't know why Donn invites him. He must do. He just walks in whenever he likes.'

Nancy said nothing but her breathing sounded weird. For days we wouldn't see him, nearly forgot about him, and then he'd be back. But never when Dad was here.

I said, 'I wish Dad would come.'

'Oh, shut up, Bernadette,' she whispered, but I could hear that she'd started crying and I didn't say anything back.

If he made Mum cry that meant she must be scared of him too. I turned my back on Nancy and, to stop myself imagining Tommy coming up the stairs instead of Mum, I picked out the shape of my little pot on the mantelpiece, full of special shells.

2

Now

Her uncle pulled up in the back yard and let himself in by the back door. Elian had been trying to catch her eye the whole journey, but now he looked back from the front seat with mock surprise.

'He does talk, right?' he said. 'He didn't say a word!'

Nancy snapped, 'Not everyone has to fill every second with words. Everything you were asking was a yes or no question anyway.'

'I thought it seemed safer.' Elian opened the door and stretched his arms above his head. He looked around. 'So, we're here.'

Nancy groaned. 'Really?'

She opened her door and looked around the yard. She couldn't spot anything different at all, but then she hadn't expected the concrete to be painted with anything but mud, or the ravaged garage doors to be anything but stuck open, not quite flush to the wall, forever. The well was still locked with a padlock that also served as a major tripping hazard, right at the bottom of the wooden steps to one of the many high barns that no-one risked entering even when she was a child. She couldn't believe that they still looked like steps, that they hadn't crumbled through lack of use into kindling. And under the steps, where there are used to be one sheepdog, was another. Another black and white border collie. She wished Donn was there to tell her

6

its name. It lifted its head, yawned and stood up, shaking out his fur.

'Come here, boy,' she said, stretching her hand out. Dogs were always boys, even when they turned out to be girls. The dog didn't move.

Elian opened Hurley's door for him and walked around to the rear of the car.

'Dog, eh?' he said. 'That's great, isn't it Hurley?'

Hurley was still in the car.

Elian struggled to work the lock and Nancy opened the boot for him. He stood with a case in his hand, uncertain where to place it. He decided against putting it down anywhere and carried it to the back door where he left it on the step. He came back for the other case and Hurley's backpack and banged the boot back down. It sprang up again, and again, until it caught the third time.

'Goddamn it! What is wrong with this trunk?'

Nancy winced and hoped Agatha hadn't heard.

'Could take your damn head off. Remind me again why we didn't hire a car,' he said. 'A shiny, clean one.'

Nancy didn't remind him of the reasons she'd given him, sensible ones about being unused to driving on the left and insurance. She hadn't wanted a car because she didn't want this to turn into a touring holiday, a jumping off point for more interesting places. She wanted Hurley to have a holiday like she'd had, of boredom leading to investigation, of imagination.

Elian deposited the second case next to the first, both newly acquired for the biggest journey of his life. It had taken months to persuade him and she could feel the last of his enthusiasm shrivel up. But they were there now. What could he do?

She smiled and walked towards the dog. 'Come on boy.'

The sheepdog didn't look upwards for affirmation, like Bruce used to. It stared straight at them in turn before fixing on Hurley who hadn't moved from the side of the car.

'Ah, it's smiling at you,' said Elian.

'No, it isn't,' said Nancy, putting a protective arm around Hurley. 'Sit!'

The dog turned its attention to her. The slender muzzle grew large with teeth and it barked before resuming that smile of domination.

'Let's get inside,' said Nancy, the tremor in her voice causing Hurley and Elian to scramble for the door. She didn't turn her back on it, but edged away, avoiding eye contact. Hurley hadn't encountered more than two dogs in his life, but she was surprised at Elian running like that. She picked up the cases and backpack and took them into the lobby.

'Don't put them down in here,' said Elian, 'it's even muddier than outside.'

'Don't worry about me.' She put the cases down hard and handed the bag to Hurley. 'Don't you know you shouldn't show a dog that you're scared?'

Elian picked the cases up as she closed the back door. The round handle needed to be turned both ways until it hitched closed. The lobby. She couldn't remember whether that was what they'd called it or what her mother had called it. The black and white tiles were uniformly grey, the deep sink chipped and the taps rusted red around the base. There was a selection of rainproof jackets and stinking hats hanging from hooks on the wall, steel capped boots and wellingtons on the floor. She sighed. Why hadn't Donn allowed them to come in the front? That would have impressed Elian, the double frontage and front door so big it was two doors. The hallway, the wide staircase, that would have made him feel that he was having a historical experience rather than a grimly farming one.

'Okay,' Nancy lightened her voice, pointed to the right and smiled for Hurley, 'that is the downstairs toilet, and this is the parlour. Like a big kitchen, but not a kitchen. Well it used to be. Anyway.' She opened the door on the left, waited for them to enter and closed the door behind them. 'You need to remember to keep all the doors closed to keep the heat in and the animals out, OK?'

They turned to the fireplace.

'And this is my aunt, Agatha.'

Agatha put her tea cup on the side table and stood. Elian walked over and shook her hand.

'It's so good to meet you. How are you? I'm Elian, this is Hurley.'

'Hello.' She sat back down again. 'He's tall for ten.'

Elian said, 'He's fourteen. Might explain it.' He smiled.

'Small for fourteen,' said Agatha.

Elian opened his mouth, closed it and turned breezily around. 'Wow, what a room. High ceilings.'

Agatha picked up her tea cup again. Donn came into the parlour with a single cup and poured himself tea from the pot on the table by the window.

'Help yourself,' he said to Nancy.

'Thanks. A cup of tea would be lovely.'

Donn sat in the matching armchair to Agatha's in front of the fireplace and Nancy took three cups from the cupboard in the small kitchen and used the strainer while pouring from the pot.

'It's been a long trip.' Elian was still addressing Agatha. 'But it's super to be here. It's so green. It's just so . . . green.'

She nodded.

'And after all the troubles, it's great to be here. I've read up on it all.'

Nancy looked away. 'Elian.'

'All that bombing and everything, I wasn't sure if there'd be anything left.'

'Elian.'

'But you always had our support in the US. Any oppressed people get our support. And there have always been great

9

ties between the US and Ireland, all the presidents and stuff. Kennedy is a good Irish name, isn't it?'

Nancy shouted, 'Elian, come and get your cup!' He came to the table and Nancy hissed, 'Stop talking. Please. Don't say anything until you're asked. And then just one word will do.'

He frowned and whispered, 'They're so quiet it's making me anxious.' He took the tea and raised his voice again. 'You're not going to give Hurley tea are you? I don't think caffeine will do him any good.'

'I'll ask him.' She turned to him, 'Hurley?' He edged away from the door towards the table, 'Would you like to try some tea, or would you prefer water?'

He shrugged, dragged a chair from beneath the table and slumped so he could look out of the window. His bag was on his lap. Nancy poured him a cup with lots of milk and placed it on a saucer in front of him.

She bent down to whisper, 'Don't drink it right to the bottom. It has leaves.'

'So, it's been a long trip,' Donn said.

'Oh yes,' said Elian. 'We left Detroit yesterday. Was it yesterday? Tuesday, whenever that was. Then we changed in London, which was great, really great. Nice airport.'

'Did you call on Nancy's family?' asked Agatha.

Elian, delighted to be having a conversation at last, set his cup down and pulled a chair up in between Agatha and Donn.

'No, no time for a stopover. We were just so eager to get here after all that getting ready, sorting out the packing and stuff. It took us about a month, getting the house sitter organised and, wow, just choosing what to bring. We're here a while, I know, but it's always an upheaval. Holidays, why do we do it to ourselves?' He laughed his tight, nervous laugh. 'But it's going to be great, seriously. It's going to be great.'

Donn held his cup out for a refill. 'It will be busy when Bernadette gets here.'

Agatha snorted.

'What?' said Nancy. 'What do you mean, she's coming? After us?'

Donn shrugged and held his cup out. Nancy took the teapot over, filled his cup and returned with the milk. She sat down heavily at the table and held her hands together. Elian started coughing and spitting tea back into his cup.

'God, sorry. There's something in the bottom of this cup. What the hell is it?' He spat again.

Agatha crossed herself and looked up to the ceiling.

'It's tea leaves, Elian,' said Nancy, quietly.

'Oh.' He flushed.

'Does your boy not talk?' asked Donn.

Hurley kept his face turned to the window.

'Not much,' said Nancy.

'Doesn't take after his da then.'

Elian tried to laugh but it turned into a nervous cough. Nancy wanted to hide somewhere and cry all the tiredness and disappointment away.

'I think we might have a lie down before dinner,' she said. 'Where are we sleeping?'

'In the best bedroom. Bernadette's family can have the girls' bedroom.'

'All of us in one room?' asked Elian.

Agatha nodded, 'All of you in one room. The house hasn't got any bigger.'

'But Bernadette isn't going to be here at the same time, is she?' asked Nancy.

'How would we know?' said Agatha.

'Let's get the bags upstairs,' said Nancy. They must have got it wrong. They were confused. Bernadette couldn't be coming at the same time. Someone would have said something.

11

Elian held the bags and gestured with his head for Nancy to open the door. Hurley followed them out of the room and up the stairs.

'Hurley, go back and close the parlour door, please.'

He frowned, but he did it. The hallway that Nancy had thought would impress Elian wasn't commented on. She'd forgotten how dark it was when the outer door was closed. The large, peaked glass panel in the ceiling above the stairs was covered in leaves and moss, giving a green undersea tinge to the stairs. The stair carpets were worn to creamy threads in the middle, still brown and red at the edges. Nancy led them in silence to the best bedroom, and hesitated before she opened the door. It wouldn't strike them as the best bedroom.

She pointed back down to the first, smaller landing. 'The bathroom is there, if you want it.'

Elian and Hurley looked blankly back at her. She opened the door.

The room had two windows, one facing the front drive and the other facing a field on the left of the house. Or the right as you approached it. She wondered how she had described this room, if she had at all. Her parents had slept in this room and she didn't really come in here much. The one thing she remembered was a commode hidden inside a normal looking chair.

'Wow, what an old chair,' said Elian, with no enthusiasm at all.

She decided not to tell him. The bed had fresh bedding on, at least. She didn't remember the last time she'd slept in a bed with sheets and scratchy woollen blankets. If Elian called it quaint she might thump him, but looking at him he didn't look like he was going to say anything else for quite some time.

'Where am I sleeping?' asked Hurley.

'They didn't mean we should sleep in the same bed, did they?' asked Elian.

12

'No,' said Nancy, unsurely. She noticed a fold down bed next to the wardrobe. 'There's a z-bed. But I think you could stay in the girls' bedroom.'

'You want me to sleep in a girl room?' said Hurley.

'I mean the kids' room. It used to have the girls because there were more of them. The boys were in one room, but Donn sleeps in there now. There were four boys in one bed, so you could always share with him if you're going to be picky.'

'No, thanks.'

'I'll show you the room,' said Nancy, picking up his backpack.

He took it and slouched behind her. She opened the door to the much larger room, one double bed facing the large bay window also overlooking the drive like her room, and the other single bed against the left hand wall. Another window faced the paddock at the side of the house.

'Pick a bed, any bed,' said Nancy, wondering why she was talking like that. Tired, probably. She needed a sleep, but had to face Elian on his own first.

Hurley put his backpack down and jumped onto the bed by the window. She thought of telling him it was wrong, that wasn't the bed she'd slept in, but decided to say nothing.

When she got back to the best bedroom she was relieved to see that Elian was asleep. She didn't want to talk about Bernadette again. Not yet.

3

Then

They looked like two cupboard doors either side of the fireplace. The one on the left was forbidden. The one on the right was a larder built into the alcove. This was where we got the glacé cherries from. Sometimes Sister Agatha gave them to us when we'd behaved ourselves and let us pick one out, stickily pulling it from our fingers before chewing it quickly and hoping for another. More often we dared each other to climb on the armchair and fetch them down two at a time. That was mostly me, even though Nancy complained that I'd had my fingers on them. How she expected me to balance on the arm, open the door and hand her the clear, plastic pot to choose her own, I'm not sure. That was only giving me more of a chance to get caught.

This time I did get caught. The sound of the door opening and Nancy's gasp made me twist and I fell from the arm of the chair onto the cracked, brown tiles of the hearth. My arm hurt like Nancy had kicked it with both feet at once and I cradled it like a baby until Mum came to see why Sister Agatha was shouting. I could hear Florence crying in the distance so knew she was already in a bad mood.

'She's a thief,' said Sister Agatha, shaking her head. 'Stealing from her own family. I don't know what you've been teaching that child. I knew someone was, but I'm not one to point the finger. And,' she pointed at Nancy, 'that one's no better. She knew exactly what was going on.'

I thought later, after I'd stopped crying, that they played with blame like me and Nancy. That when me and Nancy were old and grumpy, we'd still be the same and try to wriggle out of getting told off. Adults got told off a lot in this house. Every time Mum was angry she called her Sister Agatha, and she did now.

'Oh, you're so much better than the rest of us. If only you'd had children you could have shown us all how it was done. What a shame you married Jesus instead, Sister Agatha.'

Sister Agatha drew her black cardigan around herself and stood, arms crossed. 'Agatha. And I know your children call me Sister Agatha too, just to be offensive.'

'Look at you, all in black, just like a pretend nun. It's no wonder, is it? Except they chucked you out.'

'I left, and you know full well why, Eithne.'

I had quietened now and watched with amazement as they argued above my head. They'd forgotten I was there, sitting in the white ash that surrounded the fireplace. Nancy was long gone.

'I know it was nothing to do with me. I don't know why you're so touchy about it, it was your decision.'

'When your ma asks you something on her deathbed you don't have any choice.'

'It's not my fault you had nothing better to do than move back in here. I had a family of my own. I had a life.'

'You –' Sister Agatha looked down at me. 'Get out of the fireplace so I can clean this mess up.'

I tried to get up without using my hands, but the brush was underneath me, my legs arched over the fire surround.

'I can't get up.'

Mum came over to me and pulled me up by putting her hands under my armpits. I cried out.

'Where does it hurt? Can you move your fingers?'

After a physical check she took a tea towel from the kitchen, tied it around my neck and helped me place my arm inside it.

'We'll talk about this later,' she said, and sent me from the room.

I looked at my sling proudly. This would impress Nancy. I was officially injured and must look sad and remember not to use my arm until at least the next day.

By lunchtime I'd forgotten and picked up my fork in my hand.

'If you can do that, you don't need a sling,' said Mum.

Reluctantly I slid it over my head but was pleased to see a large blue bruise marking my fall.

'You were very lucky,' said Mum. 'The fire could have been lit, you could have bashed your head open, all sorts of things. You must never do that again.'

I felt like telling her how many times I had done it without anyone knowing at all, but decided against this. I nodded and Mum's eyes fluttered.

'I know a very silly girl who stood on the side of the chair and fell into the fireplace and had to stay in hospital for three days because her brain had been squashed. You wouldn't like that, would you?' She seemed very cheerful about telling this gruesome story, her face tight with the effort not to smile.

'Was it Nancy?' I said, breathlessly.

'No. I can't tell you who it was as you would only think badly of them. You might even think that they had forgotten what it was like to be young and excitable.'

I scanned the faces at the table, all blankly looking at Mum apart from Sister Agatha who was biting her lip, her face flushed.

'I'm not sure concussion is a laughing matter, Eithne. No wonder your children are so badly behaved if that's the kind of thing you think is funny.'

Mum spluttered into her tea and took a few minutes to compose herself before she could finish her dinner.

'As a punishment, Bernadette can help me prepare the dinner,' said Sister Agatha.

16

I looked pleadingly at Mum, but she shrugged and the subject passed for everyone but me. A whole afternoon spoiled by having to stay in the kitchen with long, black Sister Agatha instead of racing Nancy down the driveway to see who was quicker, or seeing who could cross the cattle grid quicker without letting their feet slip between the bars. I was getting good at that, although I had twisted my ankle twice getting good.

'Can Nancy help too?' I said, not looking at Nancy.

'No,' said Sister Agatha, 'I have to keep my eye on you.'

I didn't have to look at Nancy to know I would pay for that, but it would have been worth it to have her there.

When Sister Agatha took the plates into the kitchen Nancy leaned over to me.

'Bern, I dare you,' she said, 'to call her name three times without stopping.'

My eyes widened and I shook my head. Sister Agatha came back in with afters and I couldn't look at her because I was thinking about it. Nancy knew I was too and was giggling too much to say thank you for her slice of cake.

'Nancy,' said Mum, 'what do you say?'

Nancy opened her mouth and laughed long and hard. When she got her breath back she managed to whisper, 'Thank you,' but by then I'd started laughing. I always took much longer to stop. That meant I usually got the blame. Every time I felt nearly in control I caught Mum or Sister Agatha's disapproving stare and that was it for another few minutes.

'Eithne, I don't believe either of those girls deserves cake.' Sister Agatha was poised to snatch them back. '"Set a guard, O Lord, over my mouth; keep watch over the door of my lips."'

'They can just sit there until they say thank you properly,' said Mum.

Sister Agatha sat down, cringing at each new burst of

laughter. Florence looked from one face to another as she ate half her cake and sprinkled the other half in crumbs around her.

I tried to stop. Sister Agatha had caught us and specifically banned us last week from saying someone's name three times even though we explained that Nancy had jinxed me for saying something at the same time as her, and you can't break a jinx without saying a name three times. And if you couldn't break a jinx you couldn't ever speak again.

'What a blessing that would be,' she had said. 'I can't believe your ma encourages all this devilish talk of jinxes.'

'She doesn't mind,' swaggered Nancy.

'But, as she well knows, calling someone's name three times can be fatal. Why would you want to draw Satan to you, that's what I don't understand.' She shook her head, 'And when your mammy recites the rosary with you, do you thank God for the time she gives to you?'

I knew that was a trick question, but Nancy went, 'Oh, we ever don't do that.' That had been the end of that afternoon. Learning the rosary gave me very sore knees, and I didn't want to spend another afternoon in penance, especially when I had to do the dinner anyway. But Nancy asked me to and I liked to make her laugh, especially about Sister Agatha.

Now she scowled at Nancy instead of me, for a change.

'Nancy, you'll be washing up,' said Sister Agatha, 'after both meals today.'

Nancy looked at her and appealed to Mum.

Mum shrugged. 'If you find everything funny you have to realise it irritates people.'

'But it isn't fair!'

'It stopped you laughing.'

Nancy scowled at me and picked up her cake.

'What do you say, Nancy?' said Sister Agatha.

'Thank you.' Nancy scowled at me again. It had definitely become become my fault. Everyone was waiting for me to beg for my cake too, but I couldn't. I would laugh again, spit crumbs everywhere probably, so I sat and watched them eat and kept my fingernails deep in my palm.

'Just say sorry, Bernadette,' said Mum.

Sister Agatha shook her head, 'Never has the phrase blue-eyed girl been less fitting, Eithne, than with that one there.'

I hung my head. I hated being the only one with blue eyes, the only one with dark brown hair. I told friends at school that my dad had blue eyes but it wasn't true. It was just me. And Uncle Ryan, but we never saw him now.

4

Now

Elian looked so disappointed that Nancy became quite enraged with him.

'No, it's not quite the European experience you had in mind, but it's important to me. It will be sold, sooner or later, and I might never be able to come back.'

They were having a hissed argument across the emptying suitcase, even though Elian was clearly trying not to.

He spread his hands. 'It's fine. I'm just tired, and it isn't quite what I was expecting.' He hesitated. 'Is it what you were expecting?'

'Kind of,' Nancy hedged. 'I thought they'd be more pleased to see us, I suppose.'

'That's all I meant.'

Elian crossed to her side of the bed and put his arm around one shoulder. Nancy shrugged it off.

'It wasn't quite what you said.'

'We've got a month and we can stay a month. I was just saying, I've never been to Europe and Italy doesn't feel so far away now we're here. It was a suggestion, nothing more.'

'Well, it wasn't what we agreed and I'd rather you didn't just say it again.'

'Fine,' Elian backed away with his hands raised. 'No problem. Just saying. It might get a bit cramped when your sister gets here with everyone. Is it the family? Or just her?'

'I have no idea. I think they're just confused.'

The sun was filtering through the thick tree canopy. It was the only sun they'd seen all day. When they flew in the cloud was thick and low. When they waited for Donn to pick them up outside the airport it had started to drizzle, and their drive to the farm was in full downpour most of the way.

Hurley walked in.

'Why didn't you knock?' snapped Nancy.

'They said to get you right away for dinner.'

'We're coming,' said Elian. 'Have you been having a nice talk downstairs?'

Hurley looked at him and then left.

Nancy said, 'Can you just not talk at dinner?'

'You can't mean not talk at all.'

'I do. Just slow down and speak when spoken to. You're very overbearing at times.'

'Would you like to pick any more holes in my personality?'

'I may do later. And for God's sake, nothing on the oppression of the Irish people.'

Nancy left the room to go downstairs and realised that Hurley had been standing just outside the bedroom door.

'I thought you'd gone down.'

'I was waiting for you. I don't understand them.'

'You understood that they wanted you to come and get us.'

'They did this.' Hurley mimed eating, walking upstairs, the number three and walking downstairs.

'Wow. Complicated.'

They waited for Elian and went downstairs, Nancy noting all the familiar creaks. They let her go into the parlour first and sat around her at the table. Agatha and Donn had started to eat so they helped themselves to the soft potatoes and slices of chicken. The light had faded from this side of the house, not even hitting the high roofs of the garage and barns opposite. They had managed to sleep through most of the day's sunlight. There was tea on the table and Nancy poured for them.

'Tea leaves,' she said, as she handed one to Elian. He nodded and mimed zipping his lips.

'When are you going to the retreat?' she asked Agatha.

'Agatha isn't sure she wants to go anymore,' said Donn.

Nancy choked on her chicken and made an effort to swallow it down.

'Why's that?'

'I am sure,' said Agatha. 'I am going.'

'You said that with a houseful –'

'Never mind what I said in private to you,' she interrupted Donn. 'I'll be off in a couple of days, I expect.'

'What time?'

Agatha snapped her head up. 'You're in a rush to see the back of me, Nancy.'

'It's only I was going to ask to borrow the car so we can get some juice and things that . . . things like that.'

'We always used to walk,' said Agatha, 'didn't we Donn? Five miles to school and back. No-one thought twice about it.'

Nancy looked at her and thought about asking when she'd last walked to the shops and back, but changed her mind.

'Maybe there's a bus we could catch,' said Elian.

Agatha shook her head, 'By the time you get to a bus stop you're in the village.'

'Can we hire some bicycles, maybe?'

Nancy, Agatha and Donn all stared at him. He seemed to remember that Americans shouldn't talk and put his head down. He ate studiously for a while but no one else spoke.

'How far is it?' he asked.

'Two and half miles,' said Donn.

'That's why I said it was five miles there and back,' said Agatha, slowly.

'Sure, thanks.'

Nancy looked at the clock. It was nearly seven and she wondered how early they could all go to bed and start again tomorrow. Or maybe they should take a walk after dinner. It was the countryside that people came for, after all. And it wasn't raining for once. Elian could use his smartphone to navigate a route somewhere and then he could feel a little bit in charge of events. That would make him happier. She would feel happier when Agatha was off being holy and Donn might be a bit more talkative.

Nancy kept her voice light. 'Has anyone heard any more about when Bernadette is coming?'

'I thought you'd all worked this out months in advance,' said Elian. 'Didn't you speak to your mother about it?'

'I did. I thought it was all arranged.'

'No one arranged it with us. We weren't told,' said Agatha. 'Your ma just said that you were all coming over to say goodbye to the farm, for some reason, and could we air the rooms. We weren't so much as asked, were we, Donn?'

Elian and Nancy looked at each other.

'We could stay somewhere else,' Elian said quickly. 'We don't want to intrude.'

Nancy clenched her hands around the cutlery.

Donn said, 'It's all arranged now and Bernadette is coming.'

Nancy said, 'But you really don't know when?'

'We didn't know when you were coming until this morning and we get our orders to collect you.' Agatha cut her chicken but didn't seem to be eating much. 'Your ma would know when. Haven't you spoken to Bernadette herself?'

Nancy shook her head. 'Not for a while. It's expensive.'

It had quickly become a Christmas and birthday card relationship, friends on Facebook to catch up with the basics and little other contact. Her mother still used the phone, and even sent letters with funny little stamped heads.

'You should phone her,' said Elian. 'Then at least we'll know what's what.'

'I will,' said Nancy. She didn't want to and wondered how

23

she could persuade someone else to do it for her. 'I might phone Mum tonight, just to let her know we're here safely.'

The rest of the meal took place in silence and Nancy relaxed. She looked around, spotting the familiar corners, and noticed how the door to Cassie's room framed Agatha at her end of the table.

Walking down the driveway, Nancy didn't know which way to take them. She knew which of the nearest fields belonged to the farm, but she somehow thought Donn rented most of them out now.

'Let's walk along the road,' she said.

'There's no sidewalk,' said Elian.

'If a car comes, just get on the grass.'

Hurley stumbled on the cattle grid and Elian picked his way across before losing a toe between the bars.

'What the hell is this, a man trap?'

'It's to stop the animals coming this way.'

'Jesus, you could break your legs.'

She was hoping that when they came to the peat bog, part owned by the farm, she'd spot it and they could talk about bog men dragged from the depths, stained black by the peat and rigidly clinging on to their past and the way they died. More likely though, Elian would question whether it shouldn't just be left for future generations, rather than burned on the fire. She had liked digging the peat blocks and turning them to dry out quickly. It seemed a better use than crumbling it into pots of tomato plants, which always seemed to want more water than she could remember to give them. She had no green fingers, unlike her mother, or patience, but in that she and her mother were quite matched.

The sky was still a pale blue in the west. The rain from the day was scenting the earth and grass, so the smell seemed stronger than on the hottest days. When they came to an aluminium gate at the entrance to a field the trampled and darker mud pooled around the entrances. The sheep stayed well away from them, despite Hurley's insistence on climbing onto the lowest rung to dangle longer, juicier grass from the roadside. The sheep bleated a warning to each other and retreated well away from his hand.

'Donn might ask you to help him move the sheep to a different field,' she told him.

'Why?'

'For fresher grass. I'm just saying because he can get a bit cross if you run at them. If you fancied it you could, but I'm just warning you.'

'Doesn't his dog do it?'

'Yes. Most likely.'

That dog. She'd forgotten about it. Unlike Bruce it hadn't run around to walk out with them, but lay down as if determined to herd them back into the house at the first nod from Donn. It must be a good sheepdog, or Donn wouldn't bother to feed it. She'd seen him take the leftovers, the potatoes and chicken left uneaten at the table, and tip it into Bruce's steel dish under the staircase. It had waited until he was back inside before it started to eat. It was clearly an obedient dog, when it came to Donn.

She looked behind them, but the dog hadn't followed. The grass in the verges sparkled with single strands of gossamer, stretching across and up and over, but she couldn't see any webs. Hurley probably wasn't interested in spiders any more. Elian looked at the way the landscape curved into groups of trees and pointed out to Hurley distant farmhouses. He was from a town and lived in a town. He'd taken her on road trips out into Michigan but they hadn't really got out of the car anywhere where there weren't already other people. One time they'd driven past a field of buffalo and she'd made him park up on the roadside so she could stroke their noses and take in the wilderness in their fur. Their food had been poured over the gate for them, straight onto the ground, and she could see uneaten strawberries in the mix which struck her as odd. After driving on for half a mile they'd seen a diner promoting its buffalo steak and her stomach had clenched. She knew the link between animals and meat, she'd been on a farm every summer for twelve years, but she'd never got used to it.

'Shall we turn back?' said Elian.

The breeze had picked up and his fleece was zipped up to his chin, his shoulders hunched. She looked at Hurley, jacket flapping open and his hands in his pockets. They hadn't made it to the end of the road but she nodded. On the way back she tried to conjure up memories to stick to the places they passed.

'Down there was Mary's house, that's the sheep dip. The silo is over there.'

'What's a silo?' asked Hurley.

'I don't know, really. Sometimes there were cows in there. It was next to the hay barn. We can go back that way.'

They crossed the road and took the lane towards Mary's until they got to the silo. The large barn, as high as two storeys, had holes in the corrugated roof but the smell of cow pats was as strong as ever. Elian and Hurley covered their noses. Nancy pointed to the hay barn, only half as full of bales as she remembered it.

'Hurley, you musn't go in there, OK? It's full of rats and the bales can topple over and smother you.'

Hurley looked at her as if going in there had not crossed his mind. They went through the gate, past the row of stable buildings, some of which no longer had doors.

'It's really dangerous in these buildings, too. The roof could come down at any minute.'

If it was true more than thirty years ago it must be true now. She saw the stable with the door high up in the wall and walked up to the blue door. It took a few goes to pull the rotten door open enough to look inside. She took her mobile from her pocket and switched on the flashlight app. There were glimpses of stalls, of steps and of heaps of metal that glinted. She stepped back and realised that it was nearly dark outside. Elian was waving his phone around, above his head.

'I haven't had any reception since we got here. Have you?'

She checked. 'No.'

She led them back through the mud to the next gate at the yard and, too late, she remembered the dog. They watched him for a moment before deciding to use the front door. In the space between the outside and inside doors they took off their shoes and left them, lined up and stinking, before taking it in turns to wash the mix of mud and whatever else from their hands in the kitchen.

'Next time we'll wear wellies,' said Nancy. She hoped they would say something, something nice about the farm or the fields, or even the sunset, but they both slumped down at the table.

'The TV's on in the front room,' she said to Elian. 'Why don't you watch it for a while, while I phone my mum? Hurley, you can get ready for bed.'

They went to the hall.

'Are your relatives in there?' whispered Elian.

'The TV doesn't usually switch itself on.'

She watched him tentatively turn the door handle to the front room and edge his way in.

'Close the door,' she heard Donn say.

He closed the door.

'Can I have a shower?' asked Hurley.

'There isn't one. Just have a quick wash, I'll come up soon.'

Hurley lingered and then went upstairs.

Nancy picked up the receiver of the grey telephone, the same one as she remembered from before, she thought, and phoned her mother. It seemed to take so long using the rotating dial, but it finally began to ring. Her mother answered.

'What's going on, Mum?' said Nancy, and she felt the knot build in her throat again. 'What have you done?'

'I'm fine, Nancy, thanks for asking. So you arrived.'

'Mum, they say that Bernadette is coming.' Nancy waited. 'Is she?'

'Bernie will be there.'

Nancy closed her eyes. 'When? When we've gone, yeah?'

Her mother sighed. 'You're the two who should be close and aren't. All my brothers and sisters who emigrated and I never bothered to write to more than once a year, I can't tell you how much I regret that.' Her mother breathed in to force out a fake laugh, 'Think of all those fantastic holidays we could have had.'

'You arranged this so Bernie could have a cheap holiday to the States?'

'No. You know why. Just sort it out, love, for everyone. Time goes too quickly.'

She could hear her mother's voice breaking so made hers very light.

'Agatha's not pleased to have us here. It's difficult.'

'Don't worry about that. You know what she's like. She'll be off soon enough.'

Nancy blinked back the ache in her eyes. 'Elian hates it, Mum.'

'This isn't for Elian. It's for you and Bernadette. Family needs to be close enough to say things that need to be said.'

'Elian is my family.'

'Then he'll understand.'

'But you never –' Nancy bit her lip.

Her mum coughed and then her voice was clearer. 'Bernie is coming in two days. Just hold tight and rest up. See Agatha off and then put Hurley in her room. Don't ask her, just stick him in there.'

'But, what if . . .'

'Move anything breakable, obviously. It's going to be fine, and if it isn't fine, it'll be worth it in any case.'

Nancy finally let the tears fall. 'I wish we'd come to stay with you instead.'

'I'll be over in the autumn again. Just, please, Nancy, please make it up with Bernie.'

'I don't know if I can.'

'Try.'

'I will try.'

'And tell her we still love her and always will. She can call anytime. She knows that, but tell her anyway.'

'See you soon, Mum.'

'Tell her we miss her.'

The phone tinged as she replaced the receiver. She rubbed her face with her sleeves, took a deep breath and joined them all in the front room. Just the same. Brown flowers on the wall above the dado rail, the piano against one wall, dining table in the large bay window, the settee long ways across the middle of the room so you could walk right around it, and the lace antimacassars still in place on the headrests.

She'd clearly entered after one of Elian's anecdotes as he was saying, 'Ten thousand Elvis impersonators can't be wrong.' Neither Agatha nor Donn were looking at him.

The fire was burning peat bricks and Nancy sat on the rug in front of it, exactly where she used to sit with Bernie. Donn was in the armchair, Agatha and Elian sat at far ends of the settee. There were no curtains as there were no neighbours. She shivered.

'Sit here, Nance,' Elian said, patting the gap between him and Agatha.

She sat down between them and he took her hand in his.

'I forgot to check on Hurley,' she said.

'He'll be OK.' Elian's grip started to hurt.

5

Then

At home we never had potatoes like we did here. Mum always peeled them, huge flakes of red or brown skin sticking to the sink. Here they were boiled in their skins for hours, or at least until the insides were fluffy with air. You had to weigh them down with butter balls before they disintegrated in a small breeze. I had finished washing the potatoes, but not to Sister Agatha's satisfaction. I was glad to put off the butter balls, made by rolling a spoonful between large cross hatched wooden paddles to pattern them. I could remember eating a number of butter balls, one after the other, until I threw up.

'That'll teach you,' said Mum. And I never touched butter again. My potatoes were always in danger of floating away when a door was opened.

Sister Agatha inspected my work. 'I need eight apples for the pie.'

I froze. 'Where from?'

'Where do you think? Cassie's room.'

My hands clasped each other. 'I'm not allowed in there.'

'You are when you're sent there.'

I walked slowly into the parlour and looked at the door, the pair to the larder with the glacé cherries. I'd heard things behind this door. Maybe this was my real punishment. It was waiting for me behind this door. I rubbed my hands together.

'Hurry up!'

I wasn't going to get away with it by postponing it. I reached out for the handle.

'What's keeping you?'

I opened the door and breathed out. It was how it always looked when I was allowed in. There were boxes of apples piled up in a corner, a sack of potatoes and a box of crisps that had been bought for our stay, even though we weren't allowed more than one packet every two days. We'd never finish them in time.

I stepped forward into the room that was always the coldest in a very cold house. There was a tiny window, and it was right behind the kitchen fireplace, but it never got any warmer. I crooked my sore arm and laid the apples along it, apart from three which I carried in my other, upturned hand. I became aware of a smell and stood, trying to place it. The closest I could get was the smell of a handful of coppers when you've been holding them too long. But there was something else, which kept sliding away, something I should remember but couldn't.

I left the room and pushed the door closed behind me. I took Sister Agatha the apples and she sent me back to the sink to peel them. Why would you peel apples, but not potatoes? It was all upside down. I did what I was told, the smell still nagging at me to recognise it. Maybe I was just anxious because Tommy had been here last night. I usually wasn't allowed in there when he'd been in the house. I didn't want to know why that room was his room, was linked to him.

'So,' said Sister Agatha, 'you were one of the lucky ones in May. Tell me all about it.'

'About what?'

She turned, her hands covered in flour. 'About what! About seeing the Holy Father at Wembley Stadium, that's what.'

'Oh,' I said, 'it was good.'

'What was he like?'

31

'We were very far away from him, up the top really. I saw his little car.'

Sister Agatha shook her head. 'Do you know how many people would have given anything to be there that day? And that's all you can say.'

She twisted back to the pastry and took her frustration out on it, the flour dusting her black clothes. I could hear her muttering to herself. It could have been a prayer or a curse.

'Agatha, why didn't you become a nun?'

She cleared her throat, 'It turned out not to be my calling after all. Not at that time.' She thumped the pastry.

I'd watched The Sound of Music a little while ago and I knew that nearly nuns sometimes didn't become nuns, but that seemed to be because they were summoned away by smartly dressed men to look after their children.

'But why?'

'"Even a fool who keeps silent is considered wise; when he closes his lips, he is deemed intelligent."'

'What?'

'Sometimes it's nice to stay quiet, Bernadette. God loves silence.'

'But, did you –'

'I came home to look after Da. That's all there is to it. I was never a full nun and there is no mystery to it, whatever your mammy says.'

I looked away from her and out of the window. Nancy was in the yard with Bruce, throwing a stick for him to chase down the lane and return to her. There were three ways out of the yard. If you turned left you'd arrive at the front of the house through a gateway half as high as the house itself, which led you on to the driveway and out onto the road closer to the village. If you went straight on you'd arrive on the main road much quicker. If you turned right, through the gate which was shoulder height on me, you'd pass by all the stables and outhouses, right down to the silo. There you got onto a little road which you could take left, back on to the main road, or right which led to other farms. I chose to take this route in my head as I peeled the apples: past the hedges, across the bridge over the stream and running past Mary's house before her dogs smelled that I was there. I'd only been there with Donn and I wouldn't want to go without him.

I had forgotten about the dare, but now it came back to me. The best way would be to whisper her name twice and then say it louder, but that was a bit like cheating. I glanced at Sister Agatha. She always looked so cross. I wondered what it would take to make her laugh. I wondered if she'd ever laughed. Just about anything can set me off, even knowing that I really mustn't laugh can make me. School assemblies or churches are the worst, or in the middle of getting told off. And I always felt like I was getting told off by Sister Agatha even if she was just asking me if wanted a drink.

I needed to create an emergency, one where you call for help, but I'd had enough trouble today. I decided to just give it a go and then I could swear to Nancy that I tried.

'Agatha?'

She was looking out of the little kitchen to the parlour.

'Agatha?'

She still didn't move or answer me. I moved to the side to see what she was looking at. It was the door of Cassie's room. She hadn't heard me. I felt guilty for feeling triumphant that I could do it. It would mean something different to her, that I wanted to bring her death or the devil, but I just couldn't understand it. It was like her belief that you never turned around if you heard footsteps behind you because it might be a spirit and they can kill. To me I would just think it was a person and want to know who was going to jump out at me. And shouldn't spirits be in heaven or hell anyway?

I whispered, 'Agatha.'

She whipped round and made me jump.

'What?' Her eyes looked strange and she was blinking a lot.

'I think I'm finished.'

'Right. Off you go. Oh wait, I have a gift for you and Nancy.' She put her hand into her pocket and pulled out two little plastic bags. She handed them to me. There were two strings of rosary beads, black and shiny like a line of beetles.

'Thank you,' I said.

'They're to be used. They're not decorations.'

I nodded, stuffed them in my pocket and ran out to Nancy. Bruce had gone and she was sitting on the doorstep in the drizzle.

'Let's go to the hay loft,' she said.

She jumped on a bale and pretended she was on Top of the Pops, as usual. She kept saying that she'd get there one day. Sandra's sister, a couple of years older, had gone and was going to get her in. The first our parents would know about it was when they were stunned, like the rest of the country, by her superb style and co-ordination in front of Duran Duran.

'Not Bucks Fizz, though.' She had standards. Usually they were Sandra's standards first. They were changing all the time and Duran Duran probably wouldn't cut it by the time she got to Top of the Pops. Her latest album, taped from a turntable by placing her tape recorder in front of the speakers, was 'Scary Monsters (and Super Creeps)'. It wasn't that new, but Sandra's new boyfriend was mad on it. Her favourite song had a tape of its own so they could practise their routine. Every time the song ended she would move the needle back and tape it again, so it filled the whole thirty minutes of that side of the tape. She played it on her Omega pretend Walkman that she bought from the market, but she was saving up for a real Walkman.

I didn't think she got all the words right, but she swore she'd copied them into her notebook carefully.

'I think it's "sleeping in the streets",' I said.

'Well, it isn't. Sandra checked the lyrics and she knows. She gets Smash Hits every week. She doesn't have to guess.'

34

I left her to it and climbed up three bales, challenging myself to jump off. I couldn't quite do it, two was enough, but I sat up there and pretended I wasn't scared, just sitting. Nancy was trying to do a full body jump and turn whenever she sang "do", but wasn't quite pulling it off. David Bowie was rubbish to dance to, but Nancy said Adam Ant was silly, Madness was for babies and Captain Sensible was just awful, so I didn't say what I liked. She knew what was good because she was at Comprehensive now, and they knew all of that kind of thing. I had to pay attention, so I could tell everyone at my school what they should say. It changed all the time though and made my head hurt.

'Sandra says she's getting her hair permed in the summer and dyed blonde.'

'Sandra says only have sex standing up when you've got your period.'

'Sandra says that she's going to start smoking when she's fourteen so she doesn't get fat.'

'Sandra knows these exercises that make your boobs bigger.'

I lay back on the bale, so only my legs dangled off and listened for rustling. We weren't allowed in the hay loft really. Mum always said that it was full of rats, but if it was I would have seen them. She was probably exaggerating and it was only mice. Even Donn said the bales might fall on us and suffocate us but we were super careful and that would never happen.

Sometimes there were cows in the silo next door and we could spy on them from the bales. They didn't do much. Sometimes Bruce would sit by the gate and run up to anyone coming towards us which gave us a bit of time to pull the hay from each other's hair, but not today.

I looked at the corrugated roof and listened to Nancy. She was halfway through a fresh burst of the first chorus, out of tune because her headphones were in and so that didn't count. Then she stopped. I lifted myself onto one elbow, imagining her splayed on the ground. She was standing on the bale, though, pushing at the buttons on her stereo. Tommy was standing a couple of feet away, his arms folded.

'All right, Nance?'

She nodded and pulled the headphones off. I shrank back, even though my legs were totally obvious if he looked up.

'I hope you're not misbehaving.'

She shook her head.

'Good. I'll be back tonight, so we don't want anyone creeping around when they should be in bed. Do you understand me?'

She nodded.

'Grand,' he said. 'I'm glad you remember our chat. Because little girls who are too curious tend to get their tongues cut out. Ask no questions and tell no tales, and stay out of my fucking way.' He looked up at me, 'Right, Bernadette?'

I jumped and nodded a lot, so he could see me. I couldn't believe he'd used that word. Nancy had told me it was nearly the worst one ever.

'But you're all right, aren't you Nancy?'

She nodded.

'I like your dancing. Very sophisticated.'

Nancy blushed and looked away. He walked back to the lane and we heard his car fire up and drive away.

Nancy climbed up to sit next to me. Her cheeks were still flushed and she was blinking. She blushed a lot around him. He could be on TV, she said once. I said she fancied him and she nearly broke my arm, so I just thought it now.

'We should have checked for cars,' I said. 'I didn't see him come in the house.'

'He doesn't always come in,' said Nancy. 'He came out of one of the stables.'

'Which one?'

36

'Don't know. He wasn't on his own. There were three others with him before.'

'Was that one with shiny shoes there?'

Nancy nodded and looked away. No-one else ever wore shoes out here, let alone shiny ones. I looked towards the barns and smirked.

'He said you were sophisticated.'

'Shut up.'

She blushed a bit and picked at the bale. I hugged my legs.

'Why does he hate us?'

'We're English.'

'But we're Catholic too.'

'Too English to be proper Catholics, he says.' She straightened up and tossed her hair, 'But he said I was beautiful and if I wasn't English he'd be in love with me.'

'But you are.'

She looked at me and then looked away.

'Was he talking to you when I was inside?'

'Just for a minute.'

'He said a lot in a minute,' I said. 'He's nicer to you than he is to me. Maybe I look more English.'

I was starting to try to get my head round what all the signs and symbols meant. The red, white and blue kerbstones, the green, white and gold flags. It was complicated, more complicated than saying you didn't like songs that you did like. It was knowing what shops you could go in and which streets were safe and making sure you said Derry when it was spelled Londonderry.

'Everyone hates us,' I said.

Nancy shrugged and looked towards the gate. We sat quietly, listening. Tommy had left the barn but there might still be other men, even scarier men, in there now.

Nancy shivered. It was starting to rain.

'Shall we go in?' I asked.

She nodded. We climbed down from the bales and began

to pick the hay from each other, brushing it off our own clothes where we could see it. We went through the gate and walked slowly past an old tractor and the carts which weren't used any more. I started to imagine someone leaping from one of the barns and tried to run.

'You can't run in wellies!' shouted Nancy.

I could try. I stopped, went back to her and dug into my pocket.

'Sister Agatha gave me this for you.' I held out the beads.

'Wow.' Nancy pulled hers from the bag and dangled them from one finger. 'Thanks. Hide yours so she doesn't make us do any praying.'

6

Now

It was a much longer walk to the village than Nancy remembered. Even Elian, who often walked to work on a Friday instead of paying for the gym, was tired.

'Are you sure it's only two and a half miles?' he said, twice. He frequently took his phone from his pocket to check for reception, even though Nancy had told him it was unlikely. They kept to the wet grass of the roadside although there were few cars, as when they came there was little time to jump out of the way. Their shoes were still damp from the day before anyway. The roads curved around, almost back on themselves, and Hurley was the only one of them who seemed to accept it as a walk. Both Elian and Nancy wanted more from it, both scanning the landscape for interesting things to point out. They found little to say.

They crossed the river Bann over the narrow stone bridge and arrived in the village. Nancy headed for the nearest shop, a convenience store, she wanted to call it.

'Is this it?' asked Elian. 'Isn't this the outskirts?'

'This is it. Just don't chat to anyone about anything other than the weather.'

'I got it last night. No religion, no politics. Agatha brought up religion, not me.'

'She asked if you were planning on going to mass, not what you thought about the different denominations and their role in the world.'

39

Elian sighed and looked around. A couple of roads of black and grey buildings, the police station which still, even now, looked like a well-defended fort in which secret and terrible things happened – this was it.

'I'll just go for a wander,' said Elian.

Nancy felt like saying, don't bother. The word village isn't a promise that it will look like some pretty and abandoned town of yokels in Somerset, or poets in the Lake District. Sometimes a village is small because no-one else wants to move there.

She nodded and took Hurley inside. She remembered this shop being the most exciting place in the world. They would test run sweets and fizzy drinks in Northern Ireland before deciding to roll them out in England. She liked being part of this early wave of people who got to decide things. Now, at home, she got all of these American products before they were introduced here, but that wasn't really the same. She looked around, but she didn't really know now what sweets were new and what were already sold in every newsagent in the UK. There was little that Hurley recognised but she'd long told him that English chocolate was much better than American. Sweeter and paler and easier to eat more of in one go, but she didn't say the last bit.

'Choose something,' she said, 'just remember it won't be exactly the same as at home.'

She looked around for food to add a little variety to what Agatha fed them at the strict mealtimes. She had a feeling that Agatha would disapprove of any eating outside of these times, but she was also sure that life would be easier if Elian and Hurley could be occasionally lifted by a change. A change back to what they recognised as normal, in a way. Not that their kitchen was full of chocolate or crisps. It wasn't very processed, very American at all. The doctors had all agreed on the importance of Hurley's diet being simple and lacking in colours and other additives. It was their last chance to show that he didn't need any medication, that his diet

40

could eliminate the worst excesses of his behaviour. In fact, she thought, Agatha's plain cooking was probably exactly what Hurley needed. She just wanted to add a few different vegetables and fruit, that was all. And some chocolate to hide in the suitcase, under her clothes. And beer for Elian, who fetishized European lager in the way Budweiser used to be cool in England. She chose one with monks on the front as it seemed to be even more European, although she'd never have thought that when she lived here.

Hurley had a Snicker and dropped it into the basket.

'Half today and half tomorrow, OK?' she said.

He shrugged and went to look at the magazines. She chose eight bottles of beer from the alcohol aisle and then put two back. They had to carry whatever they bought. When they brought the car they could get more.

Hurley appeared at her side again. 'That man was talking but I don't know what he said.'

Nancy looked over his shoulder. The man looked cross and was putting a magazine back into its slot.

'Never mind,' said Nancy, 'he was probably just being friendly.'

They took the basket to the counter and paid, Nancy looking at each note carefully to make sure she gave the right amount. She could have used her card but wanted the familiarity of the money, the thick, colourful notes and different shaped coins. It made her think of pocket money and how much she used to value pound coins, and weren't all the silver coins smaller, somehow thinner?

She bagged up the shopping in parachute thin plastic bags and left the shop. Elian was waiting outside.

'I finally found some reception and then my phone died.'

'I told you to turn it off. Looking for reception wears down the battery.'

'There's no point repeating it, is there? I just told you what happened.'

41

'I got you some beer.' She looked at him. 'Where's the backpack?'

'I thought you were bringing it.'

'Where,' she tried to flap her arms, 'exactly would I have hidden that?' She held out one bag to him.

'Don't they have any paper bags?'

'Why don't you go in and ask them if they supply paper bags for American tourists?'

'Well, ten thousand Elvis impersonators can't be wrong.' He looked at the bag. 'This is really going to hurt my hand.'

Hurley searched in Elian's bag and then Nancy's bag for the Snicker.

'And you thought that was a good idea?' Elian continued.

'Yes, I did.'

'Didn't the dietician –'

'Yes, I know.'

They set off back down the road.

Nearly back at the house, a plastic bag stripe scoring her palm, Nancy remembered the stones in the field. She assumed they were still there, but hadn't checked from her bedroom window. Elian and Hurley wouldn't have known, even if they were there, from the road. The hedges that lined the field either side of the gate were thick and varied. The concrete posts which secured either side of the gate didn't look like the entrance to a historical anomaly. She remembered that her father had loved these stones, had studied them and then been banned from ever coming near them.

They placed their feet carefully, crossing the cattle grid, but Elian slipped and there was a crack. Beer began to drip from the holes in the bottom of the plastic bag.

'Brilliant,' he said.

'See if there are any left.'

He lowered the bag to the ground and pulled the handles apart. 'Three down, one left.'

Nancy groaned. 'I've still got two.'

Elian pulled out a large piece of brown glass and looked around for somewhere to put it.

'You can't leave it lying around. It all has to come inside.'

He put it back in the bag and carried it at arm's length so the drips didn't land on his shoes. She went in the front door and held her hand up.

'You can't drip it through the house.'

'But, what about the dog?'

'It's a sheepdog. You're not a sheep. Just pretend that you're in charge.'

He went around the house and she took her bag to the parlour and sat down in Agatha's chair. Elian was exhausting. She assumed Hurley had gone upstairs. Nancy heard the dog barking, but the dog was always barking at birds, at visitors, at the weather. The dog stopped barking, and there was a moment of silence. That's when the screaming started. She hadn't heard Hurley scream like that, not as a toddler, not in one of his most recent tantrums. He screamed now and, tasting copper at the back of her mouth, she ran.

'It just attacked him,' said Elian, kneeling by Hurley, his hands clasped together.

Her hands slipped against the door handles, her knees buckled at the step and she half fell towards Hurley. He held his hand towards her and she smiled, for some reason, smiled with her mouth but her eyes kept sliding away from the blood. She could smell it, like a handful of copper coins held in a child's palm for too long, that stink of blood she carried with her. She shrugged her cardigan off, her elbows getting caught, and gently wrapped his leg in the green wool thinking, this isn't good for the wound, this is even worse for my cardigan, but her brain preferred the cool mint to the scarlet lacerations and she managed to block out Hurley for a few seconds to think, where is the dog?

The dog that didn't deserve a name was back below the

decaying staircase, hunched down as if it was waiting for them to move. Its mouth was curled upwards and its nose looked wet. It eyed them both, it seemed. Nancy began to walk Hurley towards Donn's car. The keys were in the ignition, as usual.

'Elian, tell Donn I'm taking the car. Tell them we've gone to hospital.'

'I want to come,' said Elian.

She half saw him closing the door behind him. The ordered way they were discussing this, somehow hearing each other's enunciations above and beyond Hurley's cries suddenly struck Nancy as funny. She kept her eyes on the dog as she opened the rear door and guided Hurley through the gap. Elian got in beside him.

Hurley was getting louder, possibly. Nancy turned the keys and backed out of the driveway, turning at the gate. She messed up her three point turn and just about missed the wall before speeding down the driveway.

Drive on the left, drive on the left, she thought, before turning right into the road. She didn't know the way to Coleraine, but she knew the general direction. With the sound of the engine making Hurley fade into the background she wondered if he had run out of fear, run out of energy or was fainting. It hadn't seemed like a lot of blood loss, but shock. Did shock kill nowadays? Elian said nothing. Maybe they should have phoned for an ambulance. She'd done it wrong, she always got it wrong. She could make it not her fault. She could, if only Hurley would stop screaming.

She drove on. Her hands started to shake as if all the action she had suppressed in front of the dog was happening all at once, the running she didn't do, the throwing things that she couldn't do. Her throat started to tighten and she counted her breaths in through the nose, out through the mouth, the techniques they'd been taught at counselling to deal with Hurley. But this wasn't him. She couldn't hear him now.

She adjusted the rear view mirror to look. His head was back on the seat, his face pale and eyes open. His chest was still going up and down. Elian was just looking at him.

A car horn blared and she swung back on to the left. Drive on the left.

'Hurley, are you feeling any pain?' she asked.

His eyes fluttered but stayed open. If he died, if he died – then what? She would never go back to Michigan, that was for sure, and would never see Elian again either. And that thought didn't bother her one bit. She hid it and focused on the road. At least it wasn't raining.

Drive on the left.

The farm was lit upstairs and down when they returned. Donn and Agatha would never have as many bulbs burning at once.

Bernadette.

Elian had got Hurley through the front door and still she couldn't force her hands from their grip on the steering wheel. It was only the thought of Bernadette coming out and being trapped in the car with her that did it. She forced herself to leave the car and climb the steps to the door. Inside the house there were two girls and a man she half-recognised from photos, and Bernadette.

'Bit of a day,' said Bernadette, and grimaced.

'Yes,' said Nancy. She'd planned to say lots of things, nice things, about how nice it was to finally be together, planning trips and food, and now that 'yes' had exhausted everything she wanted to say to her.

Bernadette said, 'I'll make some tea.'

I was going to do that, thought Nancy. She bit her lip and nodded. Her nieces sat side by side on the sofa. Hurley tried to take up a place on the rug in front of the fire, but Elian slid him into place next to the oldest girl. She shifted away from him. He laid his head back on the creamy antimacassar and closed

45

his eyes. She nudged her sister to move up, which she did, and then she moved away some more. For all that they reminded Nancy of her and Bernadette, she wanted to smack them both and send them to bed. Horrible prissy little girls. She couldn't even remember their names. She and Bern weren't ever like them. Those girls who shifted away from Hurley like he was a bad smell had no spark in their eyes at all. Their father was speaking softly to Elian, next to the piano. Nancy couldn't hear what they were saying but she understood the gestures. She looked at Hurley, eyes still closed.

'Where's Donn?' she asked, her voice croaky.

Elian said, 'He's just popped out.' He made a stopping motion with his hand so she didn't ask anything else. That's when she knew that he taken the dog out to shoot it. 'Agatha's in bed.'

She wanted to go home. She just wasn't sure where she wanted that to be right now.

Bernadette came in with a tray. The teapot had been cleaned. She set it down on the dining table and sorted out the cups and handed glasses of juice to the three children. Nancy imagined how much sugar was in it, but said nothing. Hurley opened his eyes to take his and closed them again, but held onto the glass.

'Did you have a good journey?' asked Elian.

Bernadette laughed. 'I don't think you can ever have a good journey when it involves the Irish Sea. It was almost worth it, just so we didn't have to hire a car. I always worry about the excesses and all that nonsense. And you never know what the children are up to in the back.'

Nancy looked at Bernie's daughters. She could tell exactly what they'd be up to. Pinching, sniping and moaning. She tried to raise herself into the conversation.

'Yes,' said Nancy, 'a car is useful. We could all go over to Portstewart one day, maybe. Go to Morelli's and the Giant's Causeway.'

'Maybe,' said Bernadette. She didn't look at Nancy. 'We have lots of plans too.'

Nancy smiled. She was going to be friends with Bernadette by the end of their holiday. Maybe for now they could just get on like people who used to know each other well, and that would be enough.

'So, what's the view on his leg?' asked Bernadette.

'It looked really bad, but they're not too worried. Largely cosmetic, he'll be fine. He'll need a check up.'

'Good. An early night perhaps?'

Bernadette's eyes weren't even on her when she asked questions. She was signalling something to her older girl, some keep quiet or sit still order to two children who looked incapable of making noise or moving independently. She decided to wait to see if Bernadette repeated her question.

She didn't. It had been forgotten in her little silent exchange.

'Sorry, what were we saying?'

Nancy smiled, 'I can't remember either. I think I'm going to get Hurley up to bed.'

She stroked his shoulder. He handed her his juice, which she left on the tray, and he followed her out of the room.

'Night, Hurley,' said Elian, not leaving his new talking partner.

Nancy tried to help him up the stairs but he leaned on the banister more.

'I'll make up the bed in our room. Will you be all right?'

He nodded.

'Don't forget to brush your teeth.'

He nodded.

'I'm so sorry about what happened, Hurley. I should have done something, made Donn tie the dog up.'

He shrugged.

'Go and collect your things. I'll see you in the morning.' She went into the bathroom, just for a bit of space and listened to the girls coming upstairs, complaining about sharing the

47

room, crying about sharing the small bed. She cleaned her face and brushed her hair.

Hurley was waiting on the stairs outside the bathroom.

'My bed's not ready,' he said.

'No. I'll do that now.' She carried his bag to the room and put it on her bed.

Nancy struggled with the rusty clasps and hinges, but finally got the bed unfolded for when he came in. He slowly sat down on it and they both cringed at the screaming metal.

'Just try not to move around too much,' said Nancy.

'I can feel the metal.'

'We'll see how we get on. After tonight.'

She hoped Elian would offer to swap, if anyone needed to.

Downstairs the front room was empty. She found them all in the parlour, Bernadette at the head of the table, Elian and Adrian flanking her, and an almost empty bottle of white wine in between them.

'Open another, would you, Nancy? This one's all gone. We couldn't wait all night.'

Nancy found the bottle in the fridge, among many other bottles, and unscrewed the previous cork from the corkscrew. She looked around at the many boxes of provisions, the multipacks of crisps and the family packs of Twix and Mars bars sticking out of them. How was she going to hide this from Hurley?

She scraped off the foil and reapplied the corkscrew but the cork would not budge. She refused to ask anyone in the room to help her, but strained against it until Elian came to see what the hold-up was.

'Here you go,' he said, as it popped. 'What do we do about all this junk food? Didn't you say anything to them about what Hurley can eat?'

'It's their food, not ours. I didn't even know they were coming until we got here. What could I say?'

He took the bottle back in and left her to find her own

glass. When she sat down at the table and was pouring her wine they heard the gunshot.

'Poor Donn,' said Bernadette. 'He always said that would be his last dog.'

Elian kept his head down and waited for the conversation to resume on a different subject. He couldn't hide that he was glad and Nancy hated that. She forced her attention away from him, back to Bernadette.

She seemed so much the same, bright blue eyes which smiled when her mouth did, but distant, like she wasn't really there. The weird thing was that Nancy felt the same. Nancy had never felt guilty for leaving home. She was sick of making excuses for Bernadette. It was too embarrassing to be around those hospitals and other locked places. Nancy had wondered about this inevitable reunion for so long but hadn't expected Bernadette to be so confident, so self-contained. She didn't really need Nancy at all.

In the end they had to go to bed without seeing Donn and having to commiserate with him. The longer he didn't come back in the house, the more Nancy thought that maybe the shot wasn't for the dog. What if he'd just killed himself and they were all just sitting around drinking wine? What if he'd killed his dog and they were all sitting around drinking wine?

She lay awake as Elian slept, as quiet and contained as he ever got. Hurley was curled up on the fold out bed at the foot of theirs. She crept downstairs, automatically avoiding the creaky midpoint of the steps.

In the parlour she was disappointed to see Agatha was up, too. She was talking to herself. With horror Nancy realised that she was praying, her eyes closed and hands pressed together. Nancy pulled the door to again and waited outside. Maybe she should just go to bed. Or maybe Agatha realised she was there and would finish. She couldn't decide if it would be worse to wait or to leave. She lingered, deciding to give her a couple of minutes. The murmuring stopped and she peered through a slight gap. Agatha was looking at her.

She opened the door fully and closed it behind her. 'I was thinking, before you go, you'll have to show me how to work the immersion heater.'

'I will.'

'We only have a shower at home. One click and it's heated, two minutes and you're done. They're not comfortable with baths yet. They see it as lying in your own dirt.'

Agatha tutted. Nancy wished she hadn't said it.

'Do you want any tea?' asked Nancy.

'Not at this time of night.'

The fire was nearly out, just a few embers glowing at the bottom. Nancy passed through to the kitchen and got a glass of water before joining Agatha at the fire.

'All ready for your trip?'

Agatha nodded, staring into the end of the fire. 'I'll pray for you.'

It sounded like a threat. Nancy wasn't sure how she should respond.

'Thank you.'

They sat quietly for a while.

'Did you ever regret leaving the convent?'

'I didn't have a choice. Donn needed someone to keep house until he was married. I did think he would get married but God had other plans. It's not for me to question them.'

Nancy thought about the uncles and aunts who had escaped the house. Some of them had escaped the country too, but not Beth, Donn and Agatha. One other sister, Shona, had left home to keep house for a second cousin, a priest in Cork. She was there for eight months before she stole the week's collection and ran off to Canada with a married man. Agatha didn't speak to her, but Nancy's mother wrote. She'd visited her a couple of years ago and then Nancy on her way back. Others had gone to Australia, one to London. One uncle, Ryan, had just gone. No-one seemed to know where he was, her mum said.

Nancy realised that Agatha was looking at her.

'I thought you may become a nun.'

'I never really considered it.' Nancy shifted in her seat and drank most of her water.

'Maybe you should have. I think it would have suited you.'

Nancy smiled awkwardly.

Agatha shook her head. 'That sister of yours, I pray for her most of all. Those poor wee bastards. Condemned to –' Agatha threw her hands in the air.

She meant Bernie. Nancy remembered how they always called their aunt Sister Agatha, but only behind her back. When had they stopped that?

'I'd better get up to bed,' said Nancy.

Agatha looked exhausted all of a sudden. 'Look after Donn, won't you?'

'I will.'

Nancy put her mug on the table and turned around to leave.

'Promise me.'

'I promise.'

She didn't hear Donn come in, but she heard him climb the stairs and close the door to his bedroom. His steps sounded like those of an old man. Knowing he was inside made all of the following noises, the shuffles outside, the cries of animals, more disturbing. They reminded her of something, some other night, but the feeling was vague and she didn't want to grab it properly. If she did she would never sleep again.

7

Then

Sunday mornings were different here. At home Mum didn't mind what we wore and I was always happiest in my jeans. I'd just grown out of my favourites, with the Muppet patch on the back pocket, or Mum said I had, but I squeezed into them a few times after that. It hurt, right across my stomach, but I didn't want to give them to Florence yet. One day they disappeared and I had a new pair, but no Muppets on them. That's what I normally wore, with day-glo legwarmers. Mine were pink and Nancy's were green. She asked me to swap when we unwrapped them at Christmas but I didn't. I was so happy that I had something she wanted and it was the first time I decided to keep it instead of swap like she wanted. After that she spent weeks telling me how rubbish pink was, but I didn't mind.

For church here I had to wear a nice, clean skirt. It was a dark red ra-ra skirt, and it matched Nancy's, but she hated us matching and I hated skirts.

'No leg warmers,' said Mum, and we stripped them off. It was too warm for them anyway, but Nancy complained.

'I'm not listening,' said Mum.

Sister Agatha washed our faces with the same mouldy smelling flannel, which Nancy felt she was far too old for. Florence smiled when Sister Agatha told her she looked like a little angel and gave Nancy a knowing look.

'NB,' Nancy whispered to Florence.

Florence didn't know what it meant but she knew it was bad and clung to Mum.

We got into Donn's car, Florence on Mum's lap, and drove to church and parked in the car park across the road. On the way in there was no talking. You were allowed to nod, but not smile, not that I nodded at anyone. Sister Agatha did nod at every single person she passed. I wondered how she could know all these people and be on her own all the time. She led us to the second row and shepherded us in so she could sit on the end and continue to nod. She didn't dress any differently for church, just black blouse, black skirt and black jacket, same as always. I wondered why she didn't have special Sunday clothes, or maybe every day was a Sunday when you were so miserable.

The priest was different to ours too, but a bit more exciting. He liked to scare people about hell and swung his arms around when he was in the pulpit. Our priest at home was a vegetarian who liked to talk about animals and love. I didn't mind listening about hell and devils, but Mum always twisted around and made a fuss of Florence so she couldn't listen and ask awkward questions. Sister Agatha made us sit near the front, but Donn always sat in the back row. There were always lots of men in the back rows and I wondered if it was a secret rule about men who weren't married. Tommy was often there.

Everyone was smart, even us, and sang loudly, even when they shouldn't have because they were really bad. The girl behind us kept stroking Florence's hair even after her mother smacked her hand. It echoed around the church in the quiet bit. It was always cold and always dark in there, but I didn't mind that. It made the candles stand out more, especially the one in the red glass which showed God was in, I think. The small, high windows rarely had sun to show you the pictures, not like our church with its floor to ceiling stained glass and weird pointy bits.

'A sixties architectural abomination,' my dad had said.

'It's got under floor heating,' said my mum.

I never liked going up for communion here. If you put your hands out the priest gave you a funny look. You had to kneel at the bar around the altar in a line and he'd do a circuit, popping the wafer into everyone's mouths for them. Sometimes I'd hold my hands out and sometimes Nancy did. I was always pleased if we both did because then we looked as if we knew the right way and they were getting it wrong. I didn't think there was anything sinful about my hands, even if they weren't entirely clean. Then the grim, cropped altar boy would give you a sip of the wine, but not let go of the chalice, and then you had to get up and go back and kneel. In our church there were padded cushions but here there were hard wooden plinths to rest on and my knees would ache. If I got up too quickly Sister Agatha would poke me until I knelt down again. I tried to wait for Nancy but her knees seemed harder than mine. When I sat down again they were always red, but then I could watch the men who came forward from the back of the church. I smiled if I saw Donn, but he never looked at us. Maybe he was a bit scared of Sister Agatha too.

Almost as bad was trying to get out of the church at the end. Vaguely familiar people would approach us and tweak our cheeks.

'It's not wee Nancy and Bernadette?'

Nancy had perfected this haughty look into the distance, so they fixed on me and the way I looked back and asked me stupid questions about my school, my age and my life and when my da would be coming over and didn't we miss him terribly. Sometimes I couldn't understand them and Nancy would translate for me to stop them repeating themselves over and over. Tommy would be outside the church door, pulling out people to talk to, laughing with the priest.

Nearly free, we'd have our hands crushed by the priest at the door, and then visit Gran and Granddad's grave, which they shared. I loved the drive back. It was all green fields, brown mud, small mountains and grey houses and no more church for a week. Most houses were the colour of the clouds, stippled with pebbledash against the wind and rain. Our farm was special, covered with a flat white plaster, with dark sea grey slates which glistened after every shower, signalling to the other roofs across the flat fields like dark beacons. I liked the heavy doors, thick walls and thin windows. Best of all I liked being welcomed home by Bruce, racing the car.

This Sunday when we got home the potatoes were ready to heat and the chicken smelled ready to carve, but there was already someone sitting at the table in the parlour.

'Ryan!' I said.

'Hello, girls.' He was shaved but his hair was much longer now, drifting over his blue eyes. 'Long time no see.'

I saw his long green bag on the floor and thought how he'd missed my birthday. 'Have you got me a present?'

He looked confused. I heard a gasp and turned. Mum had put her hand to her mouth. She looked down at us.

'Go upstairs and wash your hands, girls.'

'They're clean,' I said, and held them up for her. Church was supposed to be clean and we were clean when we went there in the first place.

'Wash them again. You too, Florence.' She closed the door behind us. We went upstairs slowly, trying to listen. Sister Agatha came in the front door, carrying the freshly picked peas in a basket made from her skirt. We waited on the landing while Florence stood on the toilet lid and let the water run over her hands.

'Jesus, Mary and Joseph!'

I never understood it, but when Sister Agatha said things like that it didn't count as blasphemy. If I'd said it, it would have. The door closed again, and then we heard Donn come in from the lobby.

'Christ! What are you doing here? Get out!'

There was the noise of chairs scraping and something got knocked over.

Donn said, 'You were told. He warned you what would happen.'

Then the voices went quieter.

'Where's he been?' I asked.

'How should I know?' Nancy held her finger to her lips.

We hadn't seen Uncle Ryan since he turned up in the middle of the night on Florence's birthday. He hadn't brought her a present either. Mum cried and Dad said he could stay, even though that made Mum cry more. He stayed that day, sleeping on the sofa for most of it, and then he left while we were at school the next. I asked where he'd gone and Mum said Timbuktu. I didn't think that was a real place, but I looked it up and it is.

There was a splash in the bathroom. I went in and used a towel to wipe the floor, then shook it out and laid it back on the side of the bath. Florence sat with us on the landing, smiling at us, and keeping pretty quiet for her.

The parlour door opened and Sister Agatha called us down to the bottom of the stairs. She had three plates balanced in her hands.

'Front room, girls.' We sat on the sofa in a line and she handed us our plates. Her hair looked messy and her eyes were red. 'This is a special day. You are going to eat in here and you're allowed to watch the television. Just leave the plates on the table when you've finished and behave. I'll be back to check on you soon.'

'Can I get a drink?' asked Nancy.

'I'll bring you a drink soon enough.'

'Are we allowed to go outside?'

'Nancy, listen,' said Sister Agatha. 'You all stay right here until you hear otherwise. I'm relying on you. Do as you're told, please.'

When she left the room I looked at Nancy.

56

'She said please.'

'And television on a Sunday.'

We listened from our spots on the sofa but we didn't even go to listen at the serving hatch. We picked at our chicken and butterless potatoes and watched nothing. Through the serving hatch we heard the door close to the lobby.

'I have to tell him.'

Donn was cross. Donn only got cross when we chased the sheep.

'Please, Donn,' said Mum, 'don't do it. We can get rid of him, send him away again.'

'He came back. He knew what would happen.'

'He was wrong. He gets that now.'

'I have to tell Tommy, Eithne. You have no idea.'

'It's your brother! Our brother!'

Then there was the sound of the back door and a sob. The parlour door was closed again.

I looked at Nancy. She was already looking at me. Florence was jabbing at the television, trying to switch it on.

'We need to hide,' I said.

'We'll be okay,' she said. 'Mum will make sure.' She pulled Florence onto the settee in between us.

'What about Ryan?' I whispered.

'Oh, shut up, Bernadette. Tommy won't really hurt him.'

But I'd never said he would.

8

Now

Donn set off with Agatha. Nancy and Bernadette waved her off to the retreat with rather too much smiling. This, the first moment that Nancy and Bernadette had been left together, was silent. They continued to look down the driveway towards the gate.

'Do you expect Bruce to come running down to the house?' asked Nancy.

'Sometimes.' Bernadette turned to go back in.

'Mum said to put Hurley in Agatha's room. I can't think of a better way to divide people up, can you?'

'No. That's fine with me. You can do it while we're out.'

Nancy looked at their car, a seven-seater. There were seven of them in total.

'Where are you going?'

'Portstewart.'

'I love that place. I wanted Hurley to know what holidays were like when I was a child.'

Bernadette stared at her. 'Seriously?'

'Yes. I loved coming here.'

Bernadette pressed her lips together, but then decided to say it anyway. 'You have good memories?'

Nancy paused. This wasn't how she'd imagined the conversation while she couldn't sleep. She'd thought of them sitting in front of the fire, checking if there were still silver fish underneath the rug. She'd imagined them being ten and twelve, and they weren't. She felt cross that Bernadette didn't understand what she wanted.

'So why are you here, then?'

'Answers.' Bernadette looked back down the drive. 'And knowing my enemies.'

She began to walk to the hedge on the left. Nancy clenched her fists, but Bernadette wasn't going to get away with her sniping. They were in their forties now. She caught her up.

'Look I know we grew apart, but that was decades ago. I'm not your enemy and I'm glad you seem so well and happy. I know it was really hard for you, and you went through it more than me, but it was hard to watch as well.'

'Oh, you only watched, did you?'

'Anything that happened was not my fault. You know what happened. It was the therapists, not me.'

Bernadette was on her tiptoes, but couldn't properly see over the hedge. 'It was always about you.' There was no emotion betrayed in her face at all. Her eyes were dry, her mouth making calm and considered words. 'Children are never believed until an adult believes them, like someone hearing the tree fall in the forest. You let me down really badly, Nancy, and I told you I'd never forgive you. I meant it.'

'What?' Nancy tried to control her voice. 'When did everything become my fault?'

Bernadette smoothed her hair behind her ears. 'I didn't agree to this as some kind of reconciliation. We were coming anyway. This summer isn't about you, Nancy. We're just all here in the same place.'

'What about Florence?'

'What about her? Do you even know what's happening with her?'

'Yes!' Nancy tried to think back to what she'd last seen on Facebook. Nothing came to mind.

Bernadette laughed.

59

Nancy said, 'Why is it up to me to contact everyone? You could have called me. I'd loved you to have visited.'

'You never suggested it.'

Nancy stumbled over her words. 'I invited you to the wedding.'

'Yes, yes you did.' Bernadette shrugged and looked up at the house. 'Thanks.' The paint on the windows was peeling and the cracked pane of the storage room between the two front bedrooms was highlighted by the angle of the sun. She held her hand to her eyes to glance at the few clouds. 'Anyway, we'll see you this evening.'

No offer to take everyone and Nancy couldn't ask. She would spend the day moving Hurley from her bedroom to Agatha's room and see what happened next.

The girls had been bathed and were curled up in their pyjamas on the sofa, each with a DSi again.

'Your turn, Hurley,' said Nancy.

'I only have showers.'

The girls whispered to each other and giggled. Nancy frowned, 'What did you two say?' They shrugged. She had to start thinking of them by name. Erin and . . .? She turned back to Hurley. 'The boiler has been kept on for you and you need to keep that leg clean. We're seeing the doctor tomorrow. Now upstairs.'

He grumbled but left the room. The girls looked at each other and then at Nancy.

'Should you be on those before bedtime?'

'Mum said.'

'I'll just check with her, shall I?'

They ignored her. She tried not to slam the door. Bernadette was in the parlour putting on some eyeliner. She lowered the small hand mirror.

'We're going to pop out, Nancy. You don't mind babysitting, do you?'

'I suppose not. Where are you going?'

'The pub.'

Nancy thought of the windowless bars she'd seen by the road.

'Who's driving?'

'We'll do stone-paper-scissors,' said Bernadette. She lifted up the mirror again.

Nancy couldn't remember when she'd last seen her with make-up on. Maybe it was when she was fourteen and trying to look old enough to get served in town on the infrequent holidays from hospital before she never went home at all. Everyone knew which pubs were age-blind. Nancy never took her out with her but Bernadette often found her own way to the same pubs. Sometimes they'd walk home together and decide what film they'd pretend to have seen. That was all they'd say.

'Should the girls be on the consoles?'

'Oh, I don't mind. It keeps them quiet. Just don't let them outside on their own. They probably won't even ask.'

'We were always outside on our own.'

Bernadette looked at her. 'Exactly.'

Nancy wasn't sure what that meant. Hurley had been wandering around, now that his leg felt a bit better. 'What time should I send them to bed?'

Bernadette looked at her watch. 'In an hour? Nine-ish. Let them watch TV if they ask.'

'Have you told them you're going out?'

'Not yet.' Bernadette put down the mirror and pushed the top back on the eyeliner. 'They'll be fine. Don't worry.'

Nancy nodded and went to check that Hurley was in the bath. He had turned the tap on but the plug wasn't in. She put it in place and put the cold tap on too to temper the scalding water.

Hurley was lying on her bed, next to Elian who was reading.

'Go and get your stuff ready, and stay in the bathroom so the bath doesn't overflow.'

'It's OK, I haven't put the plug in yet.'

'I have, now go. And don't pull the string that switches the electric heater on, OK?' She closed the door after him. 'Can you believe that? He knew he was wasting water.'

Elian nodded. 'Terrible.'

'And,' Nancy waited until he put the book down, 'Bernadette's going out! I don't know how to talk to those children. They're so rude.'

'I don't know if we can go around pointing at other people's children, Nancy,' said Elian. He lifted the book back up. 'You don't mind babysitting, do you? I think it'll be fun to visit a pub.'

She pulled his book down. 'You're going with them?'

'Of course. It doesn't take two adults to babysit.'

'I didn't realise.' She knelt down on the bed. 'You won't repeat anything I said about Bernadette and all that, will you?'

'What do you mean?'

'The accusations, the stuff.'

'Her being nuts? No, I won't.'

Nancy gasped. 'Elian!'

'I'm kidding, mental health problems, whatever. I won't say a word.'

'And –'

'And I promise not to ask anyone if they're IRA.'

'Jesus.'

He flipped his book back into place. Nancy went back downstairs, past the locked bathroom door where she listened to check that the water had been switched off. When she got to the bottom step she sat down. Her sister would rather invite Elian out for the evening than her. It had been years since they had been sisters, maybe, but if Mum thought it could all be fixed then she would try. But it seemed that it was only her intention. Nancy rubbed her face with both

62

hands and went into the front room. The girls glanced at her, but didn't move.

'Did you know your mum and dad are going out?'

They nodded. 'We heard.'

Nancy looked towards the serving hatch through which she and Bernadette used to listen to conversations in the parlour, if they were loud enough. There were plenty of whispered chats that they never heard. She moved to the window and looked down the driveway. The sun was nowhere near setting but had been caught in the large trees that marked the passage to the gate. She could see the sun still shining on the paddock to the right, the long grass rippling in patches. A figure appeared on the drive and she gasped, raising one hand to her chest, but it was only Donn. She smiled at her reaction, who else would it be? He looked half made without a dog next to him, looking at his side occasionally as if he could still see a black and white shape keeping faithful pace. The fields had been sold off one by one. Everyone knew it was only a matter of time before everything had gone. She needed to remember to give him some money for the food they'd eaten, for being here.

Donn walked around the side to come in the back door. It made sense with the state of his boots, but seemed to indicate that it wasn't really his house. The owner should use the front door, no matter the mud they carried with them.

Through the serving hatch she heard him come in, the shuffle of boots and closed and opened doors. Bernadette came out of the parlour and shouted up the stairs.

'We're off, let's go!'

Her husband and Nancy's husband met on the landing.

'Bye, girls,' said Bernadette.

Nancy watched them go down the front steps to the car parked out the front and saw them drive away. Someone, maybe Elian, waved to her. She turned back to the room. The girls were whispering to each other.

'Maeve wants a drink,' said Erin. She didn't take her eyes from the TV.

Erin and Maeve, that was it.

'She knows where the kitchen is,' said Nancy, and forced a smile. The girls exchanged a look. 'How about we switch the consoles off and play a game?'

'No thanks,' said Erin. Maeve giggled.

'What's funny?'

'You don't let Hurley watch TV. That's weird.'

'It's not weird to not watch a screen all the time. Look,' Nancy took each console and closed it, 'it's quite possible to live without it.'

'We'll tell,' said Maeve. 'You didn't save our games.'

'You can tell. The game is still there, I haven't turned it off.'

'But you closed it!'

'And the world didn't end.' She placed them on the table. 'So, there was always a chess board and cards in this cupboard.' Nancy moved to the dresser at the back of the room and kneeled down. There were photo albums and old Christmas cards, but underneath was the chess board, folded back on itself to hold the pieces inside. She pulled it out with one hand, using the other to hold everything back inside the cupboard. When she stood up she saw the girls had slipped out. Maybe they'd gone to get a drink. Then she noticed the consoles had gone too.

She put the board on the table by the window and used her nails to unclip the sharp piece of metal which kept the sides closed together. The wooden pieces looked unscathed, although the green felt underneath them was peeling away on a few. She placed the board upright and tried to remember which order they went in – castle, knight, bishop or castle, bishop, knight?

It didn't matter. There was a black pawn missing. She thought about delving back into the cupboard but knew

64

the girls weren't coming back. They were probably in their bedroom with their screens raised to their noses. Hurley was just absent. All the time.

Nancy rested her face on one hand and looked out of the window. It was getting dark now. The ceiling light reflecting from the window made it seem even darker and she could see herself, bored, slouched, within the pane of glass. There was half a memory of a group of people standing here, trying to see past their reflections, staring into the darkness of trees and, what was it? There was something out there that was scaring everyone. She'd been scared too but didn't know why. A shape appeared above her reflection and she swung round.

'Donn! You frightened me.'

'Sorry. I was just going to tell you that Hurley had gone to bed. He said to tell you.'

'Oh. He could have said goodnight.'

'He's not one for unnecessary words.'

'Or politeness.'

'Or pulling the plug out.' Donn smiled and sat down at the other end of the table.

'Were you talking to him?'

Donn nodded. 'He's a good boy.'

Nancy sighed, 'I know.'

Donn shook his head. 'I've seen the way you watch him.'

'I stand up for him,' said Nancy. 'I find it difficult. Trying to keep him in school, trying to make him . . .'

Donn looked at her, and then away across the darkness. Nancy watched him.

'You were quiet, but you had friends. I remember people being here.'

Donn nodded. 'Yes, I'm sure you do remember people. They weren't always friends.'

Nancy looked away. Their reflections were bright now against the black night glass. Nancy never looked out like this at home. She had the feeling that bad things happened in dark gardens. The larger the garden, the bigger the secret. But there were no people here. It made it feel safer to look.

'Have you any idea when Agatha will be back?'

He shook his head. 'She's not coming back. There won't be anywhere to come back to, anyway. Most of its sold already and someone's interested in the land that's left. They'll probably knock down the house. Who knows?'

'It's so sad.'

He looked at her and said nothing.

'Where will Agatha go? Is she staying at the convent?'

'Yes. It's not a retreat. She's becoming a nun. Again.'

'Why didn't she say?'

'You didn't ask.'

'She wanted her room kept for her. Why would I ask?'

Nancy watched him watching the night. All she could see was their reflections.

'I'll go up, too.' He pushed his chair away from the table and walked away.

She watched him climb the stairs slowly and her eyes filled with tears. This always happened. She moved somewhere and the local shop closed. She joined a group and it folded within weeks. She came back to her family farm just as it was being sold. She was always just too late, always lacking the timing of other people. But this must be why Mum had pushed for her to come back this summer, not next, or the one after. She'd known it would go, but hadn't realised how it would feel.

One tear fell and she swallowed the rest back until her throat was sore. She needed to check on Hurley, remove electronic items from the girls. The NBs she thought. What would Bernie say if she were to call them that?

Standing, she rubbed her face and walked purposefully upstairs. If the girls had heard her they hadn't cared and, again, she had to unarm them. She held out her hand for their handsets.

'We'll tell,' said Erin.

'Brush your teeth and get ready for bed.'

'We did brush our teeth,' smirked Erin.

'Then do it again so I know you have.'

They looked at Nancy as she left the room, and left the door open, and she heard them whispering as she crossed the landing to her room. With the door open she made it clear that she was prepared to wait until they had done as she said. Eventually they had each changed and each visited the bathroom.

'Goodnight,' she said, switching their light off and closing the door. She heard the pause before they switched the light back on. She opened the door and switched it off again.

'We have the light on,' said Maeve.

'Goodnight.'

She waited until they had started to be rude about her before she crept away. She realised that she was avoiding the centre of the landing and stairs, in the same way as she had as a child. So many times she had not wanted to be heard. She had been too young and scared of being caught. Now she was too old, and determined to make herself seem omnipresent. She opened the door to Hurley's room and peeped in. She'd moved all the crosses and Mary and Jesus statues to the wardrobe. It smelled of Agatha and, she suspected, always would.

'Book down and light off, Hurley.'

He placed the book by the light before clicking the switch. He didn't say goodnight either, but wriggled down beneath the sheets and woollen blankets until she could only see his hair. She paused on the small landing by the bathroom and Donn's bedroom, listening, and then sat on the top stair, consoles on her lap. She should have asked how long they had left. There were lots of things she should have asked.

9

Then

Beneath the rippled tin ceiling and supporting beams, curtains of long dead spiders hung, tatty and aged by the holes of a thousand tiny creatures. It was our favourite stable, partly because of the high, weird door to nowhere and partly because I'd noticed the door was the exact blue of the Tardis. We'd brought our rosary beads with us because Nancy thought, if they looked worn, Sister Agatha might let us off praying with her. We each rubbed our beads with our t-shirts.

'Has he gone again?' I asked. 'Ryan?'

'Bern, I don't know. Why do you always ask me?'

I whispered, 'Did he go with Tommy?'

'How would I know? I heard the same as you.'

'What do you think he did, Ryan?'

'I don't want to talk about it. Let's play hide and seek.'

She hung her beads on a nail and I copied her. I sat cross legged in the dust and covered my eyes. I could hear her moving things around, finding spaces.

'Thirty.'

I stood and looked around but I couldn't see where Nancy was hiding. I heard pebbles fall onto the roof, clanging once and dribbling down until they silently dropped to the ground. I shivered, thinking that she'd found another secret way out and I was the only one in here. Could she have slid past as I counted with my eyes closed? I had been counting loudly, like she asked, but Nancy wasn't as careful as me. She'd have kicked the rusting drinking trough or set the shovel sliding down the wall before it clanged on the ground.

I whispered, 'Nancy.'

The bendy ceiling and floor made uneven by all the rubbish over it made me feel wobbly, that any movement I made could make the stable tip. I wanted to hold on to something, but didn't dare touch the flaking wood of the stairs or the webbed walls. I reached for a metal sheet and immediately pulled my hand back. A sliver of paint had slid itself into my fingertip, right underneath my nail. I didn't cry out, but made my way back to the door where day still came through in long lines, the planks at the bottom wide enough apart that I could pass my hand through. There was a broken dresser by the door with a dozen jam jars sitting on it, cloudy with years of waiting. Maybe this was where the spiders lived. There weren't any alive in the webs so they must hide somewhere else, run out, spin a bit, and run back. I knew how spiders ran, flinging their too many legs around and making me shiver. I never admitted to being scared of them because that would start Nancy off and next thing I'd find one in my bed. Or more.

I whispered again, thought I heard a smothered laugh echo back to me.

'I'm going in,' I said loudly, 'I'm bored.'

There was no response. I pulled the door open.

'I found a spider nest in the jam jars. They've just hatched.'

Silence.

'See you then.'

I pushed the door closed behind me and stood up against the wall so I couldn't be seen through the gaps. I still wasn't sure if she was inside or outside and I half expected Nancy to jump out at me. Inside I heard something throw itself against the door and I stood back. The jam jars began to crash on the floor and I backed away.

'Bern!'

I went back to the door and started to pull at the wood.

'Bern!'

Nancy was throwing herself against the door again, but it was caught on something.

'Bern!'

She pushed again and fell out, knocking me to the floor. Nancy was sobbing, pointing her dirty finger at me.

'You locked me in there.'

'There's no lock!'

'You jammed it.'

'I didn't!'

'I'm telling Mum.'

I sat up in the mud, wiping my sticky hands on my jeans. I struggled to stand up, the wellies cutting into my calves when I tried, but I finally was upright. She wouldn't tell Mum that it was her idea to hide in one of the stables we absolutely weren't allowed in. She'd say something that made it sound like my idea. But she'd been the one who'd shown she was scared and then she'd feel bad for lying and getting me in trouble. Later she'd be nice again, not call me Bernadette for the rest of the evening, maybe. As long as I kept my mouth shut.

Another jam jar crashed inside the stable and I pushed the door back so the ghosts and spiders would stay behind the door. I crossed the yard and climbed on the trembling aluminium gate to Bryn's field and watched the sheep. They wouldn't come across for grass. They didn't really like people, as the cows did. I wasn't allowed in this field either, but didn't want to go in anyway. Sheep were a bit mad, flocking like birds and threatening to knock you over. Sometimes Donn would whisper to Mum or Sister Agatha that there was 'another one', and me and Nancy would run up to Mum's room to spot the dead one. Once we stayed to watch him drag the dead sheep onto the trailer, but I didn't want to see that again. I didn't like the way its head dangled, like it was broken, and I really didn't like the way the other sheep didn't care. Nancy laughed at the way Donn struggled with the body, and even went out later to pick some stinking, greasy wool from the barbed wire to tease me with.

'Dead sheep's wool,' she whispered as she left it on my shoulder, beside my plate, anywhere she could think of to make me squeal.

I could hear Mum shouting for me now from the house. My finger, with the splinter of paint, began to throb and I squeezed it to bring tears to my eyes. I could play for sympathy too. I would need it if Mum was going to get the tweezers and needle out.

I could have cut through the arched passage next to the garage, but that would have made things worse. You could see right through to the house but the ceiling could give way at any time, my mother said. Donn did use it, and so did Tommy, but Mum couldn't order them about. They didn't seem worried it would collapse, but then Donn only worried about sheep and Tommy didn't worry about anything, I thought.

It was probably safe enough, but this wasn't the time to get caught trying it out. I went around the garage and came in through the gate into the yard. Mum was packing a bag on the doorstep, her sunglasses on her head.

'Come on,' she said, 'I've been shouting for you.'

'Why?'

'We're going to the beach.'

I must have looked surprised.

'What's the matter with you? Get your wellies off and find your costume.'

I nodded and winced. 'I've got a really bad splinter under my nail.'

'It'll probably come out in the sea. Go on, everyone's ready.' She picked up the big shopping bag she used for towels and put it in the boot of Donn's car.

'Is Donn coming?'

'No, girls only.'

I was going to ask about Agatha, but she pointed to the upstairs of the house.

'Now, please. But, Bern,' she held my shoulder, 'only use the front door, OK?'

I ran around the house, upstairs and stripped off so I could put my costume under my clothes. Nancy was just putting her t-shirt back on and stood in the doorway. She had one hand clenched hard and she shook it like it meant something, then left the room without talking to me.

'I didn't do it!' I shouted. 'It was stuck!'

She slammed the door behind her. I stuck my tongue out at the door and pulled my clothes back on. My jelly shoes were under the chair by the bed and I carried them down with me. I was so cross with Nancy that I forgot. I opened the door to the parlour and stared. Tommy was at the table, his dark hair fallen over his face, his hands over his eyes. He slowly lifted his head and laid his hands down on the table.

'What the fuck are you doing here?'

I slammed the door shut, and ran out the front door.

Mum started the car and I got in the back with Florence.

'Hold on to her,' she said, and backed out of the yard, much quicker than usual.

I tried to forget that I'd seen the door to Cassie's room wide open, a long green bag next to a blanket rolled up on the floor, and a gun on the table.

Nancy was in the front of the car so no-one noticed her silence but me. She hadn't told Mum anything about the barn, and she didn't say anything to me until we got to the seafront.

'I don't want to swim with you, Bernadette,' she said. That was it. I was surprised to get away with it, but she'd get me back. She always did.

Usually by the time we got to the sea the clear skies had filled with clouds, but this was one of the magical days. Mum was distracted and said yes to everything. She even let us go on the pedal boats in the square outdoor pool. You could swim in it, but the floor was slimy with green stuff and I still had to put my feet down a lot. I preferred the boats, even if I had to share with Florence because Nancy wouldn't go with me. I liked the weird pool. It was too difficult to get to the sea from this bit of the coast because there were loads of sharp, black rocks in the way. Sometimes we parked on the Strand up the road and went in the proper sea, but this was where the ice cream was and the boats and bright windmills to stick out of the car window and, if we were lucky, fish and chips on the way home. There was a pretend beach next to the pool where they'd dumped a load of sand for small children. Maybe they told the little ones that this was the real beach and the actual one was kept secret until they were bigger. You couldn't even see it from here. There was a huge cliff in the way. My dad had walked around it to the Strand and back once, but my mum was angry. She said she knew someone who'd been knocked off the path and drowned, and he said it must have been a storm or high tide and don't be such a drama queen.

I wished he was here. I was sure I could walk round safely too. Mum stayed with Florence on the baby beach and let me and Nancy go to the rock pools with a bucket. She thought we'd stay together, but Nancy went right out and told me not to follow her.

I didn't care. I was much better at finding things on my own and I needed to think about what I'd seen. I felt full of words that made no sense.

I sat on a rock and dipped my fingers into a pool, warmed like a bath by the sun. Only the pools had any warmth to them although Mum said the sea was the Atlantic and much warmer than the Irish Sea which didn't come from America.

I stilled my fingers. A crab came up from the sand and moved to hide beneath a stone. I waited a little and then lifted it, to watch where it would go next. There were no shells here, and I didn't feel like putting the crab in the bucket to scare Florence.

I climbed along to the next pool, slipping on a bit of seaweed and cracking my ankle on a knob of rock. It reminded me of my finger. I examined it, pressed against the nail. Mum was right. It had come out in the water. I smiled. No needles.

I had reached the fifth pool before I found my first shell. There were lots of different types, but I only collected one of them. They were small, the size of my fingernail, curved underneath so the sides almost met, and on top they were ribbed like a finger print. Dad said they were called trivia, which I thought was a stupid name, but he also said they were very like cowrie shells which can be used instead of money in some places. I called mine cowries as well and thought of each one as a pound. I was good at finding them. I already had some in my pot on the mantelpiece, so if I got lost in one of those countries I'd be a millionaire eventually.

I picked up my shell and put it in my shorts pocket. By the time I'd found six, Nancy had realised what I was doing. She never found any. As she picked her way over to me I had to decide whether I was going to buy her silence or bank on it being too late now for her to say anything to Mum.

'How many have you got?' she shouted across to me.

'Three,' I said.

'Can I have any?'

I shrugged. She could tell me what she'd do for them first. I wanted a week off from being called Bernadette and she couldn't tell Mum anything I did for two.

'I don't want any anyway,' she said.

I looked at her. She held her hand cradled in front of her and was looking into it.

'Have you found one?'

74

'I have,' she counted, 'eleven.' She smiled at me, closed her hand and held it up, next to her head.

Eleven. That was all the ones I'd found this summer.

'Give them back.' I started to scramble across the rock. 'They're mine.'

'Stop!' She pulled her hand back. 'I'll throw them.'

'Nancy, please don't.' I felt panicky, my breath coming quickly.

'Say that you're sorry.'

'I'm really sorry. I didn't mean to shut you in, the door got stuck. Please give them back.'

'How many can I keep?'

I estimated how much it would be worth. 'Five.'

She turned and threw her arm forward. I saw them scatter and ping off the rocks.

'You should have said six.'

I watched her skirt around me and, once on the sand, run back to Mum. I headed over to where I thought they'd landed, but I couldn't see any of them. My eyes filled up and I sat down on a rock, wiping my face and trying to get just one back. They were gone.

I headed back to Mum.

'Why didn't you come back with Nancy? You know you should keep together.'

I sat heavily on the sand.

'And your foot is bleeding. I do wish you'd be more careful, Bernadette.'

'Yes,' said Nancy, 'be more careful, Bernadette.'

Mum had packed up the towels and buckets and took the last one from me.

'We're going to Morelli's now. Get your jelly shoes back on.'

I put them on and followed Mum to the car to put the bag back, and then over to cross the road. I made sure that I didn't sit next to Nancy but the ice cream made me forget for a bit, until I looked at her again. The sky clouded over as we sat there.

'We timed that perfectly,' said Mum, sitting back in her chair. She lifted her sunglasses back onto her hair and I thought how happy she looked. At the farm she always looked a bit cross or about to be cross. I thought she must miss Dad.

'Why doesn't Dad come for longer?' I said.

She blinked and then looked at me. 'He only has a week's holiday. He spends the weekend driving up and then has five days to get ready to zoom us back home again. Assuming the car makes it.' She smiled. 'I'm kidding. He misses you too, you know.'

'I know.' I imagined him getting into his car and speeding around London before releasing the brakes and flinging himself right up the country in one go. 'It's quicker flying. One year can we fly instead of taking the ferry?'

'Maybe. He likes to drive us back. And it's good to have our own car that last week.'

Nancy snorted, 'Only if you like stones.'

'Well, I do like stones, Nancy. So that's lucky.' Mum wiped Florence's mouth. 'We'd better head back before the weather breaks.'

I thought about Ryan, about Tommy. His hands over his face. Could he have been sad? Was it even possible?

'Mum?' I said.

It must have been something in the way I looked or the way I said it, but she shook her head and didn't answer me.

'Mum, I forgot to use the front door.'

She put her face in her hands and then slapped her palms on the table.

'One thing, Bernadette! I asked you to do one thing!' She rubbed her forehead. 'I'll have to go round.'

'No, Mum, you can't!'

'Bernadette!' She put one finger to her lips. 'I'm thinking.'

'Do we have to go back? Can't we stay here for a few days? A hotel?'

She stared at me and shook her head. 'Never look like you're running, Bernadette. Ever.'

She paid up and I unpeeled myself from the plastic seats, seeing how much sand I'd left behind. We crossed back to the car.

'Can I sit in the front this time?' I asked.

'Yes, that's fine. No talking, though, I need to concentrate.'

'I'm the oldest,' said Nancy.

'And that's why it would be better if you looked after Florence.'

I settled down in my seat. Out of the corner of my eye I could see Nancy frowning. I knew Mum just didn't want me to talk to her but I would have to eventually.

10

Now

Nancy was tired of everyone making pronouncements on Hurley but this was the only conversation that Bernie wanted to have. One mention of the trip to the doctor about his leg and every professional, like Bernie, wanted to discuss his life history. Nancy was used to people assuming they knew more about her son than she did. She reacted how she always did and shut down, listening to the noises in the background. The problem was that, however much they said they weren't judging her, she knew they were. She did her own research, anticipated their suggestions so she had her own list to give them.

'No, he doesn't eat processed food more than once a week.'

'No, he doesn't watch TV. He doesn't have any screen time at all, no violent video games.'

'No, he has a regular bedtime and doesn't get up until the morning.'

They had their suggestions, she'd followed them and now there were only a couple of options left. Ritalin or a special school, whatever they wanted to call it.

'So you're saying there's nothing wrong with him?' she asked Bernie.

'No, I'm saying there's nothing unusual about him.'

'At least once a week he has a violent tantrum. It isn't that usual.'

Bernadette started to look away. 'I'm interested in child-centred therapies, not ones that put the needs of the parents and teachers first.' She looked back, 'You really can't think of any specific triggers?'

Nancy could. People were a trigger. The main and only trigger. 'No. I can't think of anything.'

Bernadette sat back in her chair and tapped the table. 'He's been fine around the girls.'

'They haven't even spoken to him. They leave him alone and that's how he likes it.'

'Oh, I'm sure they have spoken to him a little bit.'

Nancy caught the slight blush to Bernadette's cheek.

'No. Not a word.'

Bernadette poured some more wine into her glass. The sun was setting over the other side of the house. Although they'd discovered that the best room was no longer locked to them they still chose to sit at the parlour table, where their aunts and great-aunts had sat and bickered like small children.

Bernadette looked out of the window as she gave her verdict. 'The problem is that the more rules he encounters, the more labelled he gets. The more labelled, the less taught he is. The less taught, the less learning he has. And then the rules become even more problematic and he becomes more challenging. Children don't want to get things wrong, they don't want to antagonise people. They'd much rather get everything right, and you have to behave as if they're trying to.'

Nancy leaned over to help herself to the bottle and topped up her glass too. 'Can you talk to Elian about it? He's entirely behind the pill route and this summer has been his cut off. Can't you tell him there are other priorities than getting him through a few exams?'

'Nancy, don't be ridiculous. He's your husband. You talk to him.'

Their first proper conversation by themselves, and Nancy felt as if she'd failed.

'Sorry, I just thought you'd be able to put it in the right way.'

'Because he thinks I'm some mental health expert?'

Nancy winced. 'Did he bring it up?'

'Just a bit.'

'Sorry.' Nancy drank half her glass down.

Bernie gave a weak smile. 'My past means I don't deserve privacy, apparently.'

'It's my past too. He's my husband. Of course I'm going to talk about my childhood.'

'Funny, because you've never spoken to me about it no matter how many times I begged.' Bernadette's eyes slid from Nancy. 'There are things I need to know.'

Nancy faced the window, still open although the meagre heat of the day had already gone. The wine warmed her though. She could feel a flush on her cheeks. Nancy looked out at the barn, at the steps, at the roof, at the open forever garage doors until she gave in and looked at Bernie. She was making an effort to think of her as Bernie, rather than Bernadette. Adrian called her Bernie. Even Elian did now. Saying Bernadette had started to sound like a rebuke.

Bernie's eyes had glazed over. She faced the door to Cassie's room and seemed to be looking through it to the room, to the window, to Bryn's Field beyond. Nancy turned to stare at the door too and started to become aware that she felt someone was going to open it. Someone was going to walk through it and into the parlour, and the thought terrified her. She quickly looked at Bernie who was already looking at her.

'Everything that happened to me, what do you put that down to? Before the therapy messed everything up.'

'The car.' Nancy tried to look definite. 'It was the shock and trauma of what happened in the car with Dad.'

'It was before that. It all happened right in front of you. What about before?'

'I know nothing more than you. We can't talk about it.'

'You don't know or you can't talk about it? Which one?' Bernie leaned over, 'We can go somewhere else. Anywhere. It doesn't have to be here.'

Nancy shook her head. 'There's nothing to say.'

'We were all guilty, Nancy, one way or another. I knew, everyone knew what was happening.'

Nancy made her voice light. 'So I don't need to say anything. Do I?'

Bernie sighed. 'What do you remember about Cassie's room?'

Nancy looked back at the door. 'Nothing much. We weren't allowed in there.' She twirled her glass and looked back to Bernie. 'What do you remember?'

Bernie looked down at the table. 'Doesn't matter.'

Nancy spread her hands out. 'I really don't remember.'

'Try.'

Nancy felt that this was a test. If she passed, a little bit of Bernie would be hers. She turned her seat to face the door. It was painted white, about a dozen times like every other door, so that there was a fat bulkiness to it. The outside handle was white.

'There's no inside handle,' Nancy said.

The doorframe was slightly lower and narrower than the other doors because it matched the cupboard door on the other side of the fireplace. It was a pretend door in a way that she'd liked as a child. It looked like a cupboard but wasn't. It was like the bell pushes in each room that looked as if they would ring like a bell, but they'd all been disconnected and didn't make any sound anywhere. She still liked to push them.

She thought her way into the room. About eight foot long by six foot across, a tiny window near the top of the far wall, no fireplace. Apart from the new little kitchen and the lobby it must be the only room without a fireplace downstairs.

'There were always boxes of crisps in there and it smelled

81

of apples, even when they'd all been eaten. Sacks of potatoes. I think there'd been meat in there once. Did it get used as a cold store for meat?'

Bernie had looked away now, her mouth covered by a hand. She was blinking a lot, as if there was a light shining into her eyes, but the sun had even left the rooftops now.

'Are you crying?'

'Go in the room.'

Nancy scraped her chair back, opened the door and walked into the room. It still smelled of apples.

'You don't remember anything do you?' said Bernie.

Nancy shook her head, 'Nothing else. I really don't, except it was kept locked a lot.' She didn't think that she'd ever looked out of the window. She'd never been tall enough. She walked across now and saw the vegetable bed, overgrown with tassels of fennel, in front of the hedge. A sparrow flew out, tweeting. In Michigan she'd been astonished by scarlet blackbirds, black squirrels and actual chipmunks which ran across the ground in front of you. She'd forgotten how pretty a sparrow was.

She turned back to the table. Bernie had gone, but that didn't surprise her. She became overwhelmed by the fear that Bernie was standing on the other side of the door, ready to close it on her. There was no door handle after all. She lunged for the doorway and stepped through with a sense of relief but, as she shut the door on the icy room, she realised that she must have forgotten something about that room. Something had made her not want to get shut in.

She sat back at the table. She would ask Bernie but knew that she had failed the test. Elian had gone on at length about how normal Bernie had been, how he'd never have suspected, how she hid or coped with her 'mental health problems' well. Nancy wasn't so sure. There were glimpses of that other Bernie, asking the unanswerable, disappearing from the room. She wasn't going to chase Bernie around the house.

She realised with a start that she didn't know where Hurley was. She checked the front room and the best room, then the bedrooms. From Hurley's back bedroom she saw them coming back through the archway. Hurley sat on the back door step watching Donn fill the peat basket outside the back door. Nancy exhaled and tried to relax her shoulders. She went back to the parlour trying to think about the last time she'd not consciously thought of him or been brought back to the thought of him somehow.

Nancy boiled the kettle in the kitchen and was about to offer Donn a cup of tea when she realised that Hurley and Donn were talking. Neither of them had said more than half a dozen words a day to her, or to Elian, unless they were absolutely forced to. What on earth could two such silent people have to say to each other?

She gazed out at them in surprise before finishing her own cup of tea. At the table she pulled the chair up by the window so it didn't squeak on the tiles and sat down as slowly as she could. And then she listened.

'I was younger than you. The warts covered my knees, dozens and dozens of them. You know we had to wear short pants then, I couldn't hide them. The warts that had everyone avoiding me at school and refusing to let me play football because they said if a wart was hit it might fly off and attach itself to them.'

'So what did she do?'

'Every first Sunday of the month, Da had a massive steak for his dinner. It was just always that way, I don't know why. So Mammy heard from someone, it might have been Mary's Ma, that steaks got rid of warts.'

'If you ate it?'

'Not if you ate it. That Sunday she was supposed to cook it, she woke me early and took me downstairs and rubbed it all over my legs. It was cold and slippery and made my legs pink. Then you had to bury it, so she did, really deep so the dogs couldn't smell it. They could smell me though. Da never quite looked at her in the same way, but as if she was touched in the head.'

'So what happened to the warts?'

'The idea was that, as the steak rotted away, they would too.'

'And?'

'They did,' said Donn. 'My legs became smooth and my knees knobbly in the normal way and I was allowed to play football. But she told everyone about the steak, my mammy. She bragged about it in the village and the news went round the parents, and round the children. And I was terrible at football. I'd never practised. When I missed the goal by a good ten feet, despite standing only two feet away, Dougal flipped.

'"You're mammy is a witch. Tell her to glue those warts back on and fly you away on her broomstick."

'That then went back round the children and up to the parents and no matter how much work Mammy did for the church after that it never got any better. I wished for my bobbly legs back that everyone laughed at because it was so much better than them laughing at me.'

'Did you have any friends?'

Donn's voice seemed to travel away from Nancy now, as if he'd sat down next to Hurley. 'Just the one. Tommy. He'd talk to me as we walked home. You know when people are only friends with you because they want something from you? It was like that. Took me a while to realise, but.'

Nancy got up to stop them talking but then sat down again. She didn't want Hurley to know about Tommy, to even know the name. It was too late now. If she made a fuss the name would stick. It was Bernie's fault, bringing up all the silence and locked doors.

They were quiet for a bit and then Hurley spoke.

'I haven't got any friends.'

'Some people don't need them. Sometimes it's better not to. I wouldn't worry about it. All you need is a good dog.'

There was a long silence. Nancy put her hands on the chair to push herself up quietly. It was time to call Hurley in. Then he spoke again.

'Do you miss your dog?'

'That one? He was good for the sheep but I always thought – well, you know, if I keeled over in the fields I thought no-one would ever find my body.' Donn laughed.

'You thought he'd eat you?' Hurley laughed too.

'I did, sometimes. There won't be any more dogs, but. There won't be any more farm.'

The girls in the front room started screaming. The door opened and they were herded upstairs to get ready for bed. Nancy closed her eyes and thought, when I've finished my tea I'll get Hurley up too. Then she heard the older girl complaining that Hurley wasn't in bed and she was no way going before him, even if he was older. She was clever and better and, and, and, and Nancy decided that Hurley could stay up for as long as he liked.

Hurley spoke quietly, so that Nancy nearly missed it. 'I like it here.'

'It suits some,' some Donn. 'I think it suits you.'

'Is Tommy still your friend?'

'He's around. I wouldn't call him a friend. He's just around.'

11

Then

Nancy made me get the biscuits. She had the ideas, I carried them out. I carried the blame, if necessary. If I got caught I knew she'd call me Bern for at least an hour.

We were getting a bit too big to sit under the table without being seen now. Nancy had to pull her feet right under her bottom and once she got cramp and had to roll out from there in full view of Father O'Shea. That time she got the blame, but I think she thought it was partly my fault. She was more careful after that to sit in a way which she could wiggle now and then.

Today our choice of shoes was our mother, Sister Agatha and Auntie Beth. We could be confident that they would talk constantly, being sisters. Me and Nancy would be like that when we were older. It was what sisters did. It was the only thing they did together, but we knew other sisters who went to the pub and things like that. One of Nancy's friend's mums even went clubbing with her sister, but she was far too old, older than thirty. Maybe she was so tarty she was allowed in so people could laugh at her. Nancy planned to go to a nightclub for her thirteenth birthday, because Sandra had her party there, but Mum said no way.

There were no laces on these shoes. I liked men's shoes best. I got a badge for my excellent knots at Brownies, but when Nancy left I didn't like it any more.

'Lord bless us and save us,' said Sister Agatha, and we knew it was about to get interesting.

'It's absolutely true,' said Beth, her left foot tapping its heel.

Sister Agatha turned her feet away from the table but didn't get up. She must have been looking out of the window because the conversation carried on with just Beth and Mum.

'They did,' said Beth. 'A herd of cows all over the garden. They'd had it designed by a proper company. Thousands of pounds chewed and trampled.'

Sister Agatha's voice was high. 'Thousands of pounds? What did they have, gravel made from gold chips?'

'Don't be silly,' Beth snapped.

My mother snorted.

'They had the topsoil brought over from somewhere . . . I can't remember where. Somewhere very fertile.'

'A farmyard? You should have brought them here.'

Agatha mumbled something. Nancy took the last biscuit and then broke it in half so we could share it. The crumbs that had fallen between us she swept roughly towards me.

My mother was talking. 'But accidents happen. Cows get out, farmers are incompetent, teenagers are mischievous. There are a million reasons that could have led to the cows in their garden.'

'True, but why not my garden?'

'Because it looks a bit rubbish? Because it's covered in thorn bushes?'

Beth's heel was tapping again. 'Ha ha. Funny. They took the bushes out and the garden was destroyed. I kept the bushes and my garden wasn't.'

'Clearly the fairies,' said my mother, and laughed, her legs swinging out. She caught Nancy's shoulder, but must have thought it was a table leg. 'Fairies, that's funny.'

'Not to God, it isn't,' mumbled Sister Agatha.

'Oh, Aggie,' said Mum, 'we remember when you thought

87

you could hear a banshee screaming out the front all night. Don't come over all holier than thou with us.'

Sister Agatha's feet turned back in to the table. 'I was six years old. And, as I remember it, it was you who put that idea in my head. She,' she must have pointed at Beth, 'is far too old for this nonsense.'

There was silence. Nancy and I stopped chewing, just in case. Beth crossed one leg over the other and starting kicking it violently towards my ear. Sister Agatha had both feet neatly paired up as if she'd stepped out of the shoes to get ready for bed. My mother pulled her feet backwards and then her chair.

'I'll freshen the pot,' she said. 'So when will the house be ready? You've been in that caravan since March. Weren't you planning to be in before the baby?'

'We've got three more weeks.'

'Maybe,' said my mother, 'but I bet it's before that. You've dropped.'

Beth hands appeared under the table, feeling her bump. 'No,' she said, but she didn't sound sure.

Now Sister Agatha's feet started to dance a little. 'That's going to be very difficult for you.'

'Oh shut up, you old prune.'

They went quiet again, apart from my mother who was making a racket emptying the pot, warming the pot, and generally banging it around to fill in the silence.

'Are you trying to break that?' said Beth.

'Yes,' said Sister Agatha, 'she never liked that teapot.'

'Not stylish enough for her, like her London china.'

They did this, rounded on each other in turn. There didn't seem to be any natural pairings, maybe because there were three of them. There had been two other sisters, but they didn't talk about them. That's how they got the bigger room though, when there were four boys.

We hadn't seen Donn all day. It was a bit of a relief after

what happened with the sheep yesterday. I didn't know how cross he could get until we finally stopped running and listened to him shouting, 'Stop running!' He looked at us like I'd seen him look at a dog worrying the sheep.

I shivered. Nancy nudged me and I turned to say sorry. She pointed out, from under the table, towards the dresser on the other side of the room. I looked at the dresser and shrugged. She poked her finger across and then bent it downwards. I saw a pea pod and it made me think of Ryan, of the peas falling from Sister Agatha's skirt. I made myself not look at the place beyond the table where the blanket had been. I'd tried to tell her about the gun and the blanket, but she didn't believe me about the gun and said a blanket meant nothing. She hated being left out.

Then I saw the mouse and turned to smile and nod. Nancy gathered up some of the crumbs between us and flicked them across the floor. She clicked her finger together silently to attract the mouse. And then Sister Agatha screamed. I slapped my hand to my mouth. Had my mother flipped and thrown the teapot at her? Nothing fell, nothing shattered. Sister Agatha just pushed her chair away from the table and then her feet disappeared. I saw a bit of a horror film once and when that happened the person had been eaten by a dinosaur insect. I squealed a bit. Nancy swore that I screamed louder than Sister Agatha but sometimes she's wrong.

My mother was pulling up the tablecloth to poke her face beneath it and there was a sudden groan from Beth. She stood up and water poured on to the floor, down her legs. My mother jumped away. We scrambled out from under the table. Sister Agatha was pointing at the mouse from on top of her chair.

'Has it started?' shouted my mother.

'Those girls have brought mice in!' shouted Sister Agatha from near the ceiling.

The house was a sudden whirl of closed doors, which we

were put outside, and panicked voices with Auntie Beth the loudest of all.

'You need to find Jackie!'

We sat on the stairs, out of sight of the phone, so we knew what was happening. Florence was crying and Auntie Beth was crying and Mum was phoning people and Agatha was making tea. It was better on the stairs.

'Oh my God,' whispered Nancy, 'you made her baby come! You're in soooo much trouble!' Her eyes sparkled and she hugged herself.

'I didn't!'

She smiled at me. 'It's the funniest thing ever.'

I tried to smile back but couldn't.

Mum put the phone down and saw us.

'Go and find Jackie!'

We had wandered around the barns and then settled back to making bows and arrows under the monkey puzzle tree.

'Victorians thought that their baby would look like the last thing they saw,' said Nancy. 'If the baby has hairy, pointy ears it will be your fault.'

'You're making it up,' I said.

'I'm not,' she sang. 'They wouldn't go to the zoo if they were pregnant.'

'But I didn't put the mouse there. They've had mice before, I've seen the mousetraps.' They were grey and spiky with half an Opal Fruit that had gone hard. Mum caught me trying to set one off with a matchstick.

Nancy took her penknife from her pocket and cut off another springy sapling. She made a show of stripping off the leaves with the knife, even though it was dull and took two or three energetic swipes for each side.

'How do you know that anyway, about the Victorians?'

'Sandra's mum told her. That's why her younger brother looks different to her and her older brother.' Nancy lowered her voice and I leaned in. 'Sandra said that her mum was really pregnant and she opened the door one night and there was a black man standing there with a basket of kittens for sale and she got such a fright her waters broke there and then.' Nancy's voice returned to normal. 'And that's why her brother looks coloured when he's not.'

I thought this over. 'So why didn't he look like a kitten?'

'Well, I don't know. He might have done. Maybe they were brown kittens.' Nancy went back to carving her stick. 'Turn back, don't watch. I've never seen a brown kitten though.'

'Do you think Auntie Beth will keep it if it does look like a mouse?'

'She'll have to. What else is she going to do with it?' She signalled with her stick. 'You can turn back round now. I need the string.'

I pulled the ball of string from my pocket and handed it to her.

'You'll have to help me knot it. Hold the stick for me.'

Nancy did terrible knots. I held the white, skinned stick and imagined a white, mousy baby. It could have a tail, and then Auntie Beth would make a fortune from charging people to look at him and she might give me some. I wouldn't mind a tail.

'Turn it this way.'

I turned it.

'Hold it tighter, dumbo.'

I frowned and held it so that all of her pulling to make the string taut hardly moved my hands at all. She was finally happy and took the bow back. It didn't twang much but she started to search for a good arrow. I sat down on one of the hummocks that I knew had a tractor tyre underneath the grass because I remembered when you could still see the tyre. Now it was completely greened over, with some longer, feathery grass growing from the middle. I thought that Donn had just wanted to hide the tyres instead of taking them wherever you take old tyres, but now I liked these soft stools. I lay down, around the edge, and looked up at the sky beyond the pale grass feathers. It was cloudy. It was usually cloudy, but that was fine. We would have gone out even if it was raining because we liked it. At home Mum would keep us in but here it rained too often so we always had our wellies on and then she didn't mind. I worried that one day Nancy would be too old to come out and make bows and arrows, but there wasn't anything better to do, she said. I was so pleased every time she came out because after a year at comprehensive I thought she might say it any time. When she got too old I would have to be too old because Florence was small and awful.

'Accidents,' Nancy had said, before she told me how babies were made. I called her a big, fat liar so I didn't have to think about it right then. I didn't think Florence could be an accident or why didn't everyone have twenty accidental babies. And Mum seemed to like her anyway, and Dad avoided her as much as he did us. Nancy said she was an accident because she was a girl, and they must have wanted a boy. I thought that meant that we must be accidents, but she said one girl was just a girl and a second girl should have been a boy. I cried then and we just called Florence the Not Boy so I could feel better.

Nancy had trimmed her arrow, leaving a bit of leaf at one end. The wood was too green to go to an actual point, but it splayed out more every time she drew the knife across it. I'd read a book where they made bows and arrows that actually worked, but I couldn't remember what kind of wood you were supposed to use. I didn't know what kind of wood she was using either, in any case. I rested my cheek on the grass so I could see Nancy. She stood side on to the tree, pulled the string back and the arrow fell to the ground.

'It's not long enough,' I said.

'Thanks, smarty pants.'

She knew worse words than that, so I knew she wasn't really angry. She untied the string on the bow, sawed at it for a bit before giving up and snapping a bit off. She gave it to me to retie the string. She had to pull it tighter this time because it was shorter and took ages to do the knot how she wanted it.

I looked over her shoulder towards the house, but Jackie's car was still there. I felt guilty now that he was missing the excitement of his mouse-baby. Nancy took the bow and I climbed onto the hillock.

'I think we should find Jackie,' I said.

She shrugged. 'Go on then.'

He wasn't in the paddock by the house and, although I could see over the hedge, I couldn't see into the field properly because of the massive rhododendrons. I jumped off and found a hole to look through. It was like using a telescope, moving around to see different parts of the field. I saw him and opened my mouth.

I ran back and sat on the hillock, my arms around my knees.

'What is it?'

'Tommy's over there.'

Nancy dropped the bow to her side, stood on the tyres and looked across. She looked like a hunter. She jumped down and smiled.

'Let's go upstairs and watch him.'

She ran inside. I thought about it and then followed her.

Mum's stuff was everywhere in that room. By the time Dad arrived she'd have sorted it all out for him and would be using the drawers, instead of leaving the suitcase open on the chair. We crept over her pile of clothes because we knew that, however much there seemed to be no order, she could tell when we had been in. She liked having a room to herself, she said. She hadn't had it as a child, she didn't have it as a married woman. She only had it for the first five weeks of the summer holiday before our dad arrived for the last. We didn't have a room to ourselves either, I shared with Nancy at home as well as here, and the NB had the small bed because she still sometimes wet herself through the nappy, so I could understand this. I would keep my room tidier if I had it to myself, though, so it seemed even bigger.

Nancy had made it to the window and had crouched on the commode chair. It didn't smell or anything, but I just didn't like touching it. If this was my bedroom I'd put it somewhere else. Like the silo.

I bent down behind Nancy and lifted my head to the same height as hers, but just to the side. We'd crept in here before, mostly to look in Mum's suitcase, but there was a great view from here of the monkey puzzle tree. The one in front of our window had become familiar, but this had different twists. As from our window, there was no good view of the driveway, because of the trees. But the field to the left of the house looked wide and sloping in a flat way and we could see the stone pile in the corner, and Donn, Jackie and Tommy standing near it. There were sheep in the field as well, of course, and Bruce had lain down, almost flat to the ground, watching them.

'Can you see what they're doing?' I asked.

Nancy had her head just to the left of me and I was sure she could see more.

'They've got a bag on the ground,' she said.

I said, 'That's Bruce.'

'Behind Tommy, not in front of him. It might be black, but I can tell the difference between a bag and a dog.' She rolled her eyes. 'I can't see what's in it. Tommy looks angry though.'

He did. His arms swung between Donn and Jackie, over to the road and back to the stones. None of the sound of his voice travelled to the house, or not through the shaking glass, in any case.

'Should we tell him? Jackie, I mean?' I said.

'I'm not interrupting them. You can.' Nancy looked as if she was going to dare me. 'I think you should.'

'Not a chance.' I tried to make it sound as final as I could because once she started to push I found it really hard to say no. 'You're the one he likes.'

She sat down on the commode chair and I stayed in a half bent position.

'I think you're wrong about seeing Ryan's bag.'

'Yeah, you said.'

'Mum said he phoned from London. Ryan is totally fine. It was just a bag.'

'And the gun?'

'I don't think you'd recognise a gun. It was probably a spanner.'

Nancy smirked. I knew that was the version that Sandra would hear. Clever Nancy and stupid Bernadette. I think if Ryan had phoned – well, I would just have known.

She turned to look out of the window, her head recklessly higher.

'They'll see you.'

'They won't.'

Jackie was talking the most now, but his palms were upturned. He didn't look angry. Donn was still standing with his arms crossed, one foot in front of the other. I couldn't see him rock his weight from one to the other, but I would bet he was. I had seen him do that when priests were in the house, especially when Sister Agatha had abandoned him in a corner with a particularly cross one.

Tommy was pointing to the bag on the ground now. Donn put his hands up, palms towards Tommy, and started to nod. Jackie shrugged, like he was sorry for something, and picked the bag up. It only went up a little, like it was really heavy, and he put it down again. We heard Sister Agatha calling his name from the gate near the back of the house, next to the cows. He turned and Donn put his hands to his mouth.

Jackie held his hand up to Sister Agatha and began to walk, backwards, to the gate. Tommy and Donn stood still for a while. When Jackie and Sister Agatha were out of sight, they quickly acted together to drag the bag into the hole between the stones in the corner of the field.

'Come down,' I said. 'They'll be coming back now.'

Nancy pushed me out of the way a bit to stare down. 'I don't think Bruce likes Tommy, you know.' Then she gasped and ducked too quickly, banging her head on the arm of the chair.

'He saw you?'

She nodded, one hand to her head. She checked for blood on her fingertips, but there was no cut, no distraction. We'd been warned and now we'd been caught. I bit my fingernails and we then we both jumped as we heard Sister Agatha's footsteps on the stairs.

'Where are youse?' she shouted.

We left the room, our heads low. She didn't seem to notice which room we'd come out of as Nancy closed the door behind us.

'I'm off to the hospital with Jackie. Florence is in the kitchen so you need to come and mind her. Donn will be back in soon and he'll fetch your tea. OK?'

We looked at her.

'OK?'

We nodded.

'Agatha,' I whispered, 'is Tommy staying?'

'No, he's gone. I wouldn't . . . He's already gone.' She ran back downstairs, 'And stay out of my room!'

Donn was in charge. I wasn't sure how I felt about that. We'd had dinner, but could he cook? No man cooked in this house.

'You're going to have to cook,' I said to Nancy.

'Maybe you'll have to kill what I cook,' she sneered.

Sister Agatha ran back. 'And three rosaries each to pray for the safe delivery!' And was gone.

'Bern, I haven't seen my beads for ages.'

I knew where they were, but I didn't want to say.

She kicked me. 'Bern! Where've you put it? You must have mine too.'

'We left them in the stable.'

12

Now

Bernie had laughed at the thought of retracing their dad's car wheels.

'You never liked those trips, Nancy. You always wanted to go shopping with Mum.'

'So? I'd like to see them now.'

'All that time I wasted looking at them. There's a whole modern country here and he wasn't interested in anything built less than a thousand years ago. We'll go off somewhere else. Maybe see what's on at the cinema in Belfast.'

Nancy saw her look sideways at Hurley. She was clearly conscious that it might upset him, but was it a deliberate or accidental clumsiness? Bernie hadn't looked Nancy in the eye since she failed her test.

'I'd really like our families to spend some time together.' Nancy waited. 'Maybe another day we can plan something.' She turned to Donn. 'Can we borrow the car?'

'You can,' he said. 'I don't need it today.'

'Are you insured?' asked Bernie.

'I'm sure we'll be fine.' Nancy hadn't talked to Elian about not having any insurance and assumed he had weighed up the option of staying in or risking it. She wasn't going to bring it up if he didn't.

Hurley said, 'Mom, Donn said I could work with him today.'

'Donn works every day. He'll still have work for you tomorrow.'

Hurley looked at Donn, who nodded.

'Always more to do tomorrow,' he said.

'And you should wait a couple more days before you get really dirty. The bandage is off but it isn't quite healed.' Nancy picked up her bag from the table and looked at Bernie. 'Have a good time.'

Bernie nodded. Elian and Hurley followed Nancy out to the yard.

'Got the map?' she asked.

Elian rolled his eyes. 'Map. I haven't had to find my way by map for how many years? What kind of country doesn't have proper mobile coverage? GPS isn't some strange new-fangled idea, it's vital to all sorts of things.'

Nancy sighed. 'Do you have the map?'

'Yes, yes, I do.' Elian lifted it from the floor of the car and slowly began to open the pages with a rough flick.

'Do you know where we are?'

'Yeah.' He kept on flicking.

Nancy started the car and pulled out of the yard.

'We'll be near enough to Belfast to get some reception, I guess. You can get all of your emails through in one go, and I bet there won't be more than one that's worth replying to.' She stopped at the end of the lane. 'I'm turning right, if you want to find us on the map.'

'Great.'

'I'll just wait till you're sure.'

Hurley sighed, 'Can we just go?'

She pulled away. The sky was bright, although there were thin clouds, and the wet roads shone. At the end of the road she turned right again, not bothering to check with Elian. She knew the way to Belfast roughly and hoped that their destination would be signposted so that she didn't have to ask him anyway. He was flicking randomly through the pages now. It covered all of Great Britain and she was pretty sure that he was in Scotland, now Northumberland. She tried not to look, tried to keep her eyes on the road. Drive on the left. The hills swelled and subsided to the right, mists formed and cloud shadows thickened. It was green, as Elian said whenever anyone asked him how he was finding it. Very green.

Hurley was slumped against the window, looking up at the sky. What would he say? Very grey, it's all very grey. It was good how he'd started to talk to Donn. He hadn't exchanged a word with the girls and seemed to take all of Bernie's questions as part of a test he couldn't possibly pass so wouldn't bother. Nancy didn't blame him. He was fine though. He seemed fine. At home there was so much tension, so many questions to ask him at the end of every day – did you get in trouble, did you manage to stay in class for a whole lesson? It was nice not having to check on him, but she felt as if she didn't really have anything to say either.

School was stressful and knowing that he had no friends made her cry at night. Doctors and behavioural therapists and educational psychologists made up the majority of her contacts. Work had slipped from her mind and she sat for days at the workbench without picking up a pencil or a pair of scissors. Her ambitions had become fuzzy and the less she talked about it the less Elian remembered that she had a job too.

'No, I can't take him for that appointment. And it's not like you're busy.'

I am, she wanted to protest, I am busy. There's so much to do and organise and I'm disappearing into the role of carer.

'I escort Hurley and I justify Hurley and I apologise for Hurley, but there are other things that I want to be doing.'

'But they can wait, can't they? If I don't go to work we don't eat. That's what it comes down to.'

Soon she needed the car so much that she had to drive Elian to work, Hurley to school, pick him up and drive him to one appointment or another, and then collect Elian, who was too tired to cook, again. Her time, the time that really belonged to her, had shrunk back and back until she didn't know what to do with it anymore. She was just a facilitator for their lives.

They walked across to the Giant's Ring from the car park. Elian read aloud to Hurley from a brochure he'd borrowed from Bernie.

'It's about two hundred metres across with an internal ditch. That's what makes it a henge, Hurley. Late Neolithic or Early Bronze Age. What does that mean? How old is that, Nancy?'

Nancy walked away. 'Same as Stonehenge.'

'When was that though?' Elian shouted after her, 'It's your history! How would I know?'

Take away his phone and suddenly Elian's stupidity was revealed. It reminded her of the days before smartphones. What was that? When did that happen? Strings of questions emerged which Nancy wouldn't have minded answering so much if she had any certainty that he would remember the answers. Instead the same question came up again and again.

'You've asked me that,' she'd say.

'No, I don't think I have,' he'd reply, quite certain.

He clearly hadn't had any questions to ask at the farm, his mind stilled with Bernie's noise, Bernie's children. Now he started on Hurley.

'Surely you've done this period at school, Hurley.'

Hurley shrugged. 'No.'

'You must know. The Neolithic, what do you think? You've heard of Stonehenge, right?'

Hurley shrugged again.

Nancy walked towards the stones to get out of hearing. She could picture the pages her father had shown her, of the wooden posts driven into the ground in circles around the stones. Two hundred and fifty trees, making a new, manmade forest to denote new, manmade ideas. Maybe they would have made a ritual pathway and instead of jogging for the stones as she was now, the approach would be made indirect, respectfully circling them before arrival.

She touched the stones. There was nothing magical in the contact, it was just an acknowledgement of their age and her presence. This is why she would never return to Stonehenge, fenced off, precious, but would willingly go back to Avebury. It wasn't communion or prayer or magnetic powers, but just being through touching.

She walked around the side of the chamber. She could probably fit in there, between the stones. The thought of hiding from Elian, watching him look around for her with increasing anxiety made her giggle. When she crawled out or, worse, was found, she'd feel bad, though. Especially if Hurley was worried. She didn't think Hurley would be worried. She turned to watch him now, leaning with her back against one of the upright stones. He was separate from Elian who was holding his phone above his head, as if it would be any use to get a signal so high that he couldn't read what was on it. Hurley was walking the embankment, slowly as if he was the only person there. He was, she supposed, as far as he was concerned.

Nancy ran her hands over the rock and laid her head against it. She remembered this silent touching from other stones she'd visited, other outings she'd been dragged to, complaining that 'stones are all the same'. She missed this random and thoughtless history when she was in America. They despised ageing and erased it, claiming newer was bigger and better. It wasn't. How long would her house last when they left it? A decade or so, and then the nineties would become a vilified period and the new thirties or forties would offer something more sprawling or more compact, more insulated or weather resistant. She would never get used to the lack of bricks in their houses, those strange American people she was still bewildered by. The thunderstorms shook the walls and the roof jumped as the massive raindrops hammered against it. It was a house that denied the outside. The windows weren't designed to open – that's what air conditioning was for. She'd set up her separate space in the basement, refusing all of Elian's desires for a rumpus room for the boys. Elian built a man-shed instead.

In the basement the only electric outlet fed a single lamp, angled over her workbench, and a radio tape deck. That was it – no TV, no fridge for beers and no pool table. No rumpus. If it was hot she opened the window and if it was cold she wrapped up. If it was really cold, as those Michigan winters often were, she might swap the radio for a small electric heater, but usually she moved her current projects to the kitchen table where they could be examined better. Only since all the trouble with Hurley, there hadn't been many projects. Her source of ideas, her love of shape and colour, had faded into ideas that were half formed and then discarded. The thought of planning ahead, crafts for Easter at Christmas, for summer at Easter, for Halloween and Thanksgiving and Christmas in the summer, made her feel vertiginous. She began to dream of falling, uncontrollable plummets into nothingness. And all the time, the thought, what do I do next, what can I do next, what comes next?

The plan for this trip came out of that, if she was honest. Maybe she needed to see trees that weren't pruned, grass that was not cut. Maybe she needed to walk out of her house and keep on walking without being made to feel odd or weird or some kind of socially incompetent reject. They'd been for drives in the countryside when she first met Elian and she thought he was joking when they didn't arrive anywhere, but home. A 'road trip' was just that, a trip along roads, to look at what they passed, like the buffalo. She asked if they could go somewhere and get out of the car. He drove her down the I-96 to Canada and let her get out of the car just long enough to realise how much more she liked Canada than the US. He hadn't told her that she needed a passport to get back into America until this point because 'he'd never been stopped, not once'. And they had ended up in the only queue that was being stopped and she had to attempt an American accent. Elian laughed all the way home and she thought she would never forgive him.

Another time, when Hurley was a baby, they took the I-96 in the other direction. At Lake Michigan they stood on the shore, and that's when she realised it. There was nothing she wanted to see here. The land around the lake was flat, the view went on for miles. Behind her were forests and swamps all the way to Canada. She was with a man who thought a fun day out involved cruise control and seat-belts that rode over her to do themselves up. I have no choices, she thought. I want to go home. Elian told her that would be the worst time to go home, that she had to ride it out and wait until it didn't seem home anymore.

For a while she clung to the way she initially liked the weirdness of drive-in banks and sushi and massive shopping malls bordered by even larger car parks. She'd liked the way that everything in America was exactly how she expected it to look from watching TV, all the low slung eateries along the endless straight roads. By the time Hurley was three she found herself paralysed in supermarkets unable to buy any food because the choices seemed too many. An hour and thirty minutes were wasted in front of the milk aisle, trying to find a bottle that didn't have added vitamins or reduced fat or extra cream. She was still standing there when Elian arrived. She never found out who'd phoned him to tell him where she was.

'I'm allergic to America,' she said.

'Don't worry, we have pills for that,' she heard.

The noise of children drew her back. Hurley had left the wall and was heading towards her. A group of boys headed over the embankment and formed goalposts with their jackets. She shivered to see their bare arms. Now she saw, too, the half dozen dog walkers and the child climbing up the stones behind her. Elian was still waving his phone at the clouds.

'Shall we go?' she said to Hurley, head bent down to his chest. He nodded. He was so quiet, so calm. She could relax and just like him here. This place suited him. She wanted it to last forever. With or without Elian.

13

Then

Donn did make tea, kind of. Ham sandwiches weren't quite the same as what we normally ate, and I wondered what Bruce would eat if there were no leftovers. He looked quite pleased with himself until he got the phone call about six o'clock from my mother.

'She says the baby is taking ages and you all have to put each other to bed.'

'Are you sure she didn't say you should put us to bed?' I asked.

'No.' Donn was a terrible liar. 'Youse two have to put the wee one to bed, and then Nancy has to put you to bed.'

'Mum would never say that, not in a million years!'

Nancy smugly agreed with him. 'We can do that.'

'And who puts Nancy to bed?' I demanded.

'Your mammy says she's quite old enough.'

'That is completely unfair.' I stamped as I jumped off the chair and folded my arms.

'Shall I call her back?' asked Donn.

'At the hospital? You can't.'

'Oh yes I can, because I forgot to ask whether I was allowed to smack anyone who was really naughty.'

I examined his face. Sometimes he lied so badly it was almost like he was telling the truth.

'Fine!' I waited for Nancy to give me my instructions. I would memorise them and tell Mum exactly what she'd told me to do, and what I'd had to think of myself. Like brushing Florence's teeth. I hoped she'd forget that, and then I'd be the best. 'Now what?'

'Nancy is in charge,' said Donn.

I mimicked him, 'Pantsy is in charge.'

He held a finger towards me and mimed a smack. Nancy glowed, then grabbed Florence by her arms and said, 'Bedtime.'

She looked surprised, and started to follow her but Nancy stopped at the door.

She spoke hesitantly, 'Who is going to change Florence's nappy?'

'You're in charge, Nancy,' said Donn.

I hugged myself. 'I'll make sure she cleans her teeth.'

Upstairs she tried every bribe she knew, names, birthday money, sweets, but none of it was worth it. I knew her. I'd be pooey, stinky, nappy hand Bernadette. She knew it and I knew it. My trump was that I could promise not to tell anyone about it.

She did the nappy, I had to do teeth, pyjamas and stories. It was worth it.

When Florence was in bed, not asleep, but in bed, we had a quick root around in the drawers of the dressing table. Usually when we started to do this our mum or an aunt would walk in and tell us to get out and stop being so nosy.

The last time we'd just found some sanitary towels and neither of us knew we shouldn't be flapping them in the air. Now Nancy had started her periods she treated them with proper reverence. Behind them were some things with American flags on, from the siblings who'd gone to America, and some with Australian flags from the other sibling.

We vaguely remembered those lost siblings. Really we remembered how there was suddenly more space in the beds as the aunts left, and less of a feet smell by the fire when the uncles left. There were books as well, bad books. Nancy had

107

taken *Jaws* out before and hidden it under her pillow, but someone found and replaced it. She didn't really want to read it, I think, just show me the cover and then watch me run back from the sea to Mum. I did think I might have seen a fin, but it was a bit too small to be a man-eater, probably.

After we'd had a good, thorough look, we gave the NB dire threats of punishment, and went downstairs, like the grown-ups.

'You don't have to put me to bed until Donn tells you, really.'

She tossed her hair back. 'I'm not sure that's what he meant, Bernadette. He said that I was in charge, so it's my decision.'

I knew I was quite safe. However much Nancy was desperate to send me to bed, I was more fun than Donn. I saw her struggle a bit with the choice though. She settled on bossing me about.

'You can stay up five more minutes if you get me a biscuit. Ten minutes if you manage a slice of cake.'

Beth's cake that she'd brought round for the afternoon hadn't been finished yet. Donn wouldn't have put it away, so it would have been easier, really, than finding where Sister Agatha had hidden the biscuits this time. That just meant getting around Donn. I assumed he was in the kitchen. It was very quiet, though.

'Nancy, do you think Donn knows he can't go out and leave us on us own? You don't think that, when he said you were in charge, that you were really in charge, do you?'

'Oh, God! Did you hear him go out?'

'No, I can't hear anything. I'm scared to go in the kitchen by myself.'

'Don't be silly,' she said, but her hand was near her mouth like she didn't want to scream too loud.

I said, 'If you want some cake you have to come with me.'

She nodded and we crept towards the parlour door. As

108

my fingers touched the handle we heard the lobby door to the parlour close and Donn's voice. I breathed out in relief.

'Who's he speaking to?' asked Nancy.

We waited for Donn to stop talking so the other one would speak.

Donn said, 'Just the girls.'

Another voice said, 'Those bitches definitely in bed?'

Tommy's footsteps came towards the door and we had no chance to run away. He opened it and looked down at us.

Nancy gabbled, 'We were just coming to tell Donn that we're going to bed too. Florence is asleep.'

'And how are you, Nancy?'

She looked at me and then back. 'Fine.'

'Not hearing anything you shouldn't?'

She shook her head too hard. I saw her cheeks start to redden.

'No bogey stories to keep you up, no?'

His eyes had moved to me now and I felt the blush heat my own cheeks.

'That's enough teasing, Tommy,' said Donn.

Tommy stood to the side for Donn to talk to us.

'Good girls. I'll see you in the morning.'

Tommy said nothing more to us, but closed the door hard. We knew he hadn't moved away. He was listening for us to go upstairs. We trod on each step as heavily as we could and sat at the foot of our bed without getting undressed. The massive picture of Jesus, with his red heart hovering outside his body, hung above our bed. The heart had a cross stuck right through the middle of it. There was a golden halo around his head and he looked up to heaven without lifting his head, so there was lots of white in his eyes. I wondered whether Sister Agatha had put it here, and the statue of Mary on the bedside table and the cross on the mantelpiece, just for us, or if they were here before her.

We got into bed without brushing our teeth because we

didn't want to get caught on the landing. My teeth felt furry and I knew Mum would be cross if she found out. I promised myself to brush twice as long in the morning. I wished she was back. The sheets felt uncomfortable and I spent ages trying to straighten out the wrinkled blankets on top. I lay down but couldn't settle. I turned towards Nancy but she didn't look at me.

'You won't ever, ever tell him that I said anything, will you?'

She shook her head.

'Do you really think Ryan is okay?'

She closed her eyes and faced away from me. I turned the other way and looked at the fireless fireplace. I wished there was a fire now, but there had never been any fires upstairs. If I could watch the flames I might go to sleep. I thought about the way Father Christmas always knew how to find us even though we didn't really live here. It always amazed me, but Nancy wouldn't talk about him anymore. She just smirked when I said anything.

Neither of us said anything now. We were too busy listening and waiting for Tommy to leave.

'Stay awake, won't you Bernie?' whispered Nancy.

I nodded. She went to sleep before me, her head angled up against my back.

14

Now

'I heard from Agatha today. Well, she mentioned me in a note to Donn. She wanted me to give you her address.'

'Yes, Beth gave it to me too.' Her mother sighed. 'That means she wants letters, doesn't it? I can't remember how to write a letter any more. Can't you tell her just to go on Facebook?'

Nancy laughed feebly and rubbed her temple. 'Yeah, right.'

'Have you ... Has ...' She heard her mother inhale, 'How's things?'

'Difficult.' Nancy lifted the phone base from the table, sat on the floor and placed it next to her.

'Is it Bernadette?'

'Yes.'

'Is she there?'

Nancy looked up to the landing, checked the doors off the hall were all closed. 'Somewhere. Around.' She lowered her voice, 'She's pretty much avoiding me. I didn't say what she wanted, it seems.'

Her mother didn't say anything. She heard her moving things, the slide and click of something hundreds of miles away. There were birds in the background. Her mother could have the window in the front room open, or maybe she was in the garden. The joys of a cordless phone. What she wasn't doing was squatting by the stairs in a dark hallway. The meagre glow from the skylight was sickly.

Her mother cleared her throat. 'This is your only chance to ever sort it out. You'll go back over there, she'll come back over here and this opportunity will be lost forever.'

'Mum, what does she need to hear? Do you know?'

'No, I don't know for sure. You know her, she's had a lot of odd ideas over the years.'

Nancy didn't believe her. There was something strained in her tone.

'Just try, Nancy. Try to make it all right.'

'I don't know if I can, Mum. I think she really hates me. I can't work out what I need to say and she won't forgive me until I do. It's an impossible situation. I can't win.'

Nancy heard a sob.

'I want all three daughters at my funeral, Nancy. I've given up on hoping that I'll see you all at a birthday or a wedding. I've given up hoping that your father will see all of his grandchildren –'

'We'll visit –'

Her strained voice was high, 'You have to sort it out.'

The phone call went dead. Nancy held the handset and imagined her mother crying in her front room or the garden, just quickly, before wiping her eyes and pushing it all back down again. That's what she'd seen before she left, that's what she'd seen in her mind during every phone call.

She heard a voice and put the phone back to her ear.

'The other person has cleared. The other person has cleared. The other person has cleared.'

Nancy put the phone back and placed it back on the table next to the same oriental vase with the same silk flowers and peacock feathers next to the same grey phone and small lamp that had always been there. The Bakelite door handles and finger-plates, white on the hall side and black on the room side. Empty locks with swinging covers to stop spying eyes, all the keys lost except the one for the best room. The same house that it had always been. And different.

112

She pushed up from the floor, leaned back against the stairs and looked up at the skylight. She saw the thick banisters and could almost hear small footsteps avoiding the squeaky boards, hugging the dark corners. Bernadette had been the braver, had never said no to anything. Nancy had been egged on by this knowledge time and again to try harder, do more, fear less. She could follow in her path and Bernie would still think that Nancy was the leader. Surely it had been both of them together giving each other the confidence to try everything? But now Bernie and her mother were making it entirely Nancy's responsibility.

She heard movement in the lobby and the parlour and ran upstairs. Her hand was on the handle to her bedroom when she noticed Bernie's door was open and the room quiet. She looked around and then went in there instead. She wouldn't be long. Someone was bound to come up soon.

From the way clothes were thrown on the floor and beds it was clear Adrian was sleeping in the single, Bernie and the girls in the double bed. She was pleased by this. It was still a bed for girls to whisper in at night and make unsuitable plans.

Nancy saw that Jesus with the glowing heart was still hanging above the headrest, solemn Mary was still on the mantelpiece. She'd imagined that Bernie would have hidden them somewhere out of sight. She walked to the fireplace and sat on the bed. This had been Bernie's side and she had envied it during the day, and then been grateful at night that she was that little bit further away to the gaping hole in the wall, the shadowy chimney. One night a bird had become stuck inside and sent soot ghosting around the room. Nancy had screamed. Bernie had covered her mouth and frozen upright. Nancy had teased Bernie about it later, about how it was a banshee trying to get in, even though they'd both seen Agatha pull the dead bird out in the morning, her arm blackened and her dress made grey by the ash. Nancy didn't

113

look but Bernie did, and it was only then that she cried. She'd got into Florence's bed for a few nights after that until Nancy refused to go to bed at all because she didn't want to be closest to the chimney and whatever might come down it.

Nancy looked at the single bed. Bernie had often ended up with Florence when she was upset or scared. She'd always thought of her and Bernie being much closer than Bernie and Florence, but when it came down to it she suspected Florence was Bernie's favourite. And Bernie was Mum's favourite as a child, with her blue eyes and infectious laugh that triggered something in everyone, except Agatha. And there, behind her, Nancy had been pushing her, provoking her to create new boundaries and new levels of naughtiness that she could hide behind.

She stood up and noticed the small enamel pot still on the mantelpiece beside Mary. She lifted the lid to see half a dozen tiny shells, the ones that Bernie was so good at finding. She lifted one out but couldn't tell if they'd been found last week or thirty years ago. Some things didn't age.

She touched the bell push on the wall next to the fireplace and turned to leave. Bernie made her jump.

'What are you doing?'

Nancy thought of the shells, the bird, the nights of whispering.

'I don't know really. Thinking about what things were like, before.'

Bernie closed the door, 'Before what?'

Nancy walked to the window. 'Before. When we were small. This room is one of my strongest memories but we can't have spent that much time in here. We were always outside.' She looked down the drive. 'I still expect to see Bruce.'

Bernie sat on the end of the single bed and said nothing.

'Remember how we'd feed him Sugar Puffs in the parlour? That must have been terrible for his teeth. And he stank, greasy like a sheep, but it didn't bother us at all.' Nancy rubbed her hands, thinking of how she could roll off his dirt in ribbons, but not the smell.

Bernie pointed down. 'Why do you let Hurley out by himself?'

'He's fourteen. He can't walk around where we live. There's nowhere to walk to and he hasn't got any friends to visit. I like it that he wants to.'

'There are murderers here, bodies right here.'

Nancy watched her rub her hands against each other. What would happen if Bernie fell into madness again? Would Adrian wait for her or take her children?

'Bern, everything's fine. Hurley's quite safe.'

'He got away with it again and again because no-one listened and no-one saw and no-one said.'

'Bern, Dad didn't do anything. You have to accept that.'

Bernie snapped round. 'Not him. Tommy.'

The sound of footsteps on the stairs made them both jump. Erin and Maeve ran in, slammed the door open and then stopped when they saw Nancy. Nancy looked at Bernie. Her face had changed, become relaxed and normal.

'Everything all right, girls?'

Nancy walked past the girls and noticed them edge away from her. She started shaking as she got to her bedroom. She lay down and stared at the ceiling. She felt around Tommy's image, dark hair and blue eyes, always in dark blue jeans. He'd been kind to Nancy, but she remembered being anxious around him too. But then, she usually had been anxious around boys she fancied. He was older, too old than would be normal now to be spending time with a girl of eleven, twelve, but not a murderer. Not him.

Elian came in and closed the door. Nancy bolted upright.

'Jesus! Don't creep up on me.'

He looked confused. 'I didn't.'

'Sorry.' She covered her face. 'Sorry.'

115

'What's the matter?'

'I think Bernie might be having another breakdown. She's talking about bodies. She's going to start accusing someone else, of murder this time. I don't know what to do. Should I phone someone?'

'Just talk to Adrian. If anyone will know she's in trouble, it's him.'

She nodded. 'You're right.'

But she knew she couldn't talk to Adrian about it.

15

Then

On the roof of the kitchen extension, a cold, big larder where the turkey was always left, no feathers but head still on, there were two kittens. We were desperate to coax them down. Donn was at the kitchen table, talking to Sister Agatha. If he caught our eye he would point at the kittens and shake his head. We put our heads down, walked over to Bruce and carefully ignored the kittens until we were sure he'd looked away again.

Then we made squeaky noises and clicked our fingers together and did everything but try and pull them down by their tails.

'It's your fault,' said Nancy, 'you're being too noisy. Just let me do it.'

I stood still. I wanted to stroke them more.

'Stand over there.' She pointed to the garage doors. I took a small step backwards, then another.

Nancy had no more luck than we'd had together and I was glad. She would never have let me have a go. Donn rapped on the window and signalled for her to go to the garage doors. She stood beside me and glared at him. The kittens stayed where they were.

Bruce was also unhappy about this and more persistent in distracting us than Donn. While the sulky, squealing kittens ignored us, he sat at our feet waiting for a sign that we still loved him. I gave in first, sat on the back doorstep and he came over. With a relieved sigh he flipped himself onto his back, two legs in the air, and closed his eyes. I began to tickle his tummy, his chest, back to his tummy where I found that bit that made his legs shake. It always made me feel that he was laughing. The fur underneath was softer than the wiry fur on his back, but it felt just as greasy. There were lumps of mud hanging from the softest fur at the top of his legs.

I paused to watch Nancy and he lifted his head. It was all right, there were still two kittens on the roof and none in her arms. I went back to Bruce and he laid his head back down.

Donn had given up telling us that Bruce was a working dog and not a pet. He'd had to accept that, for six weeks in the summer, Bruce was both. He never said Bruce might bite like the cows or the sheep or the pigs. I didn't believe him, not really, but even my mum backed him up on that one, which she didn't always. I hadn't stroked the pigs, and couldn't get anywhere near the sheep, only the cow and her calf in their special barn. I didn't know why they weren't in a field, like the other cows. Donn said they were a special kind of cow, but I would have thought that meant they needed a special kind of field. Maybe he was scared they'd be stolen if someone spotted them. Maybe they glowed in the dark.

I'd stopped again, without realising. Bruce was looking hopeful. I swapped hands.

'They're not coming down,' I said. 'You know what it's like at Mary's house.' We had chased the cats in her yard for years and never, ever caught one. You had to be sure to chase the small ones because the adult ones were actually really scary, and sometimes didn't even run but just hissed and stared you out.

Nancy had been thinking about her response. I could tell she was trying it out on me before Donn.

'But if the kittens don't come down, Bern, they'll starve.'

'Donn got them to kill the mice. He probably won't feed them anyway.' I got upset when I said that and put my head

118

down so she couldn't see. Bruce's leg was shaking. After this he might want a treat, even though this was absolutely not allowed. He loved them, but everyone always wondered how the Sugar Puffs emptied so quickly. Nancy knew. Sometimes we'd give him one handful each, so he liked her as much as he liked me. Sometimes, when it was both of us and we thought it was cold, we'd coax him into the house and sit by the fire. We usually got caught when we did that, but Mum wasn't ever that cross, only Donn and Sister Agatha.

Nancy had come up with another plan.

'When they leave the kitchen, you go in and get some ham or chicken from the fridge, Bern.'

'You do it,' I said. 'My hands smell of dog now.'

'You can wash them.'

I could, but I knew how long it took, and how much soap, to get the greasy smell of work out of my fingers. Hours afterwards, when I lifted a fork to my mouth, I'd still get a stink of Bruce. I didn't mind, but I was sure the grumpy kittens would.

'Even if you catch one it'll just scratch you,' I said.

'Not if I feed it.'

'And when we come back, they won't remember you. Cats aren't like dogs.' I didn't know if Bruce really remembered me or just looked happy and hopeful whenever anyone smaller than an adult turned up. But I thought he did. Dogs are clever. You'd never find a cat herding sheep or barking at cars. Not that there was much point to that, unless you were a burglar. Yes, Bruce was an expert sheep herding, burglar scaring dog, and that's why I didn't mind smelling like him. Not really.

Mum opened the parlour window and called us in. 'There's someone here to see you. Wash your hands first.'

I couldn't guess who we'd have to wash to meet, unless it was a priest, but they were always in the best room. In the front room was Auntie Beth with a blanket.

'Meet your new cousin, Sinead.'

Auntie Beth held a blanket towards us. Nancy peered into it and made a fake smile. I was more worried about what I would see and bobbed forward for a quick look.

'Careful, Bernadette.'

She pulled the baby away and made me sit down. When I was suitably pinned in with cushions she slowly placed the baby in my arms. Nancy started to back out of the room.

Beth saw her. 'Hold on, Nancy, your turn next.'

Beth hovered next to me. I tried not to look down, to just hold the thing and not wake it so all its holes opened up. It moved its head and the thought of spotting a little pointed ear was nearly too much, but I had to know. I looked. A wrinkly face with small pouty mouth. It had long eyelashes and a splatter of dark hair on its head.

'Does it have a tail?' I asked.

Beth looked confused. 'No, Bernadette. And it's not an it, she's a girl.'

I thought that girl mice had tails as well, but I nodded as if I understood.

'I've had enough now.'

Beth looked relieved and lifted the vague, airy weight from my arms. She called Nancy over and settled her in the same rigid position. She took up her hovering position, hands half extended.

'I am twelve,' said Nancy. 'You don't need to watch me like I'm a baby.'

Beth backed away and sat on the settee next to my mother. Florence was curled on her lap, unsure about this new pet.

I stood by the side of Nancy's chair and had another look.

I whispered in her ear, 'It doesn't look much like a mouse, Nancy. I think they've been given the wrong baby.'

Nancy bit her lip and then started to shake with giggles. Beth jumped up and took the baby back.

'What's the matter, Nancy?'

Her giggles grew until she was laughing so hard the mouse baby woke up and started its shaking mew-cry.

'Nancy,' Mum said, 'what on earth's the matter?'

By this time Nancy was doubled over, trying to get her breath back. I was terrified she'd tell them what I said, although I wasn't sure what bit was making her laugh. I wouldn't think it was funny to be given the wrong baby, but I'm sure it happened. Sometimes I thought that I might have been the wrong baby. I had different hair to the others, much darker and straighter, different colour eyes to everyone else's. Everyone's. That wasn't funny. Dad used to call me his blue eyed girl until I thumped him once and burst into tears.

But Nancy didn't tell for once. We sat in disgrace, Beth looking at us as if we were a danger to her baby, until a car drew up outside. My mother stood up to see who it was and sat down again. Clearly it was someone known too well to open the door for, or known too little to open the door before they knocked.

Beth resumed her 'tired but happy' new mother look and posed with the still bawling baby on the sofa, balanced with its head on her shoulder. She looked at me as if it was my fault that the new visitor would see her baby like this instead of peacefully sleeping as it should have been. I thought she'd be going back to the caravan any minute, but Jackie had disappeared off. He must have had work or something.

There was a knock at the front door, and then the visitor opened it himself. Only one person did this. Me and Nancy moved a little closer together as Tommy came into the room.

'So, where's this new arrival?'

He wasn't in his work boots and his hands were cleaner than usual. He'd not brushed his hair, but an effort had been made. And all for a mouse.

'Nancy, let Tommy sit in the chair,' said Mum.

She jumped from it and stood behind the sofa, where I

joined her.

Beth handed over the baby for Tommy to hold.

'Ah, she's a beauty, Bethany. An absolute beauty.'

Beth beamed. This was what we were supposed to say, I realised.

He reached into his pocket and pulled out a note, forcing the baby's hand around it. 'Have you chosen a name?'

'Sinead.'

'Ah,' Tommy's eyes rolled heavenward and settled back on the baby, 'a lovely Irish name. Perfect.' He didn't seem to mind the frantic squalling, but lifted the scarlet face to his mouth and kissed its head. 'I think she needs her Mammy.'

Beth lifted her beautiful baby up, the bank note floating to the floor, and placed it back on her shoulder.

'I'll just walk her a bit. The girls set her off. She's normally a very placid baby. This isn't like her at all.' She turned away and glared at us again.

'Not you, I hope?' Tommy asked Florence.

Florence shook her head and put her fingers in her mouth.

'No,' said Beth, 'those ones.'

I felt Nancy tense as he turned his eyes on us.

'Well, youse two should know better.'

Nancy looked away, but I didn't like to take my eyes off him. You never knew. He had slightly longer hair than Donn and sharper cheekbones. From behind, though, I'd sometimes mistaken one for the other, both having the same farmer's outfit and big shoulders. He waited for us to say something, but we didn't.

My mother said, 'And what have you been up to, Tommy?'

'Ah, the usual. Been spending a lot of time down at Skull Lane, sorting things out.'

He smiled. I saw my mother's hands move quickly, one onto Florence's back and one onto her head. She stroked her hair.

'Have you seen Donn?' she said. 'He's around.'

'Sure, I'll catch up with him shortly. I'd like some tea if there's any going.'

'Oh,' said Beth, 'how could we be so rude! Nancy, go and get that ready for us.'

My mother stood. 'I'll help. We'll all go, so you can have a bit of peace.'

She let us all leave before she followed us. She closed the door behind us and I wasn't sure about the look on her face.

We slipped back outside but the kittens had gone.

Nancy sighed. 'We need to get those rosary beads back before Sister Agatha asks about them.'

I nodded and we went around to the stable. Nancy stood at the door and pointed.

'I'm not going in after last time.'

'I swear I didn't lock you in.'

'I'm still not. You find them.'

I shuddered. I'd dreamt about the rosary beads, about the spiders and beetles and centipedes using them to say a little insect rosary. I pulled open the door and waited for Nancy to slam it shut behind me. I promised myself I wouldn't scream and took two steps forward. They were there, dusty and dangling.

'Don't close the door,' I said. Nancy said nothing. I picked my way across some planks, unhooked them and put mine around my neck. I saw something new, a lump in the corner. It was the green bag I'd last seen on the parlour floor. I swallowed.

'Nancy?'

Nothing. So that was her revenge, to just go off without me. Maybe she'd tell Sister Agatha or Mum where I was. But usually she took revenge pretty quickly and I couldn't think of anything I'd done today. I bent down and unzipped the bag a little. I couldn't tell if it was Ryan's.

It went dark and I turned. Tommy was in the doorway with his arm around Nancy's neck.

'See anything interesting?' he said.

I stood up.

'Nancy tells me that you mentioned what you saw in the parlour the other day.'

She bowed her head and he forced her chin back up with his hand. My heart was beating so fast I felt faint.

'But she doesn't believe a word of it because she's a sensible girl. You wouldn't be planning on telling anyone else, now?'

I shook my head.

'Sure, who would you tell?'

I saw a tear run down the side of Nancy's face. I gripped her beads tightly to stop myself from throwing them at him.

'I would tell my dad.'

'Would you now?'

'Yes.' Dad was safe, was far away and could tell anyone he wanted. 'You can't get him.'

'No,' he said, 'but I know exactly where your ma is and there's space for her where your uncle went.' He smiled. 'Still feel like telling your da?'

I shook my head. He tightened his hold on Nancy's neck until her head was pressed against his chest, kissed her head and then let go.

'I have things to do.' He stretched his arms out. 'Behave yourselves now, youse two.'

I waited for her to say something but she didn't. I stared at her but she just looked at the ground.

'You told him.' I threw her rosary beads at her feet.

She just looked at them and I went back to the house.

16

Now

She got out of bed and looked out of the side window, across Bryn's field. The draught through the window was strong although the hedges didn't move with any obvious wind. She looked at the rise and dip of the field, the stones in the corner. It wasn't that she'd forgotten everything. She just didn't have to carry it around with her, like Bernie. And look what that had done to her.

But Hurley – he was so calm here, so different. It had to be worth a go.

She hadn't talked to Elian about it yet. She couldn't until she had resolved her own thoughts, and he'd say no anyway. He'd never seen Hurley at his very worst, just the aftermath. He didn't appreciate how good things had been here.

She shivered and pulled a jumper over her pyjamas before wrapping Agatha's dressing gown around her. She pulled the door to the bedroom open and closed it gently behind her. The skylight glowed green as she padded down the stairs through the silent house, her toes rubbing against the worn carpet, and then recoiling against the cold parlour tiles.

Donn was sitting at the table with a teapot and mug. He nodded to her.

She said, 'Is there any tea left?'

He nodded again and she fetched a mug from the kitchen

and the plastic carton of milk. She shook it and then sat down next to him.

'We'll have to get some more groceries. I might pop out before they get up, if I can borrow your car.'

'I need my car today.'

'OK, it can wait.' She poured a cup, noticing that it didn't steam as much as she'd hoped, before adding the milk. 'You must have been up for ages.'

He didn't answer. His eyes were fixed on the door to Cassie's room, as if he expected someone to knock or walk through. Cassie's room, Bryn's field, all these names which held on to places long after the people had gone.

'Why is the field called Bryn's?' she asked.

'It's always been called that.' He turned his gaze to the lightening grey sky and then back again.

'You know the stones in that field, what are they?'

He shrugged, but looked at her as he did it.

She said, 'Didn't Dad think –'

'You're not to go near them.'

'Why not?'

He opened his mouth and then closed it again, looking outside. 'They're dangerous, unstable.'

'They've been like that since before I was born. I don't think they can fall any more than they have.' He didn't look back. 'And there can't be much danger if you keep your sheep there.'

'Don't argue, Nancy. It's still my field for the time being.'

'That's what I wanted to talk to you about. How much are you selling the farm for?'

He laughed. 'None of your business.'

'But it might be. I think I'd like to buy it. I think it would be good for us and good for Hurley. He's like you, he under-stands –' what, misanthropic silence? 'He understands things like you do. And you could stay.'

Donn finished his tea and shook his head. 'I have a buyer. That's where I'm going now.'

126

'I'm family. Where will you go? Become a monk? You belong here and I'm giving you that option.'

He pushed his chair back. 'I'm not staying here to see everything change. This has been my entire life, for better or worse, but there's no money in it any more. I'm selling and then I'm leaving.' He pushed himself up, using the table.

'Who wants to buy it?'

'An old friend.' He grimaced, choking back a forced laugh.

'But surely they only want the land. What about the house, your home?'

He turned away and she thought he was blinking.

'Who is it, Donn?'

'Mary's son-in-law. He lives at Mary's farm now. She's long dead, of course.'

'I remember her dogs.' Nancy shuddered. 'Weren't you going out with Mary's daughter? Dating, I mean.'

'I thought that was the case.' He walked to the lobby and opened the door. 'Turns out I was wrong.'

'Did I meet him, the son-in-law ?'

'You did. Tommy.'

He closed the door to the lobby behind him. She heard him unlock the back door and close that too. She watched him pull his smeared, worn jacket on, have another look at the sky and get into the car. The keys were always in the ignition. He backed out of the yard, the reverse gear high pitched, and turned in the gateway.

Nancy sipped at her tea, but it was too cold. She carried the mug to the sink and boiled the kettle again. She looked at the side driveway. Donn's car was sitting at the end of it, but she couldn't see any traffic passing on the roads. Maybe he was thinking it over, changing his mind. As the kettle clicked off he pulled away to the right and she sighed. She made tea in a fresh mug, pouring some of the cold tea into it. It was a trick she learned from other au pairs to save milk in their bedrooms, separated from the families they worked for. In some houses they liked the help to disappear when the parents were at home so they could pretend they weren't there at all. She only came out when they were leaving for work, going out at night, when they needed her. God forbid she should make a drink in the family kitchen on a weekend, even if they didn't give her enough money to actually go out.

She sat in front of the fire and added some turf bricks to warm herself up, then folded her cold feet underneath her, wrapped in the dressing gown so she couldn't feel them against her skin.

Tommy again. In her mind he'd become unreal over the years, but she thought she may have dreamt about him because the picture she had today was clearer. He had been handsome, had dressed like a farmer but in a nicer way than Donn. His clothes were cleaner and he smelled soaped and perfumed. Her eyes were drawn now to Cassie's room, in the same way that Donn's had been. There was a link between that room and Tommy, but she couldn't quite remember what it was. And Bernie. Of course, Bernie.

How could Donn want to sell outside the family, especially to him, given a choice? She would need to get her ideas together, get Bernie onside as well as Elian. Maybe her parents would know how to persuade him.

The fire was getting warmer now. She finished her tea and rested her head back on the headrest.

The sound of plates woke her. She lifted her head up and felt her neck twinge.

'Couldn't sleep?' asked Bernie.

Nancy yawned. 'Those rooks, crows, whatever they are, woke me. I couldn't get back off after that.'

The sun was shining into the yard now, high above the garage roof. The fire had gone out.

'Want any bacon?' asked Adrian.

'Please.'

Bernie went to the bottom of the stairs to shout the girls down.

'Erin and Maeve, breakfast!'

Nancy wondered why the house felt more like Bernie's than Donn's, or Agatha's, when she was here.

Nancy limped over to the table, shaking the pins and needles from her right foot.

'Where are you going today?'

Bernie put plates on the table. 'We're visiting Auntie Beth. Erin and Maeve, now!'

'I haven't seen her for years. Never liked her much. Why are you going?'

'It's just what family are supposed to do.'

Nancy flushed and looked away. Bernie headed back to the door.

'Don't!' shouted Nancy.

'Don't what?'

'Call them three times,' Nancy mumbled, feeling stupid.

'Seriously? What's got into you today?' Bernie rolled her eyes and shouted again. This time there were footsteps in response. 'Good grief. Three times. You won't remember anything else, but you remember that. The number of times we did it and no one died.' She paused. 'No one we did it to died.'

Erin and Maeve sat at the table and began to eat the bacon sandwiches. Adrian delivered Nancy and Bernie's and returned to the kitchen.

Nancy picked one half up and picked at the searing fat hanging out.

'Do you remember anything about the history of the stones in Bryn's field?'

'Full of questions today, Nancy? I remember Dad always wanting to go and have a proper look at them. Donn wouldn't let him.'

'What did Dad think they were?'

'Ancient. He thought they were really old, maybe a tomb.'

'Why wouldn't Donn let him go and look?'

'I couldn't say.' Bernie took a bite of her sandwich and shrugged, but her eyes stayed on Nancy's. 'Could you say?'

Adrian came in with his sandwich. 'Your granddad thought that if people knew he'd lose the field. He didn't want the council or the government coming and claiming any of his land so he made Donn swear to keep it quiet.'

Nancy tried to look uninterested. 'So they've always known they were Neolithic or something?'

'Why are you asking?' interrupted Bernie. 'Did you go into the field without asking Donn?'

'I didn't know I had to ask him.'

'We were never allowed in. I thought you would have remembered that, at least.'

Erin swallowed. 'We're not allowed either. Mum said.' She smirked.

'I don't see why I shouldn't now,' said Nancy.

'You always behave like you own the place,' said Bernie.

'That's funny coming from you. What's the problem? It's not your bloody house, Bernadette. Stop treating me like an intruder.'

'Don't you swear in front of my children.'

'Oh, send them out if you don't like it.'

Erin and Maeve were watching, mouths open and eyes glittering. Now they turned to their mother who shook her head.

'Just say sorry, Nancy, and we can forget about it.'

Nancy picked up her sandwich and took her first bite; bitter wholemeal bread, sweet fatty butter and crispy bacon. She took her time chewing it.

'I think,' she said, 'that if Donn wants to tell me where I should and shouldn't go, he can. He's selling up anyway so he can't be too bothered about who goes where.'

'Not yet though. Is he? What did he say?' Bernie spoke

quietly and Nancy had the impression this was not to alert the children. There was no way they were going to miss any of this.

'He has a buyer.'

'Who is?'

Nancy took another bite and pretended to try to force the memory to the front of her brain.

'Tommy, I think he said.'

Bernie gasped and, standing up, tipped her chair back onto the tiles. Adrian put his hand out to her, but she ran from the room.

'What's going on?' she asked Adrian.

'Just watch the girls,' he said. 'Don't let them come out.' He followed her.

Erin and Maeve watched him leave and close the door and then refocused back on Nancy.

'Eat up,' she said. The mouthful stuck in her throat. She felt guilty. She should have been more sensitive. She shouldn't even have said his name.

'We're finished,' Erin said. There was still more than half a sandwich on both their plates.

'Eat it all up, please,' said Nancy. She forced a smile. The sound of Bernie and Adrian's voices was carrying through the serving hatch into the lobby. Nancy knew that she should try to distract the girls but couldn't think of anything at all to say to them. They all ended up pretending to eat, picking at crumbs, and trying to assemble words from the noise.

17

Then

We didn't know what was happening, but the quiet voices alerted us to something so we listened extra hard to find out what it was. We didn't say anything, but slid across walls to listen at doors, inched open the serving hatch to catch any sounds. We had checked for Tommy's car, so we knew he wasn't involved. We were pretty sure, anyway. Mum was saying, 'For God's sake, don't tell the girls,' and Sister Agatha was saying, 'Don't blaspheme, Eithne,' and Donn was saying nothing.

It was when we saw Donn leaving by the front door that we finally spoke to each other.

'He's got a gun,' I whispered.

Normally Nancy would have rolled her eyes at me saying something so obvious. 'I know.'

'He's going to kill someone,' I whispered.

Nancy looked as scared as me which made me even more scared.

'Have you seen any cars? Is anyone here?' she asked.

'I don't know.'

We went upstairs and looked out of every window, except for Donn's which, apart from being illegal, stank of his socks. We didn't know how even he could bear to go in, let alone close the door. We were very careful about looking out of Mum's window because the last time we'd been seen. And by someone who we were worried about seeing us again, though neither of us said it. Nancy picked up the book Mum had been reading and put it down again. Most days she'd have moved the bookmark forward or back a few pages, but it didn't even occur to her today.

And it wasn't really Mum's room now that she had to share it with Beth and the mouse, but they'd gone off for a couple of days to test run the caravan again. Beth said Jackie missed her so, and she liked to be missed. But she left a lot of things here, just in case she had to come back. We expected her back at any moment.

We sat on Mum's bed and listened for a bit. It was the quietest room because only the best room was below it, and no-one ever went in there, unless there was an extra special visitor. Not even Sister Agatha, who spent most of her time expecting everyone to treat her like that.

'Let's ask Mum,' she said.

'She won't tell us.'

'She has to.'

We found her at the table with Sister Agatha and Florence, eating biscuits. I was annoyed that we weren't offered biscuits as well, and then I realised they were a distraction. Whatever we did, we couldn't say yes to the biscuits.

'Sit down girls,' said Sister Agatha. 'I'll get some more biscuits.'

'We don't want them, thank you,' I said.

I don't know who looked more shocked, Sister Agatha or Nancy.

'We just wondered where Donn was going.'

Sister Agatha snorted. 'Did you, now? Don't you know what curiosity did?'

As we hadn't seen the kittens for days I thought that was mean. I turned away from horrible Sister Agatha and talked to Mum instead.

'Where is he going?'

She smiled at Florence. 'I don't know.'

133

'You say when people don't look at you they're probably lying.'

Sister Agatha pulled me round by my elbow. 'Don't you talk to your mother like that.'

Nancy pulled at me. 'Come on.'

'And don't go outside,' said Mum.

'Because nothing is happening out there?' asked Nancy, with her one eyebrow raised. She'd been trying to teach me that for months.

'That's right. Nothing for you two to get involved with.'

'Because we might get shot?' I said.

Mum glared at me and Sister Agatha crossed herself, then pulled her rosary beads from inside her black blouse. Florence froze, unsure whether to cry or not.

'Can I have a word?' Mum said, then dragged me into the hallway. Nancy followed. 'There is a dog worrying the sheep. You know what that means, but I thought you'd probably rather not know about it, and I certainly don't want Florence to know about it. Happy now?'

When she opened the door to go back in I saw Sister Agatha feeding Florence glacé cherries. Our glacé cherries. The door closed on us.

'You do know what that means, don't you?' asked Nancy.

I nodded. 'He's going to shoot it.'

Nancy whispered, 'It's someone's pet and he doesn't even care.'

'He's horrible sometimes.'

We looked at the closed door and went to sit on the settee.

'I hate him,' said Nancy.

I didn't really hate him, but I nodded.

'Shall we go and look out of the window?'

'I don't want to see it. What do you think he does with the body?'

'Leaves it on the road? I don't know. Maybe people never find out where their dogs went. I think he'd shoot his own

134

dogs, if they were bad sheepdogs. Or just old.' Nancy looked older again, like she wasn't shocked.

I gasped. 'He said he sent them to be pets.'

'I didn't even know he had a gun, did you?'

I chewed on my lip and decided to try out the name. 'Maybe Tommy gave it to him.'

We'd both been thinking about him, but I was the one who said it. Nancy quickly checked behind us and pulled her legs up so they were bent in half and wrapped her arms around her leg warmers. She wouldn't be caught saying his name. She didn't answer me at all.

'What did he say to you?' I said.

'I haven't seen him.' She looked out of the window. There was a crash in the kitchen and a flurry of distant movement.

'I saw you this morning. You were talking to him in the yard. You swore, Nancy. You can't tell him anything else.'

'I heard you.'

We were quiet for a bit.

'I wish we had taken some biscuits,' I said. 'Maybe the mouse will come back for the crumbs. Or the mouse baby will hoover them up.'

Nancy didn't even pretend to smile.

'It will be all right, won't it? He won't come round when Dad's here. He never does.'

'I don't care anyway,' she said, but she kept looking behind her.

18

Now

She walked down the lane, past the silo and turned right. It felt naughty, her heart beat a little faster, but there was no sign that made her turn back. She'd imagined them as a child, big wooden oblong 'Keep Out' signs on hand driven posts, maybe even a dead rabbit nailed to it. The lane was only familiar, stone walls with wild flowers creeping out from the crevices, a small hump backed bridge over a sluggish stream. There were no large trees screening Mary's farm from the road. It was low and grey pebble-dashed. It was normal.

She remembered the old woman, Mary, as she arrived at where the gates had seized open. The grass and pebbles were pushing up in front of them and the bottom hinge had pulled away from the wall entirely. She heard dogs barking and thought of Donn's last dog and Bruce before him.

Hesitating by the gate she looked for movement in the yard and barns beyond. This was a stupid idea. Elian wouldn't even want the farm and she probably couldn't afford it without him. She didn't want another farm, just this one. She knew it was silly to be so fixed on the idea, but it seemed urgent. She had to know whether it was possible before she told Elian she wanted to emigrate. But somehow it wasn't just about that. It was the name coming up after all those years. She wanted to see things from a new perspective. See people from a new perspective. She couldn't distinguish what was real and what was imagined any more.

Still, she was nervous. She'd rather have the conversation outside, or start it there and gauge the reaction where she could still see the gate. The outbuildings were right by the farm in a square as if everything was observing itself. Mary's house looked tiny compared to Donn's farm. There was something odd about the way barns three storeys high leaned over the one storey house.

A muddy jeep came up the lane, through the gate and pulled into the yard in front of her. A woman, grey haired and armed with a shotgun jumped straight out and strode towards her.

'What do you want?' She held the gun pointing down but too easily as if it would flip right into her arm.

'I'm looking for Tommy.' Nancy tried to smile.

'What for?'

'I wanted to talk to him about the farm, Donn's farm.' Nancy gestured over her shoulder. The woman didn't follow her gesture with her eyes but kept looking at Nancy. There was something there and in the long, carelessly pulled back hair. 'Are you Catriona?'

There was a flicker. 'What do you want?'

Nancy took a breath and tried to get the explanation out in one go. 'Donn's my uncle and I heard he's selling the farm to you, to Tommy, but I'd like it to stay in the family and I thought we could talk about it.'

There was a movement behind her and two red heads, one a boy and one a girl, got out of the jeep and stood by it. The girl had a long ponytail, a fox tail.

Catriona didn't turn, but shouted, 'Get inside!'

Nancy repeated although she was sure now, 'Are you Catriona? We met, years ago. I didn't know that you'd had children. I have a son.'

Nancy wasn't trying to smile any more, wasn't trying to pretend that this was a conversation. She just wanted her to know that if the gun, quite still at the moment, came up that she would be missed. She would be found.

Catriona, she was sure it was her, said nothing. What would she be now, fifty? She looked older, the wrinkles deeply set and her hair had only the barest hint of colour in streaks. Nancy had thought her so glamorous but that was before three decades of wind and sun and rain. She thought of the standing stones, their permanence. How would this meeting be broken?

The farm door opened and closed and a man walked towards them in the same quick way Catriona had before. Tommy looked like any other farmer, heavy jowls and hair cut by his wife with shears. In her mind, all these years, he had been dangerous in a Byronic way. Now he just looked like violence would come easily and she felt stupid. He stood beside his wife and crossed his arms.

Nancy said, 'I've come to talk to you about the farm.'

There wasn't a flicker. His blue eyes were flat now.

'We have an arrangement,' he said. 'He gave his word and I guess you're here because he's keeping it. There's nothing else to say. Time to go home now.'

Nancy looked from one to the other and took a couple of steps backwards before turning and walking away. She felt like running, she felt the gun pointing at her back and thought of the much improved chances of being missed if you were moving at speed, but it was a test. Never look like you're running, she thought. She had to look as if her legs weren't wobbling, as if every step wasn't a deliberate effort to keep putting distance between her and the shot.

There was no talking to them, clearly. The farm would be lost, absorbed into their land or passed to their children and her link would end.

A man was standing on the bridge. She could see his shape and thought that Tommy had called someone to cut her off already, to make her disappear right here within minutes of her leaving. She breathed fast and heavy, forcing herself to keep going and walk past him, wishing she had keys in her pocket to force between her knuckles. When Donn turned around and she recognised him she sobbed.

'What's the matter?'

She shook her head, crouched down and rested her arms on the low bridge walls. She felt her hands trembling and clamped them together.

'Are you praying?'

She shook her head. Then she thought, well of course Tommy would send Donn to kill me, who else? She lifted her head up but he just looked confused, not murderous.

'Where've you been?'

'To see Tommy.'

Donn bit his lip and turned away.

'I wanted to ask him about the farm. I thought that I could – it doesn't matter.' She pushed herself up and sat on the wall.

'You never did listen.'

'I know. I know. But it was good. Now I know that Bernie remembers him right, not me.'

He sat next to her. 'Your Elian doesn't even want to stay for a holiday. Why are you doing this?'

She covered her face. 'I don't know any more. I loved it here and Hurley's been so much calmer since we got here, so much less agitated and more focused. It seemed like a perfect idea.'

'Yeah, well, there are lots of those. Two thousand Elvis impersonators can't be wrong.'

Nancy dropped her hands and smiled. 'You've heard that too?'

'I seem to have heard it a lot recently.'

Nancy looked at him and then over the fields, his sheep, his home. A car drove along the road in the distance and she caught glimpses of it through the hedges as it passed their farm. To the right the sharp rise of the mountain was sunlit and she could see the edge of the cloud moving towards them. Soon they were sitting in sunlight too.

139

'When I married him I thought he was someone else entirely. Now that he's here, somewhere I feel comfortable, I realise that he's unbearable. He embarrasses me. Just the way he talks and sits and everything. I want to apologise for him all the time. I can't go back with him. I don't want to live with him anymore.'

'Why would you try to persuade him to move here?'

'I didn't say that. I was saying that I wanted to stay here.'

'With his son.'

'With my son.'

Donn looked at me. 'Same thing.'

Nancy looked at her watch. 'They'll be back soon.'

'Do you always have to be there, on guard?'

'Where else would I be?'

'Come and help me. I've got to move a load of sheep and I remember you used to be terrible at that. Let's see if you've improved.'

Nancy looked down at her shoes. 'I need some wellies.'

'I have plenty. Agatha could never think of anything else I might be wanting.'

She saw the car pull into the drive and turned her head into her hood. They hadn't been that long and this probably meant that something had happened. Something that Elian could deal with for now. Maybe it would make him realise what was happening, maybe he'd heard what the girls whispered to Hurley.

Donn was way ahead, being a sheepdog.

'Go out in the lane!' he shouted.

She was never any good at this. She stood in the lane, her back to the farm, and put her arms out like a scarecrow. She could see Donn rounding them into an erratic ball shape, calmly encouraging them towards the open gate and her open arms. She heard him swear and go back for one that had slipped away. The rest wandered off and he started the process again.

Her arms ached. She wished she had sticks to wave at them. Suddenly they were there, pouring out towards her and then rearing back and heading in the right direction. She'd done it. She was a lot bigger now. The stink of them hit her as Donn followed the last ones out.

'I'll stay at the back,' he said, 'you head them in.'

She walked quickly, trying not to move her arms too much and send them back the other way. Donn's car was parked across the lane but there was plenty of room for them to edge past it, through the ditch. They had started to go into the right field without her, bleating and edgy, but she stood in front of the car and pretended it was her influence. Then a couple tried to dodge past her into the ditch and she edged to the bonnet, just in time for another to skip around the boot.

'I've lost one!' she shouted, and then regretted her choice of words. The animals, devil eyed, had outwitted her for all of her ability to walk on two legs. She recognised the look of disappointment in Donn's eyes from all those years ago.

'Let's get the rest in,' he muttered.

When a couple scrambled and turned in front of the gate, ready to bolt, he was there and they changed their minds. She pulled the aluminium gate closed and secured it with the blue nylon rope. Donn was looking down the lane.

'You stay here, ready to open it up again and I'll drive round to the other end. We'll catch the bugger.'

Nancy nodded and he drove past her and the farm. She had no idea how long the lane was or how far the sheep had gone. She remembered the zoo losing its pack of wolves when she was little and worrying all night about the hedges and gardens they could be hiding in on her way to school. She had clung to her mother and kept vigilant. It was in the evening that they found out the wolves had all been waiting for breakfast at their cage that morning.

She looked out at the sheep, tried to count them and gave up. There were bits of wool tangled in the hedgerow near the gate and she reached through for some. The grease and smell made her throw it back straight away, but she remembered gathering handfuls as a child with the idea of spinning it somehow.

She heard a car and unlooped the rope. The sheep had run down to the far edge but were now returning, bleating and regretting their new home.

'Go back!' she shouted.

They didn't, but she pulled the gate across the road and hoped that the noise of the car and her bleating little voice would keep them inside. The bad sheep trotted in front of Donn's car as he swerved to guide it and she fastened the gate again. Now Donn smiled.

'You're still a terrible wee farmer.'

'Never said I wasn't.'

She got in the car next to him and he drove back to the yard. This time she didn't do her seat belt up, like him. The feeling reminded her of trips as a child, restrained only by the voices of her parents. Their car in America placed the belt on her automatically and she'd always hated it. There were no choices, so how could doing the right thing be a virtue?

She looked through the parlour window. They were all there, her families. She sighed.

'You need to go and see Agatha before you go back,' said Donn. 'You could see how she's settling in.'

'Are you allowed visits if you're a nun?'

'She's not a nun yet. They may throw her out.' Donn smiled. 'She's asked me to tell you to go, so I'm sure it's fine.'

'You're not going?'

'Not yet.'

'Where are you going to go? After it's sold.'

He shrugged, 'My cousin still has a small farm. His wife died. Not so much to do and a bit of company.' He drummed his fingers on the wheels. 'It'll do.'

'Do you have to leave now, soon?'

'Have to? In a way.' He looked into the parlour.

'Is he making you? Is it something to do with Tommy?'

'No.' He turned to her. 'And don't you be saying otherwise.'

It began to rain hard, hitting the puddles with such force that the water splashed straight out of them. The guttering along the kitchen extension dribbled out right in front of the window and joined the brown stain which worked its way up from the cracked concrete. The metal circle topping the well made the occasional clanging noise as if being pelted by gravel.

'Time to go in,' said Donn.

19

Then

Nancy kept disappearing. I'd checked all over the house and in the front, right down to the gate. Mum and Agatha thought she was with me. I checked the yard and then went down to the hay loft. She never went there without me. Sometimes I thought that she really did believe it was full of rats. She liked me to go in first and always stayed near the open edge. Today she was sitting as far in as I'd ever seen her, legs dangling off a bale, and she wasn't on her own.

'You're growing up into quite a lady,' said Tommy. 'The boys must be chasing you.'

He was leaning against a stack of hay, pulling strands out with his fingers. Most he dropped but one he placed in her hair. She moved away from him a little, but not much.

I was going to run up to her and stand beside her when I realised that she wasn't scared. She was smiling. Not a proper smile, like she found something funny or nice, but a smile that she gave to boys. Boys that she liked.

His hair had hay in it and looked messed up. Despite the hay in Nancy's hair, it still looked brushed, still in a ponytail. He leaned towards her to talk quietly so that she had to lean towards him too.

'Your Mammy probably wouldn't let you come out tonight, no?'

Nancy shook her head.

'Shall we ask her?'

'No, don't do that!' Nancy looked around and saw me standing by the gate. She hesitated for a moment and then decided to ignore me. I thought she got more cocky after that. I made her feel safe.

'Would you be ashamed to be seen with me?'

Tommy's mock annoyance made her do this stupid giggle.

'I thought you didn't like me,' she said.

'I like you, all right. It's that bratty wee sister that gets on my nerves.'

Her smile faltered and her eyes slid over to me. He looked too.

'Well, look who it is.'

I cleared my throat. 'Nancy, Mum says to come in.'

Tommy turned to Nancy. 'Does she always spoil your fun like that?'

'Yes.' Nancy slid off the bale. 'I'd better go in though.'

Tommy took her hand, bowed and kissed her fingers. 'See you soon. I'll let you know about the car, OK?'

Nancy blushed and rushed past me towards the house. To me he lifted two fingers to his head and saluted. I ran after her.

In the lobby we stopped to catch our breath and I stood in front of the kitchen door.

'What are you doing?' I asked. 'Why were you talking to him again?'

Nancy stroked her hair, catching the piece of hay sticking out. 'I thought Mum wanted me.' She pulled out the hay and held on to it.

'Well, she doesn't.' I crossed my arms. 'You're not allowed to talk to him.'

'He's Donn's friend. He talks to him. He can't think he's so bad.'

She kicked off her wellies, keeping her toes on the heel of each boot. I had to use my hands because my boots were a bit too small but I had to wait for Nancy to grow out of hers before I got the bigger ones.

145

I stood by the sink. 'I'll tell Mum.'

She stood close to me and put one finger up to my chest. 'Oh no, you won't, Bernadette. He's promised to teach me to drive and you're not going to say anything.'

I slapped her finger away. 'That's stupid. You can't, you're not allowed.'

'What's it to you? If he thinks I can, then I can.' She looked smug. 'He says I'm to keep an eye on you.'

'You won't tell him anything?'

'Bernadette, you're such a child. You make up stories and think they'll scare me. A blanket means nothing.'

She opened the kitchen door and swept through it. She'd left wet sock prints on the floor. I could hear her talking to Mum but I stayed out in the lobby. She knew that Tommy didn't like us and I couldn't understand why she believed he'd changed his mind. She wasn't that old that she could believe he was interested, but she seemed to believe that he would let her drive. I couldn't imagine Nancy behind the wheel of a car. She was nearly five foot, but she wouldn't be able to use the pedals. Or maybe she could. Maybe here, in the middle of nowhere, children did drive so they could use the tractors. Maybe it was normal. But I couldn't tell Mum without ruining everything. I had to let her know some other way.

I heard Donn in the yard, talking to Bruce, and went back outside. His head was inside the open bonnet of the car and it was starting to drizzle.

'Donn, how old do you have to be to drive here?'

He didn't look up from the engine. 'Same age as where you're from.'

'So, seventeen?'

He didn't answer. He often seemed to think that questions weren't worth answering.

'What about tractors?'

'I'm not letting you on my tractor.'

'I didn't ask to go on your tractor. I asked how old you'd have to be.'

He stood up with the oil dipstick in one hand.

'On private land you can drive at any age you like. The law only applies to the public roads.' He slid the stick back in to the engine. 'And it's still a no.'

I walked up to him so we were standing next to each other. The engine was black and sticky with grease and there was a smell of petrol stations. I looked at him and waited for him to look at me so that I could speak as quietly as I could. He looked, eyebrows raised.

'You know Tommy –'

He held up a finger. 'Don't.'

'Don't what?'

'Just don't.'

'But –'

He shook his head and I crossed my arms. Donn unclipped the stick holding up the bonnet, made me stand back and let it fall into place. He got into the car and whistled for Bruce who jumped over him and into the passenger seat. He backed out of the yard, turned and sped off down the lane.

Maybe it wouldn't be too bad if Nancy was just to drive down the driveway. Maybe even she could make a couple of turns without crashing the car into a rhododendron. But I had a feeling that Tommy wouldn't do it in the drive where Mum could see him. He'd take Nancy off somewhere and then what?

I was tired of Nancy ignoring me and so bored that when Agatha got her shopping bags together I begged to go with her. I couldn't think of anything to do except stroke Bruce's tummy, but he was still off with Donn.

'I'm bored,' I said to Mum.

'Not bored enough or you'd have found something to do.'

147

It was always the stupidest thing she said, but she said it all the time.

'But I am bored. Can I go with her?'

'What did she say?'

'That I had to ask you.' I hated it when you had to go from adult to adult, all asking what the other adults had said.

'Go on, then. Just don't be a nuisance.'

I ran to catch Agatha. 'She says I can.'

'Right, get in the back then.'

She never let me sit in the front. I wanted to ask her about Donn and Tommy, and Nancy and Tommy, but we drove the short distance to the village in silence. The engine was making strange squealing noises and I thought maybe Agatha was listening to that.

She parked up in the main street and picked up her handbag and shopping bags from the front seat. She turned round to stop me undoing my seat belt.

'You can stay in the car,' she said.

'Why? I thought you were shopping and I was helping?'

'I am shopping and you are helping. If you stay in the car, no-one will put a bomb underneath it.' She smiled thinly, reached across and locked the passenger and back doors, closed her door and locked the car.

I wondered if she was joking, although this had never happened before, and I watched her walk away, expecting her to come back for me. She went inside the butcher's and that was it. I was guarding the car. I looked across the road to the police station, barricaded and greyer than all the other buildings. Men with machine guns walked up and down the road outside it. I couldn't tell if their uniforms were army or police. I wanted to watch them, but didn't want them to see me watching in case that was suspicious, so I tried to look around in a natural way. That gave me a sore neck and I shrank back in my seat. I didn't know why anyone would want to put a bomb under the car anyway. I wasn't

148

important, the car was rubbish and Sister Agatha was partly a nun. Maybe it was because she'd parked next to the police station, but she'd done that on purpose. She could have parked up the road and I could have got out.

Then I realised she just didn't want me with her. Sister Agatha had secrets. That was quite an exciting thought, but it didn't quite ring true. Why would she bring me here if she didn't want me?

Sister Agatha didn't tend to talk about the stuff going on, other than to say 'the Troubles' occasionally and shake her head. I hadn't heard Donn say anything either, but he was friends with Tommy who said horrible things about the English all the time. But now he'd started thinking that Nancy was brilliant or beautiful or worse. I didn't know what could be worse, but I was sure it would come to me.

Nothing made sense as I sat in the back of that car, left to see off the bombers and police and everyone else by myself. I watched Sister Agatha go from the butcher's into a couple more shops, deliberately missing out others with a turn of her head. She understood how it worked. She seemed to instinctively know who was what by how they looked or how they said certain words.

Eventually she came back to the car.

'Still in one piece?'

I didn't think that was funny, but she handed me a packet of salt and vinegar crisps so I shrugged and didn't say anything.

When she started the car this time the noise was even louder. The squealing carried on at the front, but something seemed to have come loose at the back and the exhaust roared. The soldier police all turned to look at us. I cringed in my seat. Sister Agatha stared back at them before doing the worst three point turn ever, which took about four minutes and the end of which actually made some people outside the shops clap.

She roared off past the police station and back onto the road out of town. All the time she muttered to herself, but I didn't catch a single word. I didn't start to eat my crisps until we were on our road and then I ate them really quickly so I didn't have to share them. I made a sharp corner with my nails and tipped the crumbs onto my mouth.

Sister Agatha tutted. 'Gluttony is a sin, you know.'

Auntie Beth would have said to leave the crumbs for the fairies.

Mum would have said to eat up everything because there were starving children.

Dad would have stolen two crisps and eaten the crumbs, given a chance.

Nancy would have said I'd get fat from eating one crisp and spotty from eating a whole packet.

Everyone thinks they're right. I just ate the crisps.

20

Now

Nancy kept calm, like the books said. 'Did you hit her?'

Hurley held his clenched fists, like pollarded trees, by his sides and avoided eye contact. 'No, I told you, I didn't do anything!'

'I'm just asking for your perspective, not accusing you.' Nancy made sure her hands were loosely resting on her lap and not clenched. 'You need to stop shouting now.'

Hurley stood up and paced his bedroom. 'You need to fuck off!'

'OK. Time out.' Nancy got up from his bed and closed the door behind her. She thought of all the things in the room she should have taken out. The statues, the mirror, the brick hard enamel hairbrush. All normal. All dangerous.

Punishing Hurley was a tricky manoeuvre and one best left until he'd forgotten what had made him angry. But then those girls had their own responsibility for what had gone on and all they were getting was hair strokes and chocolate biscuits.

Bernie was waiting outside her bedroom door. Maeve was still crying and she could hear Adrian comforting her.

'Is that it?' she said.

'No,' said Nancy, 'he's going to blow. I need to wait until later.'

'Don't you think that treating him like he's different is counter-productive?'

'I think that he really doesn't like hearing people talk about him. He's not deaf.'

There was a bang from inside his room.

'Let's go downstairs,' said Nancy.

Nancy meant to go into the front room but walked straight out of the front door. She needed air. She needed to control her breathing.

'So? Tell me what happened, Bernie.' She walked down the drive.

'We were watching TV –'

'All of you? Hurley too?'

Bernie spoke fast, leaving no gaps for interruptions. 'I thought it would be a good way for him to bond with the girls. They're all living here but completely separately, so I said he could watch with us. And before I knew what was happening, he'd hit Maeve.'

'For no reason?'

'Would a reason make it okay?'

'I told you no TV. I told you no screens at all. You never listen. I told you how to handle him and you did exactly the opposite.'

Nancy stopped at the gate and turned back towards the house. Bernie walked along the fence and leaned against it, her arms spread out and her hands holding onto it at either side.

'I've spent enough time with parents to know that what they mean to achieve and how they act to achieve it isn't necessarily what is best for the child. It's much more about them.' She leaned her head back to look up through the trees. Nancy positioned herself in front of her.

'What does that mean? I've spent years going to a million different counsellors and they're all like you. They all think that they're the one with the only right answer, that if only I'd come to them first everything would have been fine. But they don't fix it, they complicate it.'

'Do you always refer to Hurley as it?'

'I'm not referring to Hurley, I'm referring to the situation.'

'Hurley's situation?'

'Look at me,' said Nancy.

Bernie lowered her head and crossed her arms. A breeze fluttered her hair forwards and she shook it back.

'Don't talk to me like I'm a case you can solve. I know that you know a lot about therapies but you don't know a lot about Hurley.'

Bernie tilted her head and smirked.

'Yes, I know a lot about therapies,' she mimicked. 'Elian makes it quite clear most days how completely cool he is with the idea of spending time in a house with such severe mental health problems.'

Nancy cringed. She should have known he couldn't drop it. 'I didn't say it. Why are you speaking to me like that? You did have a lot of therapy. It isn't my fault.'

'Isn't it?'

Nancy crossed her arms. 'No, it isn't. All that stuff you said, like about Dad, that was all you.'

'Oh, I've heard your thoughts on the subject from Elian, at length.'

Nancy gripped her arms tighter.

Bernie continued, 'I expect he thinks he's being open and healthy.'

'He's been in therapy too. People tend to be a little weird after that.' Nancy let her arms fall. 'Sorry. I shouldn't have said that.'

'It's nothing I haven't heard before,' Bernie said, but she turned to look over the fence, across the road and the fields. 'And it's not unexpected from you. You never did stand up for me. You never said a thing.'

'About what? And what was I supposed to stand up for? You destroyed any letter that arrived for me. You went through my stuff first and then everyone else's. You lost it.

You had it in for everybody. And then the stuff that the therapist made you come out with, no-one in their right mind could have supported you on that.'

'You could have tried.'

'Which bit? Oh, yes, the devil is definitely chasing her, doctor.' She saw Bernie lower her head and softened her voice. 'You know what it did to Dad. And you know what that did to Mum, and Florence and me. I know it was down to the therapist in a lot of ways, but it isn't my fault. None of us could help you.'

Bernie turned back. Her eyes weren't full of tears as Nancy had expected, but her cheeks were flushed. Nancy hoped it was shame and pushed on.

'Once you came out with stuff like that, really mad stuff, no-one could stand up for you.'

Bernie took a couple of steps forward and Nancy saw that her hands were clenched into fists. 'Before therapy, before all of that, before I was given memories that I can never shift now, whether they're true or not, you told them I was a liar. You wouldn't tell them about Tommy. You wouldn't tell them about the driving, even. You made me look mad long before I was.'

'I was twelve. There was nothing to tell anyway, it was all stupid stuff to get me into trouble.'

'You should have got in trouble. I was ten. You were my sister, my big sister, and you could have stopped it all.' She took another step and whispered, 'It was your fault. You are not forgiven.' She walked back to the drive and back towards the house.

Nancy shouted after her, 'Why are you here then? You hate me and you'll never forgive me. Fine. You knew we were coming, so why did you come back now?'

'For the bodies.'

'What bodies, for God's sake?'

Bernie didn't reply. Her shoes kicked up the gravel as she

walked away and Nancy had a sudden image of Bruce running alongside her.

She was right. Nancy had left her to it, had been sick of being the girl with the mental sister, the attention seeking stories of eating babies and killing cats, devils and digging up graves and being tied to crucifixes. It was humiliating. Everyone knew, everyone whispered behind her back. She'd left her to it and gone to America with no intention of ever coming back. Their father was broken, their mother cried all the time, Bernie was mad and Florence was very good at ignoring all of it. Nancy was glad to be out of it.

She walked along the edge of the garden, by the fence, until she reached the familiar space beneath the rhododendron bushes. Bows and arrows. She no longer had a penknife or loops of nylon in her pockets. She couldn't let Hurley have them either. She sat down hard on the grassy mound and pulled her feet up.

Back for the bodies, she'd said. Nancy laid her head on her knees. Mum had said on the phone that she'd come out the other side, that she was doing well. Bernie was allowing Adrian to visit with the girls now, supervised. Bernie didn't go. Not yet. She thought back to that last holiday, the last few hours they had all been in the same room without tears and accusations. Mum was the one who kept in contact, her voice inevitably wavering over the transatlantic line, her punctuation hesitant in the emails. 'Love from Dad too,' was the only contact she had had for years. Thirty years of talking which got none of them anywhere.

That was why she hadn't bothered with counsellors and therapists for years with Hurley. They just seemed to make things so much worse for Bernie, and none of it had helped Hurley anyway. She was left with drug therapies. He was left with being drugged.

This is how her mother must have felt, both protective and ashamed of a mad child, unwilling to take them out in public, tired of apologising. But what had happened to him right now was Bernie's fault. She'd provoked him, or let her girls provoke him. Nancy needed to remember that and hold her head high, at least today. He'd been doing so well.

It hadn't rained this morning but the rain of past days had soaked up through her trousers and pants. She heard rustling in the bushes and whispered, 'Bruce.' His ghost didn't come. But there were more noises, whispers, from through the bushes.

Bernie's girls never came outside, not on their own. She edged herself off the hump of grass and crept towards the whispers. A girl and a boy. Oh God, Hurley was with one of the girls. She pushed around the wet leaves, but it wasn't one of Bernie's girls. A face flashed towards her and then the girl turned her head and ran down the grass at the side of the drive, a long red ponytail bouncing behind her. Like a fox tail, thought Nancy.

'Who was that?' she asked Hurley. 'I think I know her parents.'

He shrugged. 'You scared her.'

'I thought you were still in your room.'

'It was too noisy. What were you doing, hiding in there?'

'I wasn't,' she said, knowing that was exactly what she had been doing. Adults weren't supposed to hide. 'I was just thinking. I used to do a lot of thinking there when I was little.'

'Your butt's soaked.'

'I know.' She wiped her trousers with one hand and then had to wipe her wet hand on her thigh. 'What was that girl saying?'

'Just stuff. Asking who I was and where I was from and how long I was here.'

'She asked all that and you didn't ask her anything?'

'Didn't have time.' He frowned and looked at her. 'Were you following me?'

She laughed, 'I was there first.'

'Spying then.'

'How would I know you would come and stand right here?'

Hurley tilted his head. 'Sometimes I think you've put a tracking device on me so you always know where I am. You don't trust me.'

Nancy widened her eyes. 'Why do you think that?'

'That's what they said. You always need to know where I am and what I'm doing because I'm dangerous.'

'The girls said that?'

'Bernie just laughed like they were funny. And then Maeve said that you'd said that that's why I couldn't watch TV or use a console, because if they're on you can't watch me through them. They have to be off so they record properly and you watch me on your phone.'

Nancy touched his shoulder and he moved away.

'You know that's garbage, right? You know that's not possible?'

'It probably is possible.'

Yes, it probably was.

'But I don't do that. There are no cameras, Hurley.'

He shrugged and looked down at his feet as he drew arcs in the gravel.

'Did they say this before or after you hit Maeve?'

'That's why I hit her.'

Nancy's stomach flipped. It wasn't Hurley just lashing out for no reason. Bernie was punishing her by allowing her daughters to torment Hurley. She grabbed for Hurley's shoulder and caught it this time.

'Let's get some lunch.'

'I'm not hungry,' he said, but let himself be guided up the steps into the dark hallway.

'Wash your hands and then come to the parlour.'

She watched him slope upstairs and then heard the girls

in their room above her head. She needed to watch them without making it look as if she was watching him. Even though she was watching all of them, and especially him.

What was Bernie playing at? If she hadn't just had that conversation with her she'd have put Hurley's complaint down to exaggeration or the usual made up excuses. But now it had a ring of truth. Bernie had said, 'Children are never believed until an adult believes them, like someone hearing the tree fall in the forest.' But Elian wouldn't believe either her or Hurley.

She could never tell Bernie anything at all after this.

21

Then

I decided the best way to stop her going off with Tommy was to stick right next to her. So when she agreed to go with Donn to visit Mary I had to go as well. Mary's farm was even worse than the outbuildings we couldn't go into. The farmhouse was rickety and draughty and the only good thing about it was the herds of cats that ran about outside. First we had to go inside.

Mary looked impossibly old, maybe eighty. She had white hair but it wasn't bright and clean like some old people. There were dull ends to it, like it was dusty. She always wore black clothes, maybe the same black clothes, like Sister Agatha, and had a brown shawl on. Summer and winter it seemed to be the same shawl, like she never got any colder or warmer. In summer the house was never warm anyway. The tiny windows let no sun in and the fire was always blazing.

Neither me or Nancy could understand more than the odd word that Mary said. We had to listen to Donn and guess, or sometimes he would translate if it was a question we were supposed to answer. We tried to avoid her eyes so that she forgot we were there. Whenever we answered her it meant that we weren't paying attention to her three massive dogs who snarled at us when we walked in.

'Don't try to stare them out,' Donn had said, but it was almost impossible to not look at them when we thought they wanted to tear our throats out. Nancy was better at not looking than me, but I tried to copy her, looking at the fire next to them whenever I remembered.

After a while Mary said something or other and Donn said, 'Do you want to play outside for a while?'

We nodded and walked out to the yard and that's when we started to hunt for the cats. We knew we couldn't go in any barns, so that's pretty much where they kept themselves. If we did see one walking around it hissed. If it was big we weren't interested. We were after the kittens. They were just as loud and fast as the big ones, but so much sweeter.

Me and Nancy still weren't really speaking, but we'd done this before and didn't need to talk about it until I came across the ginger one. I knew it had heard me because it swivelled its head around in my direction, but not fully. I watched it, creeping closer. Every noise made it move but not quite so it looked at me. It was using its hearing. I beckoned Nancy over. She stood at my side. I mouthed, it's blind, and she nodded. We didn't decide that she would catch it. It was always going to be her. She was slow until the last bit and then grabbed the kitten with both hands at once.

It hissed and writhed and bit at her so that she nearly dropped it, but managed to bear the pain.

'Take your jumper off,' she said, and we managed to get the legs and body still. The head thrashed about, the tiny teeth striking at us while Nancy made murmuring noises. Its eyes looked normal, but very blue, and I managed to stroke it twice without getting bitten.

'Let's ask,' said Nancy.

The scratches on her hands had turned from angry red lines into properly bleeding injuries now. I thought about the dogs and how they'd be able to smell blood and I hesitated, but she was already carrying her prize in and waiting for me by the door.

'Open it.'

'Do you think . . .'

160

'Hurry up.' The kitten was hissing again, like it could smell a room full of dogs.

I opened the door and Nancy strode in.

'We found a kitten,' she said. 'It's blind. Can we keep it?'

Mary said something but there was a lot of head shaking and I caught the word 'pet'. I noticed there was someone else in the room, a younger woman sitting in the chair that Nancy had been in.

Donn nodded at what she was saying.

The younger woman said, 'Sure, let them keep it. It won't last long out there.'

Donn smiled at her, but Mary said something cross.

'You'll have to put it back, Nancy,' he said. 'It's not yours to take.'

Nancy bit her lip as if she was going to cry, but I knew she was angry from the way her cheeks flushed.

'But it will die!' she wailed.

'Things die,' said Donn.

The woman said, 'They're too soft hearted to be farm girls, Donn. Are these your nieces from England?'

Donn nodded.

'Nancy and Bernadette? I'm Catriona, a friend of your uncle.'

Nancy tried to smile but the lost kitten was fighting to get away again. Catriona stood up, and Donn stood too.

'Here,' Catriona said, 'let me take it and I'll find somewhere safe for it to hide.'

She fumbled it out of my jumper and held it by the scruff of the neck. It hung limp and quiet. Nancy scrunched up my jumper in her hands.

'Will it find anything to eat?' I asked.

'Not if death isn't allowed,' Donn mumbled, sinking back to his seat.

Catriona disappeared and when she came back smiled broadly at Nancy. 'Would you like to try on a bit of make-up?

161

You're too old to be running around looking for kittens, sure.'

Nancy blushed and nodded.

'Come with me,' Catriona said. I stood next to Nancy. 'You're a bit young, you stay here.'

I watched Nancy smirk as she left the room. I stayed as still as possible because, now that Nancy had left, the dogs' eyes were just on me. Mary had to speak to Donn a couple of times before she could get his attention. Then she said something in a low voice which made him smile awkwardly and shake his head. He glanced at me.

'OK, there?'

I thought I was probably as uncomfortable as he was, and nodded. He smiled gratefully. Mary said something, nodding in my direction, and he shook his head. Then she laughed. Nancy came back in, scarlet mouthed, and pouted at me.

'We'd better make a move,' said Donn, standing.

'Hold on,' said Catriona, going to the table. She picked up a package and handed it to Donn. 'From Tommy. He's back from Dublin. He'll be round soon, I'm sure.'

Donn looked towards me and Nancy and nodded. I stood slowly, keeping an eye on the dogs, and began to edge to the door.

'I'll be seeing you tonight, Donn,' said Catriona, kissing him on his stubbly cheek. He raised his hand to the mark and herded us out.

In the car he handed Nancy a rag. 'You'd better get rid of that before your Mammy sees it.' He gestured to her mouth.

She took the rag and sniffed it. 'I'll use my hand.' She moved her fingers over the lipstick, making it less bright, but being careful not to smear it outside her lips.

'I like Catriona,' she said. 'Are you going out tonight?'

'No, I think she's just going to come over for a chat.'

'What, you're going to sit in the kitchen with your sisters and let them do all the talking?'

'You want me to tell Agatha and your mammy that you said that?'

Nancy ignored him. 'Is she your girlfriend?'

I looked at Donn as he tried to answer. 'Girlfriend? I don't know about that.' But his smile returned and his hand moved back to his cheek.

Nancy was smiling too, like she was one of the adults. I imagined her staying up in the kitchen when me and Florence were in bed, the children, and I hated her for wanting that. They were boring and she didn't even like tea that much. I hoped that Mum wouldn't let her, that she'd say, 'Don't be silly, Nancy, you're too young.' That might make Nancy cry and then she'd never get away with pretending to be an adult.

I reached my fingers across the back seat and pinched her hard on the leg.

'Ow! What was that for?' I could see tears of fury welling.

'It was an accident.'

She thumped me on the arm so I was next to shout.

'Youse two, stop it!'

We turned into the back driveway. Nancy was cross with me but she couldn't be all grown up when she felt like that. I didn't even mind when she kicked my ankle so hard that I nearly cried.

22

Now

She went into the parlour and found sandwiches already made and on the table.

'There you are,' said Elian. 'We're all taking a trip out. Hurley will love it.'

'Where to?'

'A science museum, about an hour away. That's one good thing about this place, hardly anything is more than an hour away. Back in the States we can drive for four hours for a day trip.'

Adrian smiled and looked at Bernie. She caught his eye, rolled her eyes, and looked away. Elian was oblivious. Hurley came in, followed by the girls, whispering behind their hands. He sat next to Elian. The girls sat down and put a DSi on the table, turned off and facing him. Nancy grabbed it.

'Not on the table, girls.' She put it on the mantelpiece.

'Mum!'

Bernie ignored them and sat down.

Elian said, 'So, Hurley, we're off to a science museum today. Pretty cool, huh?'

Hurley nodded.

'I think I'll stay here,' said Nancy. 'I'm not feeling too good. Do you want to stay too, Hurley?'

'What?' said Elian. 'Don't be ridiculous, he loves that kind of stuff. You'll come, won't you?'

Hurley looked from Elian to Nancy and nodded. 'I'll come.'

Nancy looked at Bernie for her reaction but her face was unreadable. The girls grimaced and giggled. Nancy fought the urge to shout at all of them.

She spoke to Elian, 'Can I have a word outside?'

He followed her to the hall and she closed the door behind them.

'Do you think this is a good idea after yesterday?'

'Sure.' He put his hand out to open the door again.

'You don't think we should avoid them, limit the contact between Hurley and the girls?'

'No. There'll be as many adults as children. I think it's a good idea.' He stepped towards her. 'Listen, do you really want to stay after they leave? If it hadn't been for them I think I'd have gone stir crazy.' He saw her face. 'We can talk about it, yeah?'

Nancy decided it probably wasn't the time to bring up buying the farm.

She borrowed Donn's car with the excuse that they had to visit Auntie Beth's after the science centre. She wasn't going to let Hurley go in the car with those girls, so they may as well make a day of it. She stayed next to him until they separated back into their cars.

Beth still lived in the house they had built while living in a caravan, but her two daughters and three sons had moved out. Nancy realised she could only remember the name of their first child and hoped that she could get by without making it obvious. She pulled up the winding driveway.

She turned to talk to Hurley. 'It's wiggly because Beth thinks the fairies live in those bushes.'

She pointed. He looked at them and then away, back at the sky. She turned the engine off and looked over to Elian. They'd stopped for a meal at a service station so he could fill his phone with all the information that had being waiting in the sky from him. He'd sat smirking as the email box filled up and had been reading through them ever since.

'We're here,' said Nancy.

'Just a minute.'

'No. Those can wait. She's seen us pull up.'

Elian grimaced and slid his phone back into his pocket. Beth stood at the window, not coming to the door. Nancy got out and waved to her. Beth lifted her hand.

Nancy opened the back door. 'Come on, Hurley,' she said, keeping a smile on her face. He slid out and Elian followed them. Nancy rang on the bell and only then did Beth move to let them in.

'Well, you're here at last, are you?'

'Hello, Auntie Beth. This is Hurley and Elian.'

'Well, I'd know that if you ever sent me any photos, but your mother, God save her, still sees me as family. You'd better come in.'

Nancy kept smiling.

Elian murmured, 'Are you sure we're invited?'

Nancy nodded and pushed Hurley in front of her.

'If you'd let me know a bit sooner I could have got all your cousins here, of course. But no. At least none of them have emigrated across the world, like your poor mother.'

'And how are they all?'

'Grand, grand. You'll be wanting tea, I suppose?'

'Only if you're making some,' said Nancy.

'Youse sit yourselves down. Don't worry about me.'

Beth gestured towards the front room with its three sofas and went off to the kitchen. Nancy sat Hurley down and headed towards the mantelpiece. She tried to spot which were her cousins and which were their spouses but it was pure guess work. She decided not to try to name even Sinead. The mouse, she sniggered. Each of them seemed to have at least three children each.

Beth came in with a tray.

'You've got plenty of grandchildren, Beth.'

'Not like your poor mother. Three girls and only three grandchildren to show for it. It's a crying shame.' She placed the tray on the coffee table and gestured to the cake and biscuits. 'If I'd had a bit of warning I could have got something in, but this was all I had,' she said sadly.

'That's more than enough, but thank you.' Nancy sat next to Hurley on the sofa which was surprisingly rigid.

'So, you're the American,' Beth said to Elian.

'I'm afraid so,' he smiled.

'It's nothing to smile about, as far as I can tell. All those poor wee brown babies in Iraq,' she shook her head, 'not to mention Vietnam and all those other poor wee brown babies.' She shook herself. 'You can pour.'

Elian was unsure what she meant by this, whether he was still being insulted, and looked at Nancy.

'Pour the tea,' she said.

Beth raised her eyebrows. 'Does he need translations? And I thought they spoke English over there, of sorts.' She snorted. 'So, just the one baby?'

'Sorry?'

Beth spoke more slowly, 'You only had the one baby?'

'Yes.' Nancy thought quickly to see if she could think of a valid reason and failed.

'And I hear he doesn't talk.' She looked at Hurley. 'Do you not talk, no?'

Hurley looked at Nancy who placed her hand on his.

'So,' said Nancy, 'tell me about what Sinead is up to.'

'Och, she's a wee pet. She's always round, can't do enough for me, and her with the three weans. You'd learn a thing or two from her, I can tell you.'

'No doubt.'

Elian was handing the tea cups around and caught Nancy's eye as he gave her a cup. He rolled his eyes and she caught her laugh as it bubbled up and pressed her lips together.

'Your sister now, well she's got those two wee brats, but she keeps in touch with her mother. Not your da, of course, not with everything. I don't suppose they've spoken yet?'

'I don't think so.'

Beth leaned forward and spoke quietly. 'And there wasn't anything in it, of course?'

'No. There wasn't.'

'The things she said. I'm sure I only heard the half of it.'

'She didn't just say things about him, but about Mum and me as well.'

'Yes, but we all knew those things about your ma weren't true.' Beth settled back, all hope of gossip and contradiction lost. 'Yes, Bernie's got the right idea. She'd not leave your poor mother to pine away, now. But I suppose you've got your own problems.' She looked at Hurley again.

Nancy sipped her tea. She was overly pleased at the description of Bernie's kids, but didn't dare look at Elian again in case she couldn't hold the laugh down next time. It was like being in church and being so conscious of Bernie wanting to make her laugh that she nearly laughed anyway.

'And,' Beth went on, 'you're not going to church anymore? Didn't even get married in church, I hear, like your sister.' She looked at Elian. 'Your fault, was it?'

'Yes, I expect so,' he said. 'Most things seem to be, Auntie Beth.'

'Auntie!' she squeaked. 'God bless us.' She crossed herself again.

Nancy would not catch Elian's eye, she refused. He would make her laugh and she needed to talk seriously to Beth. Hurley sighed and twisted on the hard sofa. Nancy patted his leg, noticing Beth watching her hand, watching Hurley.

'So, how is the farm?' Beth said.

'I wanted to talk to you about that, Beth.' Nancy sat forward and said, 'You know that Donn is selling up?'

Beth made no sign that she had or hadn't.

'I'd be really interested in keeping it in the family.'

Elian's head snapped towards her. Beth looked at her fingers.

'Only he seems to have promised it to Tommy.'

Beth looked away.

'Do you know why? He won't talk about it. I tried to talk to Tommy but that didn't go well. Do you think you could talk to Donn? I know how important family is to you.'

Beth laid her hands in her lap. 'I don't think so.'

'Why not?'

'Tommy has been good to us. He is family, Sinead's godfather in fact. I'm not going to be interfering in their arrangement.'

'Godfather?'

'Will you have some cake?' she asked Hurley.

He nodded and reached forward.

'I'll do it.' She put a slice of sponge cake on a plate and sat it on his lap. 'Do you need a fork?'

He shook his head.

Nancy said, 'Say thank you.'

'Thanks,' he croaked. He began to eat it and a crumb fell to the floor. Beth's eyes became fixed on it.

'I hope,' she said, 'that Bernadette hasn't been carrying on her nonsense. She'll be locked up again.'

'What nonsense?' asked Nancy.

'He's always been very good to us.' Beth pressed her lips together. 'He always was. Even when wee strumpets threw themselves at him, he had nothing to be ashamed of there. Nothing. If only we could all say the same, Nancy. We are all tested and only some of us can look God in the eye.'

Nancy shuddered. Hurley put the plate back on the table.

Nancy cleared her throat. 'I think we'll have to make a move, Auntie Beth.'

Beth stared at Hurley. 'Why? What might he do?'

169

'Nothing. He's just tired. We've been walking around all morning. Busy, busy.'

'Ah,' said Beth. 'Maybe you'd be better off visiting a church or two.' She stood up and brushed her skirt down, 'Well, that wasn't much of a visit after all these years, was it? But you were never much for family, were you Nancy? For all Bernie's faults, at least she knows where she came from and who to thank for it.'

'You could always visit both of us at the farm, while we're here.'

'I don't drive.'

'Maybe one of your children could drive you.'

'Maybe,' Beth said, looking from Elian to Hurley, 'we'll have to see how it goes.'

She herded them out of the door and closed it before they got into the car.

'Jeez,' said Elian, 'no wonder you never came back. Agatha and Donn were bad enough, but compared to her . . . Are they all like that?'

'I like Donn,' said Nancy, clicking in the seatbelt. 'I don't remember many of the others. They all emigrated when I was quite small.'

'Are you surprised? This country,' Elian shook his head, 'there's nothing here. No wonder they go on about how green it is. That's the only nice thing to say, and it's not even that nice. It's just an observation. The towns are grey, the houses have those weird bobbles on them, there's two tourist attractions and one of those is outside so it's a misery. And,' he turned to Nancy, 'I'm not counting the rope bridge. Crazy.' He turned back to watch the road. 'If it was in America the Giant's Causeway would have some great acrylic sheeting to encourage people to go and see it. It wouldn't disturb the view at all, but you'd be able to enjoy it. There'd be a nice bar so you could sit on the rocks all day, instead of having to race out and try not to slip into the Atlantic.'

Nancy checked the road at the end of the drive and pulled out slightly too quickly.

'Is that a bit of an exaggeration? And I suppose they'd just recreate the sand dunes inside a heated building with a heated, more Mediterranean sea?'

Elian smiled and rested his head back. 'Now I could spend a day there. The rain, the bloody endless rain, that's what does for the place. Anywhere that could be half decent, not from any effort from the people that live here, and the freezing cold rain gets you.' He raised his head and shivered.

'It's not raining now.'

He looked up at the sky. 'Give it half an hour.'

'But what about the prehistoric stones and graves and the history? You've nothing like that. Michigan was pulled from the marshes about fifty years ago.'

'Yeah, yeah.' Elian turned to look at her, his voice low. 'Nancy, I don't know why you keep talking about the farm. And what the hell was that about it staying in the family? The country is terrible and I haven't even started on the glum people. What is wrong with them? I thought they drank to excess and were merry while they did it. Is that just in the South? All the people I've met, I wouldn't want to see them drunk. They'd chase me down for being an American or a Jew or too short or too tall. I've never felt so completely unwelcome anywhere I've ever been.'

'You've never been outside the States.'

'So? That makes it even sadder. I can't go back and tell my friends that this is what Europe is like.' He turned in his seat. 'What do you think of it, Hurley?'

Nancy shifted her head to look at him in the rear view mirror.

'I like it here.' He was looking out of the window, not at them. 'I like the quiet and I like the fact there's no people.'

When they talked about place, Elian was talking about the strange abbreviated country of Northern Ireland. When

171

Nancy thought of it, and clearly Hurley too, they thought of the farm. They didn't need anyone else when they were there. It wasn't a plain, white house in the middle of a green landscape, but an entire world by itself. People who didn't feel that, most of her mother's generation, fled from it given half a chance. She could see her dad living here though. He'd have been happy.

'And what,' said Elian, 'was that about strumpets? What is a strumpet?'

Nancy looked at Hurley in the mirror. 'A loose woman.'

Oh,' Elian laughed. 'She sounded like she meant you. You got anything to confess, Nancy?'

'Here,' Nancy reached into the foot well, 'take the map. I know the way from here. Choose some other places you'd like to visit.'

Elian took it. 'I don't know why it's such a big book. They could have just filled it with plain green pages and no one would notice.'

Nancy glanced at him. His bottom lip had started to push out into a sullen pout. Any bond that they'd drawn in opposition to Beth had been broken. Elian liked to have people on his side, agreeing with him. Nancy and Hurley were having a different experience to him and he hated to feel left out. After a few flicks he pushed the book back down by his feet.

Strumpet, she thought. She'd been twelve. Two years younger than Hurley. Nancy bit her bottom lip. She shook it off.

Maybe she should pick up some wine on the way back and something nice to cook. Hurley could build up the fire. Hopefully Bernie wouldn't be back for hours. Then, holding Elian's hand, she would lean across to him and say, in a way which allowed him to reform it as his own idea, 'This place is great for Hurley. One bad day in a couple of weeks is something we haven't enjoyed for years. He's happy and we can all be happy. How can we not buy the farm?'

172

23

Then

Nancy had been gone about half an hour. I watched her run down the back lane to the road but I didn't see her get into the car. Sister Agatha came in the kitchen and I had to look away and pretend I wasn't watching anything at all.

'You can clean those potatoes for me,' she said.

I tried to think of an excuse but Nancy wasn't there to help me and I took them, one by one, and scraped the dirt off them with the nail brush. The water came through strong and freezing my fingertips.

'You can fill the sink, rather than waste the water, Bernadette.'

'But it comes from the well. You can't run out of water.'

'God hates waste.'

And cleanliness is next to godliness, I thought, but I didn't say it.

'I'm going to pick some cauliflower,' she said.

My heart sank. She overcooked a cauliflower worse than anything else. I stuck the hard rubber plug into the bottom of the sink and scrubbed as it filled. One of my disappeared uncles had connected a pipe to the well years ago so that they didn't have to use a bucket any more to pull the water out. My mother always said how much nicer this water was than the tap water at home, full of chemicals, but it scared me a little bubbling up under the house. I thought I heard the sound of Sister Agatha coming back, but she didn't come in.

I thought of the water welling up beneath us into the hole I could see because it was covered with the brittle metal sheet, but where was the rest coming up? The country was so wet that maybe all you needed to do was dig down a couple of feet anywhere you liked and you'd have a brand new well. This was different, Mum said, it was tested and safe and came through rocks not soil. Still, I felt the water make my hands numb and thought about it reaching up from the depths of the earth.

Potatoes finished, and determined to avoid getting any more jobs, I walked past Cassie's room. There was a sweeping noise inside it. I stopped and listened. It was quiet. I tried the door handle, making it squeak, and I heard the noise again. I pressed my ear against the wood and could hear brushing noises and a sound like a voice muffled by scarves. I took a step away, my heart thumping. There was someone in there, but the door was locked.

I heard Sister Agatha's footsteps in the hall and turned to see her come in.

'All done?' she said.

I whispered, 'Is something in there?'

She didn't even look at the door. 'Of course there isn't.'

'A mouse?'

'You and your ideas.' She whipped past me into the kitchen. 'Where's that Nancy?'

'Not sure.'

'Are you wanting another chore?'

'No.' I shrugged, trying to look relaxed.

Sister Agatha looked at me and shook her head. 'Do you know, Bernadette, the wages of sin?'

I didn't know whether she meant me or Nancy, or the answer in either case. I held her gaze and looked at the door to Cassie's room just long enough so that when I looked back she had looked away. Her head was lowered over the cauliflower as she trimmed away the stiff, small leaves and cut the green-white trees away. They fell into the pan with a little splash. I thought that her face looked a little red, her lip a little white from where her teeth bit into it. I thought, if I move away now and she doesn't say anything that means it's really bad. I took a step backwards, then another, before I turned and walked slowly from the room. When I reached the hallway and turned she rushed over, pushed me into the hallway and slammed the door.

The door didn't catch and bounced open a little. I could hear her moving away. I waited in the hall to see if she'd notice, but she didn't. I crept back and looked into the parlour. The door to Cassie's room was open and I could hear her talking quietly. She came back out and went to close it.

'No!' she said. 'You've no-one to blame but yourself. You were told.'

There was a pause.

'There's nothing I can do.' She gently closed and locked the door and stood quite still, waiting.

I walked away.

I sat with Mum in the front room for a bit. She was reading a newspaper from a couple of days ago as Florence built a tilting tower of red and blue blocks. Mum put her hand on my shoulder to show she knew I was there, but then it slipped away and I held myself instead. I wanted to say, calmly and loudly, 'Nancy is driving a car on the road right now with Tommy.' That would get her attention and then I'd get the blame for not telling her earlier, and then Nancy would never speak to me except to call me Bernadette for the rest of my life, and even then I wouldn't have said anything about Cassie's room and I could only say that to Nancy anyway. So I sat, arms around my knees, at the window in the front room and waited for Nancy to come back.

It wasn't until long after dinner that I got to talk to Nancy. Sister Agatha had made us do the washing up but stayed in the kitchen the whole time. Then she sat with us in the front room and made us watch the news. Finally, after we had got ready for bed, I could say something.

'Nancy?'

'It was brilliant.'

'What was?'

'Driving a car, idiot.'

'I don't care about that. Nancy, I need to tell you something. Something just between us.'

'I don't care.'

'Nancy!'

'If you're going to tell me just tell me.'

'I think Ryan is looked up in Cassie's room. Will you stay up with me so we can go and see? We could put a note under the door.'

'You're such a twerp. Everyone knows he left.' She looked at the bed. 'I don't want to share with you anymore. I should have the single, not Florence.' She pointed at her, arms flung out to her sides, blankets kicked off.

'I don't want to share with her!' I turned back to Nancy, 'Did you hear me? Ryan is –'

'Tommy says that I can be trusted.' Nancy sat on the bed. 'He says I know what's what.'

'What is what? What does that mean?'

'He says being an adult means knowing when to ask questions and when to let things be.'

Nancy picked up her brush and began to count strokes. I walked around to my side and knelt next to my pillow. She had to be joking. She never brushed her hair, not even when Mum sent her upstairs to do it. I just had to wait and then she'd come up with a plan. I waited and she counted. Then she got into bed.

'Switch the light off, then.'

My mouth felt dry. 'Nancy!'

'What?'

I lowered my voice, 'Someone is in Cassie's room.'

She propped herself up on an elbow. 'I learned to drive a car today. It was the most exciting thing I've ever done. You wouldn't understand but you're trying to show off, to make out you know something you don't. Do you understand what it means if you're right?'

I shook my head.

'Nothing. What could you do if it was true? Who are you going to tell?'

I blinked and looked down at my knees sticking out of my nightie. I needed Nancy to grow a bit more so I could have hers.

'I could tell Dad.'

'Tommy says he may be English but he married into this family and he knows the score. I wouldn't tell anyone, if I were you. You have no idea.'

She lay down and arranged her hair around her head. It would still be tangled in the morning. She looked at me, rolled her eyes and then closed them.

'Light,' she said.

I edged into bed but didn't lie down just yet.

'Nancy, did he tell you what Skull Lane was?'

She opened her eyes. 'As a favour, I won't tell him that you said that.'

I turned off the light.

24

Now

Nancy found Elian lying on the bed listening to music on his phone, his face lit up by the screen. She thought about turning the light on but thought this may be a conversation best held in the twilight. She signalled for him to take the earphones out. He removed one earpiece.

'I don't really want to say anything,' he said. 'It's,' he made a flat movement with his hand, 'never going to happen.' He closed his eyes.

'I'd like to talk about it.' Nancy could hear the music still whistling from the earpiece. 'I think there's a lot of potential here.'

'I don't.' He pulled out the other earpiece and paused the music. 'I hate this country and I don't intend, not in a million years, to live here. It's cold, it rains all the time. It's utterly miserable.'

Nancy bit her lip. 'When did I agree that I would always live in your country forever and ever? I never thought that my opinion would count for so little in our marriage.'

Elian laughed. 'What? You never said you wanted our family to emigrate. You never said, you know, one day, when we're all settled, we need to go back to the UK. I met you in the US, dated and married you there, had a kid there, and not once did you say anything like that. Now that I have spoken to Bernie and Adrian I wouldn't ever consider it. The things they say about London . . .'

'That's just English people. They always complain about everything. It doesn't mean that they mean it. When I talk about Michigan I'm the same.'

'Really? I've never heard you talk about home like that. Are you saying that you're miserable, that all this time you've hated our life?'

'No. I just said, it's how English people go on.'

Nancy sat on the commode chair and Elian fiddled with his earpieces, winding them around his fingers. Nancy knew this look of his. Petulant. His wishes were being ignored and he needed to show that on his face. He did it most with his mother, his eyes filling with tears, if she wasn't totally enthusiastic about what he was saying. She never supported him, he would claim, and slump from the room. She always followed him. Nancy refused to and knew how long he could hold a grudge for. She didn't have time for that.

'It's not just for me. Think about Hurley. Don't you think he's been a different child over here? He is really benefitting from the space and exercise. He had that one bad day, and God knows those girls are provocative.'

'So it would be their fault?'

'Don't change the subject.'

'His counsellor thinks that you excuse too much of his behaviour.'

Nancy looked away.

'You can't blame people for provoking him,' said Elian. 'What did we do to make him smash up his room the last time? What did you say to make him skewer the TV with the baseball bat?'

'They were problems that he brought home with him.'

Elian snorted.

'I'm serious. He needs somewhere like this.'

Elian shuffled back up the bed, pushing the cushion behind his head. 'There are farms in Michigan. Many more farms than here. You have to understand there is nothing special about this place, other than your connection to it.'

'I fucking hate America. I hate the counsellors and therapy and drugs and "special ed" and politically correct ways of naming what's wrong with Hurley. What if he just needs to be away from people? Not everyone can be sociable, not everyone has to be comfortable with public speaking. What's wrong with being quiet? Being shy and awkward have become personality defects and have to be treated with drugs. Being overactive is a personality defect and that has to be treated with drugs too. The whole way of looking at people is wrong.'

Elian crossed his arms. 'You hate America?'

'You only hear half of what I'm saying, do you realise that? You said you hated this country, anyway. I can say it too.'

'But you don't actually live here. You and your husband and child live in the USA.' Elian looked out of the window at the clouds, the monkey puzzle trees, the drive dwindling away between them. 'Are you giving me some kind of ultimatum?'

'What do you mean?'

'When I go back home with Hurley after my,' he made quotation marks with his fingers, '"holiday", are you staying here?'

She'd already said, 'Hurley's staying with me,' before she realised how the discussion had escalated. 'You expect me to ferry him around all the time because you're too busy. Why would that suddenly change? Maybe you could even get a transfer to Belfast. It's not far. We can get the broadband set up and you can have a whole bedroom for your office. I can have a whole bedroom for my crafting.' She remembered saying that Donn could stay on, but pushed that thought away. 'There's plenty of room for your parents to visit. And then we can have holidays from here to all the European

180

places you want to go. Italy and Greece and France, they're so accessible from here.'

He was staring at her but it was too late to sell him the idea. He looked almost amused.

'He doesn't even want to sell it to you.'

She walked to the side window. 'Look out here. There's a prehistoric monument that's never been excavated, right here in the field. Come and look at it.'

He wrapped the earphones around his phone and dropped his feet onto the floor with a sigh. He stood upright, stretched, and then walked around the bed and out of the door.

Nancy looked out of the window. She watched the idiotic sheep eat their way through the dusk, across the field for the twentieth, thirtieth time that day. Fucking Elian. Fucking Michigan. Fucking stupid people in general.

Somehow, accidentally, she might have just ended her marriage.

She looked around the room. If she was going to be honest with herself, she couldn't see this as her room. She couldn't see it as her house and her driveway. She couldn't buy anything without selling their house in Michigan. She had put everything on the line, maybe over the line, on an emotional whim. She was running away from being told what a bad mother she was, what an inconsiderate wife and incompetent craftswoman. She could sit in her basement for hours and come up with no ideas of her own, before trawling the internet to find other people's ideas that she could adapt.

She sat on the bed and looked at the monkey puzzle trees. Was this a mid-life crisis? Was she one of those women who went on holiday and threw everything up in the air for a sniff of youth or difference? She'd pottered along for years, doing whatever came next.

She let her body fall backwards onto the blankets, uncomfortably screwed up beneath her back. The ceiling flashed at her and she frowned, wondering what it meant, before she

181

realised. Headlights. She could hear the car now. Donn was back. She tried to summon the energy to push herself from the bed, and failed.

Nancy heard footsteps downstairs and the patter of smaller feet up the stairs. The girls had been sent to the bedroom. More steps and a door. Hurley was in his room too. The ground floor had been cleared for the adults, just like when they were children. She closed her eyes, focusing on what she could hear, but it was all vague murmurs and slight bangs. She shivered.

She pulled a cardigan from one of the drawers and tried to shake her arms through the sleeves which were folded inside. Her hands emerged and she stood still, trying to slow her breathing. Then she knocked on Hurley's door. She waited for him to answer and then went in anyway.

'Hi,' she said.

He was sitting on the bed, looking out of his window at the yard. She sat beside him.

'Everything's gone a bit funny today, hasn't it?'

He tilted his head towards her, but kept his eyes on the window. 'What have you done?'

'After dinner I wanted to talk to everyone about buying the farm. Bernie went mad and then Dad went mad. Donn said no anyway. It's all a bit of a mess, but it'll be fine.'

He looked at her now, a strangely knowing look which let her know he knew she was lying.

'Could you imagine living here, Hurley?'

He shrugged. She tried to think of a way of putting it which wouldn't sound leading if it was quoted back to anyone.

'Where would you like to live, if you could live anywhere?'

He thought about it and then smiled. 'The North Pole.'

She smiled and said, 'OK. There's not many people there. Wouldn't you be lonely?'

'You'd be there, and Dad.'

She put her arm around his shoulders and squeezed gently.

182

'I'd better go downstairs.' She stood up. 'There might be some shouting, but I want you to stay calm, OK? Practise your breathing exercises.'

He looked at her and nodded.

She left the room, closed the door, and walked down the stairs. She ran her hand along the banister, sticky with old varnish, and held onto the large ball at the bottom. Three deep breaths and she was ready.

When she opened the parlour door she saw only Donn and Bernie. They sat at either end of the parlour table, all the dinner plates still in front of them. She remained standing by the door, next to the grandfather clock. Someone had asked a question, someone was waiting for the other to respond. She couldn't tell which.

Bernie turned her head towards Nancy. 'What do you want?'

'I want answers.' She turned to Donn, 'Is the farm for sale? And can I talk to you about buying it?'

Bernie snorted. 'Go away, Nancy. No-one cares about what you want.'

'It's my business too, Bern-a-dette.'

Donn shook his head.

Nancy stood firm. 'Have you promised it to Tommy? Why him? Why didn't I know he was Sinead's godfather?'

Bernie looked back to Donn. 'Bet you wish we were all like that, don't you? Forgetful, stupid, wilfully ignorant, whatever you want to call it.'

Nancy sighed, 'Will you just tell me what you want me to say?'

'I want you to tell the truth about what happened.' Bernie turned to Donn, 'And I want you to tell me what went on in Cassie's room. Everyone clear on that?'

'Bernie, don't.' Donn's voice cracked. 'Don't ask me anything.'

Nancy thought he would cry. Her arms and resolve fell

183

away. She stood by the clock, counting the ticks and squeaks, watching them do nothing. The fire was long dead and the room was cold with draughts from the doors and windows. She could hear the murmur of Elian and Adrian talking in the front room. They were entirely still, Bernie's hands clasped in front of her as she leaned into the table, Donn's hand loose in his lap as he leaned backward against his chair. Nancy wished she could sit as she shifted her weight from one foot to the other.

Nancy spoke. 'I don't know what I can say that will make a difference. You say I didn't tell the truth. Beth says Tommy is family. Mum says nothing. Cassie's room, Bryn's field, the Tardis stable, I don't know what you need to hear.'

'That's right, Nancy,' said Bernie, 'it's all about you. Let's leave Donn to think, and go and prompt your memory.'

25

Then

The best room was unlocked. I saw the door open and close from my seat on the stairs and caught a glimpse of black walls and pink blossom. I had looked in through the front window often enough but the curtains were always pulled to stop the furniture fading. Now it was open it meant there was someone important here and I waited to see who it was.

Mum came out of her room with Florence in her arms.

'I told you to get dressed.'

I looked down at my jeans. 'I am.'

'Properly dressed. Skirt, socks and shoes, please.'

'Are we going outside?'

'You have to get your shoes on, stop arguing.' She herded me back to the bedroom.

'Who is it down there?'

'Your great-uncle, Father Seamus.'

'Who's that? I've never heard of him.'

She sighed. 'Just get dressed, please.'

Nancy was sitting on the bed, Sunday clothes already on. I fished out my skirt from underneath a couple of tops and stood waiting for her. She hummed and walked out. I dressed. She was waiting for me on the landing, dragging her hand over the bannister. She whispered right into my ear.

'Bernie, you have to cover for me. I'm going out.'

'No. If I have to go in there, you do too.'

'Bern,' she hissed, 'I have to go. I promised.'

I looked at her. She was trying to look friendly but she still kind of sneered like she was so much older and important.

'You just wait outside the door until I've gone out the back, OK?'

I shook my head. 'If you go I'm coming too.'

'You're such an idiot, Bernadette.'

Mum shouted up, 'Bernadette! Nancy!'

'We're coming!' I shouted back and pushed Nancy in front of me so Mum could see her up through the banister. By the time we reached the bottom of the stairs Nancy had her Sunday face on but I could feel she was angry and stayed out of pinching distance.

Sister Agatha was in one of the armchairs by the blazing fire and Father Seamus was spilling over the other. She gestured to us in turn.

'Father, this is Nancy and Bernadette.'

He smiled and nodded at us. 'And how old are you two?'

'I'm twelve and she's ten,' murmured Nancy.

He shook his head and held out his hand. 'The wee African children I look after are only this big when they're twelve,' Nancy's shoulder, 'and this big when they're ten,' half way down her arm. 'I hope you thank God every day for all the food you eat and all the clothes you have.'

Nancy said, 'Yes, Father.' I nodded, hoping he wouldn't ask me anything. There was a small sofa we could have squeezed onto but we carried on standing between him and the door. He smiled and nodded. I fidgeted. Sister Agatha scowled.

'Go and see if your mammy needs any help with the tea,' she said. 'And close the door.'

Nancy got to the door before me so I had to close it. We went to the kitchen where Mum gave Nancy the tray and me the plate of sliced fruitcake. She carried Florence. We walked back in silently and placed our offerings on the table. Sister Agatha poured the tea and gave Father Seamus one of the best side plates with the biggest slice of cake. The rest of us helped ourselves. Mum and Nancy sat on the sofa. I sat at Mum's feet in kicking distance of Florence's legs.

Father Seamus said grace. I bit my lip to remind myself not to look at Nancy because I could feel the laugh bubbling in my stomach and hear the flicker of Sister Agatha's eyelids as she watched me from the corner of her eye.

'Amen.'

His cake disappeared in three wet bites. Sister Agatha kept hers on her lap, to show him she could resist temptation probably. I picked at mine, fingertip sized crumbs, trying to make sure there wasn't so much in my mouth that I wouldn't be able to swallow it down before a giggle. I didn't trust myself to look up from my plate.

I couldn't help it, whatever Sister Agatha thought, but I was supposed to be ashamed of it. My teacher complained that I did it at 'totally inappropriate moments,' but that was probably what had made it so funny. Mum got it. She hadn't forgotten how to laugh.

It felt a bit safer so I looked around, keeping my head down. There was a wooden box with a record player in it, but it looked different to ours. There was a handle on the side so you could wind it. I could feel Florence wriggling on Mum's lap and she caught me on the ear with her hard red shoe. I rubbed my ear, but still didn't dare turn round.

Father Seamus talked so much that Sister Agatha had no excuse not to eat.

'The only way,' he said, 'to properly eat a mango is waist deep in water. It's true, Agatha, you wouldn't credit it. The fruit of God's gardens out there,' he pointed to hot countries, 'is so fecund and ripe and juicy that a knife and fork are just impediments to joy. Of course,' he lowered his voice, 'these low moral standards for civilised behaviour come across in other, less welcome ways. But you haven't eaten a mango properly unless you've stripped off in a hot lake and torn it apart with your teeth.'

187

Sister Agatha crossed herself. I felt a bit sick, thinking of the unleashed stomach of Father Seamus bobbing in the water.

Father Seamus and Sister Agatha moved onto sinners. Sister Agatha liked her world to be full of sinners and Father seemed to be enjoying making her gasp and call for heaven to help them. I didn't think she meant it. Mum said nothing, except the odd whisper to Florence.

Sometimes the relatives visited us in England, missionaries from far away breaking their journeys back to a 'home' they expected to be forever unchanged. Except for the Protestants. They always expected them to have fled in the meantime and were surprised to find them still there. I quite liked Protestants secretly. There was only one other Catholic at my school and he was an idiot, but I didn't think I was allowed to say that so I didn't.

The sinful Africans or whoever were quite boring and I began to play with my heap of crumbs. If I crushed them under my fingertip I could nearly cover it and I tried to see how many fingertip gloves I could make before one fell off.

There was a noise in the hallway and the door opened.

'Hello, Father,' said Donn.

'Good to see you, Donn,' said Father, but he didn't look pleased at all. 'Will you join us?'

'I'm a bit busy at the moment, Father.' Donn turned to my mother, 'Eithne, can I borrow Nancy for a couple of hours?'

I looked at Nancy, trying to hide her delight.

'What for?' asked Mum.

'Donn,' said Sister Agatha, 'Father was just about to lead us in the rosary. I was just about to send the girls to get theirs.'

My stomach plummeted. I knew where mine was, for once, but I wished I didn't.

Donn shrugged, 'You can't deny people in need, Agatha.'

Her lips went tight.

He said to Mum, 'Catriona's locum hasn't turned up yet and she needs someone to mind the phone in the surgery.'

Mum looked at Nancy who nodded. Mum looked at me. I begged with my eyebrows.

'She can't go on her own. But if Bernie could go with her, I'm sure they'd cope.'

Sometimes I loved my mother more than anything. I did try to make my smile look a little bit saintly as I ran from the room to change.

'Take your rosaries with you!' shouted Sister Agatha after us.

The vet surgery was full of dangerous things that we must not touch. Only the phone, the pen and paper. I didn't know why Catriona had directed all the instructions at me when she'd asked Nancy in the first place.

Nancy answered, 'I'll make sure she doesn't touch anything.'

'And I'll make sure Nancy doesn't,' I added.

Catriona looked at Donn, 'Are you sure this is a good idea, the both of them?'

'Of course, they'll be fine.' He gave us a warning look and walked her out.

I looked around the shelves at all the fatal white boxes with unreadable labels.

'I didn't even know she was a vet,' I said, 'did you?'

'Yes, she told me at the farm.'

I slipped off my chair and walked over to the shelves. 'I hope no-one comes in. I can't read these let alone say them.'

Nancy span her chair around. 'No-one will come in. It's not like a shop. We're just here to answer the phone.' She caught hold of the counter to steady herself. 'Isn't he boring, old Seamus? Do you think his little African children like him? Maybe they can't understand a word he says so he hits them with his Bible.'

I shuddered. 'I bet he doesn't speak African.'

'That's not a language,' said Nancy, but she didn't sound sure.

I sat down again and twirled on my chair. 'When's she going to be back?'

'Not for ages,' Nancy bit her finger. 'We should have brought some cake with us.'

I went around the counter to the small high window. 'There's a shop across the road. Have you got any money?'

She shook her head, then rested it back and pushed as hard as she could. She went around four times and then grabbed for the counter again.

'Go back the other way if you're dizzy.'

'I'm not,' she said. But she didn't do it again.

The cream phone began to ring. She looked at me. I shook my head. She scooted her chair next to it and picked it up.

'Hello, vet surgery.'

There was silence as she listened, a look of horror on her face.

'I'm sorry?'

Silence again and she twisted the pencil around in her fingers.

'Can you say that again, please?'

Silence. She held the phone out to me. I shook my head and she shook the phone at me. I took it and listened to the voice. It was a man who sounded just like Mary, just noises and the odd pause in which I was supposed to say something. I gently put the phone back on the cradle.

'Did you understand anything?' she whispered.

I shook my head. 'Let's not answer it again.' I leaned against the filing cabinet.

She smiled and rested her head back.

'What's Catriona doing?'

Nancy shrugged. 'Vet stuff. She's nice. She's not a bit like scary Mary.'

190

'And what's happening with the driving? Got your licence yet?'

Nancy frowned. 'I'm not allowed to talk about it.'

'But you can to me. I know already.'

'It's not just driving now. Tommy –'

'Tommy what?'

She span her chair again and stopped it, facing away from me. 'Nothing.'

The phone rang and she span back. 'Don't answer it!'

'What if it's Catriona?'

Nancy bit her lip. 'Okay, answer it.'

'Not me! You're her best friend.'

Nancy looked at me like she wanted to say something. The phone stopped.

She started again, 'Tommy –'

I waited. The phone rang again.

'Never mind.'

The phone stopped.

'Nance?'

She looked at me.

'You really won't tell him what I said about Skull Lane, will you?'

She looked at me like she was really sad and span her chair away. She stayed like that for ages. I thought she was wiping her face. The phone stayed quiet. I could hear heels tapping along the street, cars driving by. A car stopping. I wanted to say something but there was nothing left. She didn't trust me not to do something stupid and I certainly didn't trust her not to tell. The door to the surgery banged open. Tommy stared at me and then watched Nancy spin around in her chair. I could see that man with the shiny shoes standing outside. I recognised him from the farm. He looked at me and moved away from the doorway back towards the road.

Tommy hissed, 'Why are you not answering the phone?'

Nancy gaped, closed her mouth and looked down.

191

Tommy pointed at me. 'What's she doing here?'

'Mum wouldn't let me out without her.'

'Jesus,' said Tommy, turning to the still open door and then back to Nancy. He walked up to her and pointed two fingers. 'You promised me.'

'I know! I meant it! Some priest turned up and I couldn't get away. It really wasn't my fault.' Nancy couldn't even look at him but she looked at me, all right. I could see her thinking how to blame it all on me. 'Bernie made Mum send her too.'

And now Tommy looked at me as well.

'Another time, then?' he said, and banged the door shut behind him.

Nancy, pale and arms crossed over her body, kicked at the desk for a bit. That was when I first felt scared of her. I was going to pay for this. It wasn't my fault, but he was angry with her, so she was angry with me. I didn't look right at her, just from the corner of my eye, and waited for her to do something.

26

Now

She followed Bernie down the driveway, feeling the roll of the white gravel under her feet. In the dusk it seemed to glow under the thick trees. She pulled the front of her coat together and zipped it up, anything but think about where Bernie was taking her. She felt her eyes start to fill now and began rapidly blinking.

'Bernie, I know where we're going. Do we need to do this?'

Bernie was waiting at the end of the driveway, the setting sun making her hair glow a little. She didn't answer. Nancy caught her up and they walked along the verge together. Nancy thought of Bruce, running alongside them. She shook her head and focussed on the landscape.

Bernie lifted the nylon rope and opened the gate. She walked through but Nancy stopped. The mud was thick around the opening with the footprints and sheep shit. A few steps out, in which she nearly lost a boot, and she'd reached firmer ground. A sheep bleated at her and trotted away.

Nancy felt sick. 'I know, Bernie. I know what I did. You know what happened. Can we go back?'

Those stones, which she'd only seen from here in the dark, seemed the centre of the field from this perspective. The pitch and dip of the field further up wasn't straight across, but more circular, curving in a wide arc. She stood upright and backed away from the stones to have a proper look. There were four large oblong stones, three lying long and upright, and one on top but pushed to the side. Christ. It really was a circle with a tomb.

'It looks different from here,' Nancy whispered.

'It looks different in the light, you mean? You've seen it from here, Nancy.'

The sheep, which had been so still she thought they were asleep, broke like a wave and ran either side, back up the field. She never quite liked sheep.

'So?' said Bernie.

'What?'

'Just say it. What you did right here. I know we both know but I've never heard anyone say it. Just tell me why you did it.'

'I don't know why I did it. Children do stupid things, you know that. I'm going back.' Nancy walked slowly back to the gate. It felt the same, walking away from Bernadette in this field. She felt the horror of what she was doing echo back, and stopped.

'Oh fuck!'

Nancy turned. Bernie was standing at the open side of the stones. Nancy heard her cry, tiny like a kitten, and Bernie fell to her knees. Nancy ran towards her but waited just short of the stones.

'What is it? Is something there?'

'He's still here.'

'Who is?'

Bernie covered her face and sobbed. Nancy looked back to the gate and up towards the house, her bedroom window. There was no-one there. She slowly walked behind Bernie and saw the gap between the stones. She couldn't see anything. She got right behind Bernie and looked down into the ditch below the stones. She gasped.

'Is that a body?'

The bones weren't exactly where they should be, but it

194

was clear enough. The sun shone through the far gap created where the stones didn't quite create a corner. A skull. A corner of a ragged blanket.

'That blanket.' Nancy fell to her knees as well. Her stomach felt heavy, the base of her throat tight.

Bernie shook her head. 'I can't believe they left him here.'

Nancy could feel her hands trembling. Her words came out too quickly. 'Who is it?'

'What?'

'Who is it?'

Bernie wiped her eyes and looked at Nancy. 'It's Ryan, of course.'

'No.' Nancy stumbled to her feet, 'It's not him. He left. We know he did, didn't we see him leave? Mum said. I'm sure Mum heard from him.'

'It's him.'

'I can't –'

Nancy staggered away, trying not to be sick, looking for something to lean on. There was nothing. She pulled herself to the top of the bank and sat down heavily. She focused on her breathing, on looking normal in case Hurley looked out of her window, in case anyone looked out. Bernie was bent over. She looked like she was praying. Nancy wanted to tell her to get up, to run, but she couldn't. All she could do was watch.

The sun was almost set, filtered through far off trees. Bernie forced herself up and sat down next to Nancy.

'I didn't know,' said Nancy. 'Ryan. I didn't know.'

'I know. I can tell.'

'Some things are so vivid. Even what was missing is vivid. Like when you got back you didn't speak for a month. That was the beginning of the end.'

'I didn't die, Nancy.'

'In a way, you did. And then you started talking and you never stopped. But you weren't you anymore.' Nancy looked back to the stones. 'What do you want me to say?'

195

'I just want you to admit what you did. I want you to acknowledge how it all started. No-one believed me. It only got so bad because you wouldn't tell them what you knew. When I wasn't talking you should have been.'

Nancy closed her eyes. A plan, a night time escapade after everyone was asleep. Bruce and the stones. She looked at Bernie. She wanted to tell her it only gets worse and worse. Bernie could only hate her more. Words were dangerous.

'Why did you come back here?' she asked Bernie.

She raised her palms and spread her arms wide. 'Mum told me you were coming here. She wants us to make things right before she dies and all that. But that's not it. That's not why I'm here. I knew it was my last chance. It seemed like the last ever chance to find out.'

'Find out what?'

'What you know. It was the only time I could ask you.'

Nancy could smell blood and apples.

'This is what I know,' Bernie whispered. 'Uncle Ryan came back and Tommy killed him. Then Tommy started to flirt with you, all the driving lessons and make up, and you took his side, and I knew and no-one would ever believe me. You gave me up and then you gave up on me. No matter who I tried to tell, they thought I was mad because you never said a word.' Her voice dropped almost to a whisper. 'Say it now. Just say it.'

Nancy kept her eyes on the stones and thought about nothing but breathing until she was sure she wouldn't be sick.

'Can we leave the field?' she asked.

They helped each other up and walked up the field towards the house. Nancy tugged at the string, then gave up and climbed over, followed by Bernie.

Bernie looked away, back towards the stones. Nancy wanted to look anywhere but at her. She didn't want to remember. Too late. It was coming back, Cassie's room, keys in locks, silences, footsteps and, everywhere, Tommy.

Bernie spoke, 'You always hated getting into trouble.'

Nancy closed her eyes. 'I don't understand how these things are connected. It was at home when it all got really awful. You can't find anything here to explain what you did. You blamed everyone. You even blamed Dad and he even wasn't here, was he? He didn't know anything.'

Bernie barked a laugh. 'Anything? Do you believe that? And even if you do, that means that you know Mum did.'

'You took it out on him more. I never understood that.'

'He was the one who could have said something. Why didn't he? It wasn't his home, or his family. He should have done something.' She pointed towards the stones. 'He's the one who made me go there.'

'It wasn't his fault. He blamed himself more than Mum did. You know what it did to him.'

'Nancy, getting someone to admit the truth has become absolutely vital to me staying alive. He knew something. Everyone knew something. Everyone suffered.'

'Don't you think-'

Bernie interrupted, her eyes narrow. 'Do you seriously think you're going to suggest something that hasn't been covered in the last thirty years of being committed, therapies, analysis, drugs, all the rest of it? If you do, please say it.'

Nancy shook her head. 'So, what do you need now?'

'Tell me what I don't know.'

Nancy sighed, 'Bernie –'

'Anything. I've wanted to ask you again for so many years, but I couldn't do it by phone or email. I know you. It had to be us and it had to be here. You spent so much time with Tommy, you must know something.'

Nancy looked around for something to give her. 'They used all of the barns, just about. There was a large metal case where they buried the guns.'

'You saw that?'

'I wasn't supposed to. When they realised –' Nancy covered her mouth. She still couldn't say. 'It was real, wasn't it?'

197

Bernie eyes were wide. 'Anything we can find, any information can help me get one over on him. Knowledge is power, Nancy. I want to have the power, for a change. Where did they bury them?'

Nancy held her hand over the wasteland between the barns and the cow shed. 'Here. Somewhere here.'

The rain was starting now, falling from the dark blue sky, tapping on Nancy's raincoat and making it bloom blotches. She pushed her hands further into her pockets and picked her way across the yard. She climbed over the bits of metal and lumps of grass which had grown over other, unknown rubbish. Her wellies slipped on something wetly sheering from the ground, but she didn't fall. She took in the gate at the end which led to the field behind them, although she couldn't see it, and the open gate leading to the silo and hay loft, which she could just about see through the thin trees. Turning right around she saw the cow shed and, turning right again, the brick shed with its passageway to the yard, the garage, and then two further sheds. So many hiding places.

Bernie was still standing by the gate, waiting. She seemed to have decided something and walked to Nancy.

'If no-one is going to tell me,' she said, 'I'm going to find proof I can hold in my hands.'

'Proof of what?'

'Proof of anything they were doing. Proof that I'm not mad.'

'You're not. What will you do with it? You can't go to the police.'

'Why not?'

Nancy thought of Hurley. 'It goes too deep. What about Donn and Agatha? What about Mum?'

'What about you?'

Nancy nodded. 'What about me?'

Bernie lowered her voice again. 'Nancy, I won't ever tell. I can keep my mouth shut.'

'Bern, you have never once kept your mouth shut! You have always told and talked and shouted. You have always told at least one person and I know because that person used to be me. You will talk. You can't help it.'

'Nancy, you owe me.' She touched Nancy's arm. 'Will you help me look?'

'For what?'

Nancy tried to turn away and Bernie pulled her back.

'Will you?'

'I can't, Bernie. I don't think I want to know.'

Bernie grabbed Nancy's hand.

'If you do, I'll try to go home. I'll try to visit Mum and Dad.'

Nancy looked at her eyes. Bernie had never lied to her, not on purpose. She talked and talked, but she always meant what she said. Nancy owed her.

'I'll help.'

27

Then

I was given the job of making afters for tomorrow by Sister Agatha. I wasn't happy about being so close to Cassie's room but couldn't get out of it. And it was my favourite. At home I always begged to make the jelly. I loved the feeling of breaking off each slippery cube and dropping it into the bowl. One always got sneaked back to my mouth, and I had to chew it too quickly so Sister Agatha didn't notice.

She brought the boiled kettle over to fill the bowl and I stirred until the cubes were cherry globes and then peas and then sherbet pips. I wiped my hands on my jeans but it didn't quite get rid of the film of strawberry. I tasted a finger, but only the smell was still there.

When I went back through Catriona had just arrived and we were sent up to bed.

'Second visit in a week,' muttered Sister Agatha.

Nancy tried to argue to stay up later but Mum wasn't going to shift, even after Catriona took Nancy's side. She didn't argue for me. I don't think she even looked at me to say goodnight, but Nancy got a promise of some makeup.

'We'll see,' said Mum.

Catriona tossed her thick, brushed hair and made a sad face at Nancy. Her lipstick glistened. Nancy lowered her eyes and punched me on the way up the stairs.

'It's all your fault. I'm sick of babysitting you.'

Nancy got ready first and by the time I'd finished brushing my teeth she was in bed reading.

'What's that?'

'I got it from the drawers.' She turned the cover towards me. *Jaws*. She was actually reading it.

I lay back on my pillow and pulled the sheets and blankets up to my neck. Nancy had passed some marker I couldn't see. Catriona liked her. She was ready to read scary books. I tipped my head back to look up at an upside down Jesus with glowing heart and sighed.

'Shut up,' she said.

'Can I read it after you?'

'It's way too scary for you.'

The end of the sunshine, filtered through leaves and twigs, was making the curtains glow. I could hear distant words from the kitchen and the flicking of pages. Florence shifted in her bed.

Sometimes the dusk was full of the shudder of shotguns. The dawn too. Rooks roosted in the trees in the front of this farm and every other, and they were bad, we were told. Like dark, evil spirits, they would peck out the eyes of the new-born lambs and eat them. I hated that image, the small boiled eggs of eyes leaving bloody holes in the heads of the fluffy lambs. We were never here for lambing, but I felt as if I'd seen it. The sudden bangs in the evening made me jump and in the morning they woke me with a jolt. Mum hated the noise of the rooks coming home in the evening and cawing at each other across the treetops. I didn't mind it like I minded the shooting. After we heard them we'd hunt for the cartridges in the grass and leaves and sometimes we'd find live ones. Mum or Sister Agatha would take them off us and tell us off for picking them up, and then we'd look for more.

'Nancy?'

She didn't answer.

'Do you want to listen from the stairs?'

201

'No,' she said, as if it was the silliest thing I'd yet come up with.

I closed my eyes. A low sound made me open them in time to see lights crossing the ceiling. Bruce barked a couple of times and I imagined the reckless race he ran against the car wheels. My heart began to beat fast and I raised myself to look at Nancy.

'Is Tommy coming?'

She shrugged, but put her book on her chest to listen. The car went quiet and the door closed with a dull slam. Then the footsteps, kicking up stones, came to the doorstep and the front door opened. We never heard the knock from up here, but he always did that. I lay down again and pulled up the sheet. The kitchen door opening let voices out. They were suddenly quiet and a number of footsteps went to the front door which closed with a bang.

They were out the front now, kicking stones towards the car. Nancy picked up her book again but I knew she wasn't reading it. I listened for a sign that they were leaving. It went on too long.

I peeled back the blankets and began to creep towards the window.

'Get back into bed,' hissed Nancy.

'You just don't want Catriona to see you.'

I reached the curtains and began to edge away the material from the far left corner. It was quite dark in the sky, but the light from the front room lit them up – Tommy, Donn, Catriona and, a few steps back from them, my Mum stroking Bruce's head. They were looking at something in the boot of Tommy's car. Their voices were low and I couldn't really catch anything. Tommy, as usual, was doing most of the talking. At one point he took something long from the back seat of the car and hit it into the boot really hard.

My mother shouted, 'No!'

I couldn't hear the impact so thought it might be something

soft. Then he pulled it out again, leant on it and I recognised it as a shotgun.

Tommy walked up to my mother and spoke quietly. He turned away and slammed the boot shut. I looked to see what my mother was doing and saw that she was looking straight at me. She looked away. I let the curtain slip back into place and ran back to bed.

I let Nancy pretend to read for a bit longer, breathing slowly to calm my heart down. She flicked another page.

'Who's out there, then?'

I turned onto my side, away from her. 'Go and see for yourself.'

I felt like crying. What if it was Ryan? I thought Ryan was in Cassie's room, but maybe Mum had let Tommy take him, which was bad, but he was alive, and that might be good. But if Mum had let him that would be the worst. Maybe Catriona had smiled and told her that she was brilliant too and gave her lipstick to stain her mouth. Mum wouldn't do that. She wasn't as silly as Nancy.

They were still outside. There was a bang, a shotgun. It didn't sound right outside but, from the way the blood was pumping inside my ears, I couldn't be sure. Nancy shook my shoulder and I sat up.

'Who is outside?'

'You'll tell Tommy if I say anything, you said so.'

'I won't, I swear.'

I lay back down. I hadn't seen what it was or who it was. She wouldn't be able to either. But I thought if I said it anyway it could be the thing that made her stay away from Tommy.

'You have to actually swear not to tell Tommy this time, Nancy. And if you break it I will never forgive you, not ever.'

She paused, but then she said it. 'I swear.'

'Tommy put Ryan in the boot. I saw him. Definitely.' I leaned across, 'And he's got a shotgun.'

Nancy bit her lip. 'Turn the light off. Quick!'

I turned it off and we lay side by side, listening for everything outside, hoping it would stay outside. I began to believe that I'd actually seen Ryan for real.

'I told you,' I said. 'He's been in Cassie's room all this time.'

'It can't be him,' whispered Nancy. 'He left. He was only here for a couple of hours and he left. Mum said.'

I didn't feel like arguing. I was just glad she was talking to me.

I wondered where Sister Agatha was. She could have been standing on the doorstep, I wouldn't have seen her, but I became convinced that she was standing outside our room. We weren't the only ones who knew which steps made a sound and which didn't. I wanted to sit up and look for feet shadows under the door, but I didn't want to see that they were there, only that they weren't there. So I didn't look at all. After a while the car started up, but it only sounded as if he drove through the archway and paused. There was the loud squeak of the gate into the yard and then it drove off again.

No-one ever used that gate to drive through. The tractors always came up from the bottom, next to the silo. I didn't think it even opened more than the width of a person.

I felt sick. I wanted Bruce. I'd let him into the lobby and the kitchen, but never any further. I wanted him to lie down here in the bed, or I'd lie next to him on the floor next to the fireplace that never had a fire in it. I bundled some blanket into my arms and made believe until I could feel his doggy breath on my face.

28

Now

'There's really nothing you can do to help,' said Bernie.

'But it looks fun. We're bored.'

'Not bored enough,' said Bernie. 'It's raining. You hate the rain.'

'No, we don't!'

Nancy watched the to and fro of the argument knowing full well, as her children clearly did, that Bernie would back down. She admired their persistence and Bernie's self-delusion. Adrian and Elian didn't look keen on an afternoon in the rain and said nothing. Hurley said nothing but Nancy knew it was because he didn't want to ruin their chances. He was no good at arguing.

'I think,' said Bernie, 'that you lot should go off in the car and do something fun, while me and Nancy just do some tidying up for Donn.'

'No!'

'You can tidy inside.'

'No!'

Hurley cleared his throat. 'Please can I help?'

Bernie covered up her surprise pretty quickly. 'Sure,' she said, caught off guard.

And that was that.

'What are we going to tell the children?' Nancy asked.

'We'll get them to tidy up and we can get a long piece of metal and work out where it's buried. It's big, right?'

Nancy nodded. 'You know it's probably long gone, don't you? They won't have left anything after all this time.'

'So we don't need to say anything.'

The children and Adrian found boots and coats and were outside first. Nancy was surprised by Hurley's urgency. Elian stayed inside for a while and then came out and stood on the side lines for as long as possible, but the rain was too cold to stand still for long. He soon joined Adrian and Bernie in dragging the large pieces of metal and wood to the sides of the square.

Nancy told Hurley to look for some shears in the garage to cut back the grass and weeds. He ducked through the archway before she could stop him and came back with a scythe and a rusty pair of shears that he soon gave up on. Erin and Maeve had the job of moving whatever he cut to the gate of Bryn's field.

'Can't we just feed it straight to the sheep?' asked Maeve.

'No, there could be weeds that are poisonous to them,' said Hurley.

Nancy didn't know how he could know this. Maybe he'd spent more time with Donn than she realised. She looked round to all four gates but Donn wasn't there. She went over to the others, nearly snapping her ankle twice, and helped them to clear the side nearest the silo around the immovable tractor.

Elian's jacket wasn't even water resistant and she could see him getting increasingly grumpy. She took off her jacket.

'I'm too hot,' she said, 'you wear it.'

He shook his head but the next time she looked he had it on, zipped and hood up, presumably over his already wet clothes. She was so warm that the occasional trickle of rain down her spine felt quite pleasant.

The rain was constant but not too heavy. It made a slight sound on the roofs and metal scrap, a rustling in the grass. She looked over to the kids. Hurley was sweeping the scythe,

the girls either side of him. She took a breath to shout at him, but Bernie put her hand out.

'Don't. He's fine.'

'It's dangerous. They're standing very close.'

'That's their lookout.'

Bernie turned back to the tyre she was rolling. Nancy watched her. She couldn't get a handle on Bernie's rules. The girls were never unsupervised, but she was willing for them to learn a lesson from a scythe.

'He's very careful,' Bernie called, coming back. 'He thinks about things.'

Nancy tried not to look surprised. No-one said that about Hurley. They said he was too rough, too angry, too slow, too erratic.

'If you're just going to stand there . . .' Bernie was waiting with one end of a plank lifted. Nancy took the other end. When they had come back for the next plank Bernie stamped on the ground. It sounded metallic.

'There's something buried here,' she whispered. 'Some kind of container.'

Nancy shuddered.

Bernie dropped her end of the plank and listened for the bang again. She raised her arms, stretching her spine. 'Tea break!'

Bernie and Elian went inside to make drinks. The children carried on. The girls were always together, she realised. Not just next to each other, but a team, supporting each other. She and Bernie had always been in competition, trying to get each other in trouble, trying to seem the best. She'd been truly horrible to Bernie, even before that summer. Nancy knew she owed her, but it could be more than she had to give.

Nancy went up to the barn with the blue door and tried to open it again. It was still wedged closed with age and rain. The last time it had opened may have been the final time.

Adrian said, 'I think it's a bit late to be looking for shelter.'

His jacket was waterproof but he'd unzipped it and the hood was back. The water on his face could have been rain or sweat but he didn't look tired.

'I can't believe they're all still standing, these buildings,' she said. 'Once the rain got in, you'd think that was it.'

'They're stone,' he said. 'The roof and windows will go, but there'll be here for centuries.'

Like the standing stones, thought Nancy, our monuments.

The others came back and they all found a tyre to sit on.

Nancy sipped the tea as the rain dripped into it. 'Watery.'

Elian sipped his. 'I miss coffee. What this place needs is a good Starbucks.'

Bernie snorted, 'And a McDonalds? And maybe a drive-in movie? And,' she added, 'God, we've adopted everything else anyway. Except the drive-ins. Wrong kind of rain.'

'It does rain in the US.'

'Yeah,' said Bernie, 'when it's supposed to.'

'There's hardly a monsoon season.'

'Just a tornado season.'

'Not in Michigan.'

'The thunderstorms are amazing though,' said Nancy. 'The houses shake like they're going to collapse.'

'Because they're made of wood. Like the Americans have never read the Three Little Pigs.'

Nancy laughed. 'Ridiculous, isn't it?'

Elian smiled uncomfortably. 'Well, ours hasn't fallen over yet.'

Bernie and Nancy spoke at the same time. 'Ten thousand Elvis impersonators . . .'

The girls were squatting under the archway. Hurley was still harvesting the weeds.

'Shouldn't we tell them they're not allowed under there?' asked Nancy.

'Why?'

'Because we were always told that.'

208

'And has it fallen down yet?'

Nancy shrugged. 'A monument.'

Bernie leaned over to Elian, 'Made of stone, you see.'

He half smiled and put his mug down on the path. He wandered off to survey their work.

'Doesn't like feeling he's the butt, does he?' said Bernie.

Nancy said, 'Americans are like that. Like to take themselves seriously. They really believe that they're misunderstood superheroes. It's weird. And I know it's a big country but, I swear, one year the only news I saw about the UK was a farmer electrocuting his herd of cows. All year!'

'I never heard about that. Maybe they made it up,' said Bernie. 'What keeps you there?'

'They do.' Nancy pointed to Hurley and then hesitated when she looked at Elian.

Bernie raised her eyebrows. 'Would you ever come back?'

'Not on my own.'

Adrian joined Elian.

'Do they get on?' Nancy asked.

'I think so. Don't you?'

'I have no idea what they think of each other. I've got so used to people being polite rather than honest.'

'It's like that here too.'

'It's different there. It's an art, saying just the right thing for how it sounds. I'm terrible at it. Sometimes, if people ask me how I am, I tell them.'

Bernie laughed, 'Social suicide.'

'Not in detail. Just like, tired or not very well. And they seize up because then they feel committed to hearing all about it. And I don't want to tell them all about it, I just want them to know I'm not great, fine or super.'

Bernie lowered her voice, 'You don't have to stay there.'

Nancy stood up. 'I feel my options are limited.' She peeled the t-shirt from her back and shook it. 'Come on, then.' She turned back to Bernie and then followed her gaze. Tommy stood at the gate nearest them, next to the silo. He had his arms crossed on the top bar and one foot resting on the lower one. A dog sat by his feet, head lowered, watching.

Nancy whispered, 'What do we do?'

Bernie opened and closed her mouth. Nancy looked around but everyone else was busy looking at other things, normal things.

Nancy said, 'We have to say something.'

Bernie shook her head. Nancy, stomach turning, walked around the rubble to the gate.

'What do you want? I seem to remember being turfed off your farm.'

'But I consider this as part of my farm and I wonder what you're doing to it.'

Nancy took a breath and lifted her chin. 'We're clearing the rubbish and sorting it out for recycling. You can get money for scrap metal and we thought Donn would appreciate it.'

'And maybe my agreed price took that into account. And maybe I'll have to lower it. Considerably.'

Nancy crossed her arms to try to control the shivering. 'Right, well we can leave it here if you really want it.'

'You're looking a bit cold, there.'

'I'm fine.' Nancy held his gaze.

'There's been talk of bodies, would you believe?'

Nancy raised her eyebrows. 'Really?'

'And police. Now, that interests me and it interests my family. If you liked I could give you a few phone numbers. My brother is in the police. So are two uncles, three nieces and one of my nephews. And that doesn't even start to cover it. Any of them, any time, would be happy to come and have a wee chat with you. You, or Hurley, over there.'

Nancy felt the rain run down her back. 'I know your daughter talked to him. I know that's how you know his name.'

'Do you know there are some far flung people who believe

210

you have power over someone just by knowing their name? And it's true. Just imagine this.' He leaned over a little further and dropped his voice. 'You're crossing the road. You've waited until there's a space and it's safe to cross. So off you trot. And you're halfway across when someone shouts your name. Really shouts, and you know it's just for you. Now, do you wait to look until you're safely over the other side? You do not. You stop and look right then and for as long as that person shouts,' he whispered, 'they've got you.'

Nancy shuddered.

'Now some people are more easily led than others. And I hear that your boy, Hurley, over there, is, well . . .'

'Is what?'

Tommy smiled, straightened up and touched two fingers to his forehead, like a salute.

'Is what?' said Nancy.

He turned and walked slowly towards the lane.

'Is what, you coward?' shouted Nancy.

She felt hands on her shoulders and span round. Bernie was pale. Adrian, Elian and the children had already gone.

'Let's go in,' Bernie said.

Nancy nodded and let her lead the way around the debris which filled the path. Bernie stopped.

'What is it?'

'Look.' Bernie pointed.

It wasn't white, more browny grey, but it was recognisably a bone. Nancy felt faint. Bernie knelt down in the mud and began to wipe the mud away. She took small handfuls and threw them behind her. Nancy held her arms across her chest as Bernie gently followed the line of the body. So many tiny bones, then larger ones, began to make a rib cage. Nancy felt sick. She turned away, focused on the blue door and the empty gate and the missing glass from the windows and the door to the first floor which had no reason to be there. She heard Bernie's small cry above the blood rushing in her ears.

Bernie was sitting back on her heels, her hands loose on her knees. Her head was bowed and she was crying quietly. Nancy forced herself to look down at the corpse.

'It's Bruce.' Nancy knelt down too. Bruce, buried with the rocks and concrete and metal and bits of rubbish from decades of waste.

'We're not going to find anything, are we?' said Bernie. 'Nothing I can take away with me.'

'I don't think so.' Nancy looked at the bones. 'Are you going to be okay?'

'I'll have to be.'

But the way Bernie looked at her made Nancy anxious.

29

Then

The farm was a funny mix of old and really old. The thing that Donn went on about most was how right they'd been not to allow pylons onto the farmland, preserving the landscape and its value. My mother groaned when she remembered how long they'd waited for electricity to arrive as a result. Not quite in time for the moon landings, not that they had a telly to watch it on. That didn't arrive until the seventies. And I thought waiting till 1980 for a colour telly was bad.

'What did you do?' I asked.

'Read books and worked hard.'

To get to go somewhere else, I thought. So many of them, their brothers and sisters and aunts and uncles, had left for other continents. I thought Ireland grew so many people that they had to fill up other countries. I liked it at the farm. To me it was a different continent from the south London suburb where I lived. We even had to take a boat to get here, like it was a million miles away.

When Dad brought the car when he came to collect us we would be free to travel around the countryside. Dad showed us a different Ireland to the one we saw for those first weeks of the holiday. Where Mum would drive us to the seaside, or Sister Agatha might agree to an outing to churches with holy springs and wells, he might take us to the same places and their pagan springs and wells. He always had a compass with him and sometimes included it in the photos so he could orient himself with the maps at home.

Nancy hated going to the stones, but I didn't. The Giant's Ring and the Giant's Grave were places I could understand. One time I picked up the largest quartz stones from the driveway and made my own stone circle on the edge of the driveway, where I'd trimmed away the longer grass with the kitchen scissors. I took Mum's camera from her suitcase and tried to take a close up but it was probably going to turn out blurry. Most small things I tried to photograph big turned out fuzzy blobs on a shiny new photo. Mum would pick up the packet from Boots and complain about the number of bad photos. I said she could always get me my own camera. She said I'd have to pay for them to be developed and she'd think about it. I waited, and used hers while I waited.

Dad's stones were bigger, much bigger than him sometimes. They would sit on top of each other, looking like strange airy houses. They didn't look safe to me, but as long as he went in I would follow him. He would call them tombs but they weren't anything like what I thought of as a tomb. Tombs were in churches with statues of sleeping dead people and metal fences around them to make sure no-one mistook them for seats. Or they were miniature houses in the biggest graveyards with roofs and doors even, but I didn't want to think of who might want to use the doors. I could see how those house tombs looked a bit like his stone tombs, but I just thought of them as special quiet places. Usually we were the only people there. Sometimes they were circles of standing stones called things like Ossian's grave and he encouraged us to sit and sketch them in the drizzle while he took photographs of them and sometimes measured them.

The Giant's Ring was Dad's favourite and he used to complain, to me, to the air, that it should be as well known as Avebury. He also complained that I was usually the only one who had agreed to go. It was a bowl in the earth with steep sides and Dad liked to sit there and try to find evidence of holes where stones had been.

If we weren't out, finding stones, he was in the house, reading or drawing. He had so much he wanted to do that those last few days of the holiday when he'd arrived went past the quickest. They seemed quieter too. What I liked best was that he seemed to keep Tommy away. No-one even mentioned his name and I never had to listen out for his car in the dark. Books and stones and quiet and no Tommy.

On our last holiday Dad had made tracings on greaseproof paper of some old maps he found in Coleraine library of the land where the farm now stood. He spent ages matching up rivers and tracks and then took out his pencil to find other markers to look for. The stones near the Coleraine road, the bridge that led to the village. He smiled as he found matches, getting closer and closer to where the farm had been built, until he arrived at the fields either side.

Nodding to himself he rolled up the combined maps and waited for Donn to come in. Sister Agatha was there, but Dad waited for Donn. I didn't know whether it was Donn's farm or belonged to both of them, but I wouldn't have tried to ask her either. She didn't like questions.

I was sitting by the fire when Dad called Donn to the table. He rolled out one map, then another, my father in his slippers which he always brought with him, and Donn in his socks stained brown by overspills into his wellies.

'You have to tell someone so they can research it. It could be a really important discovery.' He waved a book at Donn, 'I haven't read anything about a cairn in this area. Not ever.'

'No. It's a working farm, nothing more than that.'

'Can I just tell the University in Belfast? They'd just take some measurements.'

'No way.'

'But why not?'

'Not everything has to be measured. It's my field and I'm not moving the sheep.'

'What harm could it do? I can think of all the benefits, the way it could expand prehistoric knowledge of the area.'

Donn nodded outside. 'I don't care about that. I'm not having strangers trampling round my farm.'

'I do care.'

'Shame it's not your pile of stones then.'

'In a way it isn't yours either. It belongs to everyone, the world, as a little piece of the puzzle of all of us.'

'If you, or anyone else, tell anyone about that cairn, whatever you want to call it,' he lowered his voice and raised his hand, 'I can't answer for what will happen. You know what I mean, I hope.'

My father drew back and then flushed red. 'No, Donn. I don't. You'll have to spell it out to me because all I know is that an ancient and possibly sacred site is going ignored.'

Donn walked out of the room.

'It's wilful ignorance!' my father shouted after him, but he didn't turn back. Dad slapped the book against his thigh and sat down again.

Sister Agatha came out of the kitchen with a pile of plates. 'Sacred,' she spat, shoving his papers and books to one side. 'You wouldn't know sacred if God himself spoke to you from a burning bush.' She stomped away.

I could see Dad's expression, eyebrows raised and mouth open, and started to giggle. I forced two fingers between my teeth and bit down hard. Dad talking to a bush! It was too funny. He looked at me and rolled his eyes. I took my fingers out and let myself laugh properly.

Sister Agatha came back empty handed and picked up the maps as if tidying them away. She slapped away Dad's hand as he tried to re-roll them. I stopped laughing. Holding them all in one hand she placed them in the centre of the fire. Dad stood beside me, his hand on my head, as we watched them burn.

If my dad had protested, Sister Agatha might have beaten him around the head with her leather bible. She'd threatened me with it enough times. That's maybe why they didn't speak other than around the dinner table, although that could be a dangerous place with all those knives. He read everything differently and if I wanted a clear answer on the bogs and stones and flags and kerbs I had to wait until he got there. He was the only person who would tell me what things meant, and he knew because he was always looking. He looked for markings in the ground on aerial maps, he looked for stones in groups, or on their own if they were big enough.

That last year I'd found something amazing for him and I waited four weeks for his arrival and didn't even tell Nancy. In the white, angular gravel at the front of the house I found fossils. Loads of fossils, but my favourite was the heavy ammonite, maybe because I knew the name for that one. It sat heavily, too big for my palm, half excavated from the stone in which it sat. It was a dull grey in the quartz-like gravel and the first one I saw. I felt like my dad as I looked for more, and found them.

In bed at night I imagined scouring the whole driveway with my dad, cataloguing our finds. So far I hadn't found any more than a foot away from the house, but as a team we could look properly. I thought up how it had arrived in the driveway, how in mining the gravel the diggers had hit a seam of fossil rich rock and not noticed, just emptying it all the way from the large white gates to the large white house.

When he turned up in our car I ran out and grabbed him first. I sat on the steps to the house with him and handed him my finds one at a time and showed him where I found them. By this time my mother and sisters and Sister Agatha were all on the steps too.

217

'Do you know why you found them there?' said Sister Agatha. 'It's because that's where they landed when I threw them out the window.' She laughed to herself and went inside.

I watched her go and then looked at the window. Dad tried to make me feel better by saying what a brilliant collection it was, and it didn't matter how they'd got there, but it did to me.

I walked around through the garage to the cow shed and pulled myself up on the gate. It swung a little, but the blue nylon stopped it from opening. I could see the dip of the land, but not the stones. I climbed higher and had one leg over the top bar when I heard a man's voice. I couldn't hear what he said, and I couldn't tell if he was talking to me, but I scrambled back to the cow shed and ran back through passage to the yard.

Sister Agatha caught me.

30

Now

'Nancy!'

It sounded like the last in a line of shouts, exasperated.

Elian was at the bedroom door. 'Your mother wants to talk to you.'

Nancy looked away from the window, confused. 'She's here?'

'No, on the phone.'

She went down the stairs and rubbed her face before picking up the phone.

'Mum?'

'What's going on, Nancy?'

'What do you mean?' Then she realised. Donn had told her.

'Why are you doing what you're doing, that's what I mean.'

Nancy closed the parlour door behind her and stood awkwardly. She tried to think of what to say. Why was she doing what she was doing?

'It's Bernadette.'

'I realise that, but I didn't think you'd encourage her, let alone help. This could set her back years. Why are you attracting attention to yourselves?'

Nancy took a deep breath. 'You told me to sort it out with Bernadette. I'm sorting it out.'

'Not like this! Nancy,' her mother spoke loudly and

clearly, 'go and see Agatha. Don't do anything else, just talk to Agatha. Promise me.'

Nancy carefully placed the phone back in the cradle. It dinged. She remembered hearing that ding from the other end, how abrupt and rude it was.

She opened the parlour door.

'Are we going?' asked Erin.

Nancy paused. The phone started ringing again.

'Yes, let's go. I can phone whoever back later.'

Bernie followed her to the hall.

Nancy sighed, 'Can you guess what Mum wanted?'

'Bernie's mad, stop facilitating her delusions?'

'Something like that. Not quite that bad.'

'Not quite that direct, you mean?'

'She loves you. She wants you to be happy and she thinks this won't make you happy. That's not a bad thing, or a strange thing.'

'Forgetting doesn't make people happy.'

It did, thought Nancy. Forgetting was fine.

The sky above Portstewart was cloudy but they hadn't seen any rain, so that qualified as a beautiful day. The two girls sat in the rear of the car. Elian, Hurley and Nancy sat in the middle, Elian angled so he could talk continuously to Adrian.

'Why Portstewart and not Portrush?'

He'd clearly been studying the map.

'Catholics go to Portstewart, Protestants to Portrush,' said Bernie.

'Are you serious?' he said. 'But none of you are even Catholic.'

Bernie intoned, 'Once a Catholic, always a Catholic. Sand or town?'

'Let's try sand first, in case it does rain,' said Adrian.

They took a turning to the left and drove through the dunes onto the beach, a wide arc of deep yellow sand.

'Um, you're driving on the sand,' said Elian.

'Really?' said Adrian, and he drove on, smiling to himself.

Elian looked at Nancy and then back out of the window.

'Have you ever had to dig your way out?'

'It isn't a marsh,' said Bernie.

Adrian pulled up and they unloaded the blankets and buckets from the tiny boot space behind the girls' seats. Nancy marvelled at Bernie's preparedness. They spread out the blankets. Nancy sat down and patted a place for Hurley to sit beside her.

'Want to make a sandcastle?' she asked.

Elian said, 'He can come up with me and Adrian to the sand dunes.'

'But he's never made a sandcastle.'

'I need to keep moving. It will be better for his leg, too, than sitting on the damp sand.'

Elian, Hurley and Adrian strode off, up the nearest dune, and the genders were decisively split. Bernie tried to get the girls to move, pointed out that there was a tennis set and a Frisbee in the boot, but they glowered and stayed close to each other. Nancy took a bucket and spade and began to make a castle.

'Do you want to find me some stones or shells to decorate it?'

Erin rolled her eyes and Nancy realised she had made it to embarrassing older relative status. Or just old.

'I don't think they're going to be persuaded,' said Bernie, 'just leave them to get bored first.'

'We're already bored,' said Maeve.

'Not bored enough,' said Nancy and Bernie simultaneously. They looked at each other and smiled.

She finished her castle, lacking in turrets, brushed off her hands and took her phone from her pocket.

'I seem to have a signal, but it thinks I'm in Eire. I'm going to look for some shells,' Nancy said.

She got up awkwardly, brushed off her skirt and walked down to the water. It was out a long way and the sand became too wet for her canvas shoes before she got there. She'd forgotten how far the sea retreated on this wide, flat beach. The best beach in the world, she thought, if it wasn't for the weather. Had her dad said that? Someone said it. It reminded her of sitting in the farm parlour, warming up in front of the turf and worrying about Bruce outside.

She couldn't see any shells, but if she stood still too long her feet may sink down, then her legs and torso. Her arms would extend above her submerged head and her fingers would wave like discoloured seaweed.

She exhaled and turned back to the shore. She had wandered at more of angle than she thought. She could see the blanket and the three people on it, but the three people in the dunes were hidden. That dune grass, was it razor grass, was violent. She'd had thousands of whip wounds from it as it caught her as she scrambled up or rolled down, squealing either way. Hiding at the top of the dune felt safer than in the bottom of a valley. It was possible that no-one would find her and sometimes dusty whirlwinds struck up and forced her to hide her head inside her t-shirt. Bernie was always there, though. She could hide anywhere if Bernie knew where she was because she thought she was amazing and brilliant for the longest that anyone ever had. That ended. She knew that it had, and wasn't going to get better. But it was still twice, three times as long as Elian had thought she was flawless. It was nice to think that once she was worshipped.

She wandered back. The girls were back in the car, heads bowed together.

'No stamina, these young people,' said Nancy.

Bernie smiled and lay back on the blanket. She looked like she was sunbathing fully clothed, but there was no sun at all now. She looked relaxed, but Nancy could see a tension in

222

her face from trying to be normal, trying to be sisters. Trying not to ask again.

'A proper British holiday,' said Nancy, and lay down next to her. 'I forgot my sunglasses.'

'I forgot my sun cream.'

'Do you think the boys will get heatstroke out there?'

Bernie smiled, but it faded quickly. 'I think we'll give town a miss today. We can do it another day.'

'Please,' said Nancy, 'can't we stay out a bit longer? I don't want to go back yet.'

'OK. The causeway, maybe.'

'Maybe. Listen, Bernie, I need to talk to Agatha before anything else happens.'

She sat up, 'Why?'

Nancy couldn't tell her what their mother had said. Agatha might just know something that would mean she shouldn't or couldn't say anything. Then she wouldn't feel so guilty. It wouldn't be her fault. She looked at Bernie.

'It just feels wrong. Donn, Mum and Beth know what's happening, or a bit of it, but she lived there for years and she needs to know too. It will affect her, one way or another.'

'She knows. Someone would have told her.'

'It just doesn't feel right not to see her.'

Bernie lay back. 'Do it if you want. I'm not going.'

Nancy looked back to the dunes. If Hurley and Elian knew what she'd done – Bernie couldn't be trusted not to say. She could never be trusted with a secret.

The clouds had cleared above them and the sun crept across the sand towards her.

31

Then

He handed me the pole near the end when there were only a couple of sheep left. The sheep which had been through looked utterly exhausted and miserable, but he was letting me have a go, so I tried not to look sad. Nancy was off again and I had to prove how old and responsible I was so I could get to go with her. But I didn't want to do this at all.

He pushed the sheep into the long, deep pool. It was full of a milky liquid but with quite a lot of mud now.

'Push it under with the pole!' he shouted.

I tried to get the pole on its head but I couldn't seem to push it. I kept thinking about how it would sting its eyes or it might swallow some. Maybe it would drown and it would be my fault.

It was halfway now, struggling to the other end.

'Do it now, Bernie!'

I lifted my end of the pole but it didn't go down at the other end. The sheep clambered out and began to bleat and shake itself.

'Oh, for God's sake. You eejit!'

Donn jumped into the pen, grabbed the sheep by its head and got it through the gate, pulled it down to the other end and pushed it in again. It really struggled this time and I knew it was my fault. It had used all its energy to get through it the first time. Donn grabbed the pole and pushed it under, deeply and properly. I couldn't wait to see if it got out again. I couldn't see properly anyway. I walked back to the house.

It took forever to force my wellies off and by the time I had I was crying properly in the mud on the floor. I didn't want to speak to anyone but there weren't many places I could go to be on my own. There were voices coming through the kitchen door and the serving hatch which opened into the front room. I could risk running up the stairs, but would be caught and questioned and made to feel an idiot. I decided to lock myself in the downstairs toilet until I was back to normal.

In there, door locked, I remembered how much I hated this room. The tall, dappled window was covered in flies, the windowsill covered in their husks. No-one knew where they came from. They were just always there, always dying. It was a big enough room to have a spare wardrobe in there and still feel big. There was a coat rack with lots of hats and raincoats that I'd never seen Donn wear, wellies in a variety of adult sizes that still carried the fields in the grooves underneath. I didn't look at the flies and sat in the corner until they began to land near my feet and head.

Nancy was gone and too old for anything now. Donn was angry with me. Bruce liked Donn more. My mum was always busy and Florence was stupid. Sister Agatha hated me.

I washed my face in the sink, dried it on my sleeve, put my wellies back on and went outside again. I climbed over the gate into Bryn's field and ran right across it, scattering the sheep. I ran from the hedge back to the house, then from top to bottom and corner to corner. When I'd finished all the lines I could think of, pretty out of breath, I went back inside. This time I went straight into the parlour.

Tommy was sitting at the table. I was surprised because I thought Nancy was with him, having more driving lessons.

'You seen Donn?'

I tried to control my breathing. 'He's outside. At the sheep dip.' I pointed in the direction of the dip and went to open the door to the hall.

'Hey. Wait a wee minute.'

I looked back. He leaned forward and smiled.

'We need to have another little chat.'

I stayed by the door.

He beckoned me over. 'Quickly now, I haven't got long.'

His hands dropped between his legs, his elbows resting on his knees. I edged towards him, to what I hoped was out of grabbing range.

'How old are you again?'

'I'm ten, and Nancy's only twelve.'

'Ah, ten. That's a nice age. Nothing to worry about when you're ten, is there?' His hands flickered. He was speaking strangely, like he thought someone might be listening. He raised his eyebrows. 'You get out and about a lot, eh?'

I shrugged.

'You're getting big.' His smile faded, 'But you're not that big in the scheme of things. You're just a wee girl, your mammy says. No problem, I say. But there are places you shouldn't go. Did your mammy not tell you this?'

I thought through all the places we shouldn't go but did. 'Like Skull Lane?'

He cocked his head on one side. 'And what would you know about that?'

'Nothing. Only what you said.' I lifted my chin up. He was just an idiot who liked Nancy, a dirty old man. Up close I could see there were even wrinkles around his eyes.

'It's where you'll end up, at this rate.' He laughed. 'I'm just reminding you of a few things, now your sister's not around to keep an eye on you. The field here,' he gestured with his thumb behind him, 'is one of those places that I never want to see you. Got it?'

I widened my eyes as if I had no idea what he was talking about. 'Bryn's field. The one with the stones?'

226

'That's the one.'

I felt my face get hot.

'I don't even want you looking at it. Or going in it. Again.'

I flushed even more. He'd seen me. I knew he had.

'I don't even want you talking about it. You don't even mention this to your sister, just keep away. This isn't the first time I've said it and I don't like repeating myself, so you tell me now if there's anything you don't understand.'

I shook my head.

'Grand.' He sat back. 'You do as you're told and we'll have no more problems.'

I backed away to the door and tried to feel my way to the handle. I couldn't get it and glanced around to get hold of it.

'We don't want anything to happen to Mammy, now, do we?'

I looked at him again, but he was just pouring his tea from the pot as if he'd said nothing at all.

I opened the door and ran to the front room. Mum was sitting at the table with Florence and half a jigsaw. Mum saw my face.

'What's wrong?'

'Nothing,' I said and looked behind me.

'Did Donn say something?'

'I was rubbish at the dipping. He got cross.' I sat at the table with them.

'Where's Nancy?'

'Don't know.'

'Want to help with the jigsaw?'

'Mine!' shouted Florence, grabbing at all the loose pieces.

'OK, sorry,' said Mum. She shifted them all over to Florence and looked at me. 'You look hot,' she said. 'Do you feel OK?'

I looked out of the window. I could see Tommy's car now, in the drive by the archway. Mum must have heard him pull up. She got up and closed the front room door gently.

'Are you sure nothing's happened?' she whispered.

I nodded and then a question burst out. 'Where did Ryan go?'

'Just away.' She spoke quietly.

'When's he coming back?'

'I don't know.'

I felt that Tommy was in the room with us, listening at the door or the serving hatch, hearing things from Donn and Agatha and everyone. But not Mum, please not Mum.

But the longer I sat there the more cross I got. Why did he get to come in my family's house and tell me which rooms and fields I couldn't go in? He'd taken my sister away and then acted like he was in charge of me. Why did I even listen? He was horrible to Mum, but she let him be in the house. That was her fault. If I said someone was horrible she always said to keep away from them, but she didn't do that. She just hid with Florence all the time. I wanted Nancy back.

32

Now

She jangled Donn's car keys. She fetched them from the car just to jangle them. She didn't want them to stay around the farm at the minute. She tried to sell the trip but it wasn't working.

'It's a convent. When are you ever going to visit a convent again, Hurley?'

Hurley didn't look at her. Elian snorted.

'That's not helpful,' she said. She tried to speak more brightly, 'Road trip! You love road trips, come on.'

'I want to stay here,' said Elian.

'Me too,' said Hurley.

'Fine,' she said, 'what are you two going to do?'

'We're making a camp,' said Hurley.

'Oh.' Nancy looked at Elian, 'Just you two?'

He nodded. 'Boys only. Adrian's going to join us later.'

Nancy smiled. 'Good. That sounds really good. I'll leave you to it then.'

She walked out to the lobby feeling pleased that they would be spending time together, and then hesitated by the back door. There was a feeling, a bare suspicion, that she'd missed something, not asked the right questions. She opened the back door and got into Donn's car. She tucked the directions into the visor and turned the car around in the yard.

Adrian and Bernie were standing by the gate to the barns. They waved as she drove past.

The sun was shining on the mountains as she pulled into a parking space in front of the shop in the village nearest the convent. She went inside and bought a sausage roll and a packet of crisps. She added a Mars bar as it was being rung up.

Outside she looked for somewhere to sit and eat, but ended up getting back into the car. The street was empty and, it struck her, very plain. There were no adverts in the shop window, no colour on the houses. A dog barked in the distance and a door slammed. She saved the Mars bar for the journey back and drove on to the convent.

It looked like a small, religious country house, a statue of Mary fitted into the arch above the gates, a black cross above the door. The pebble dash was flaking from the walls and the window frames needed painting. She parked with the three other cars and walked up the steps. The paint on the cross was peeling away too, the steps speckled with dark flakes.

The door opened and a nun greeted her. She wore a black blouse and long skirt, her hair hidden by a veil which fell to her shoulders.

'Ach, you must be wee Nancy, all the way from America.' She guided Nancy in by the elbow and closed the door. 'Your aunt is so looking forward to seeing you again.'

Nancy's eyes widened. 'Is she?'

Guided through the corridors, past ten closed and silent doors, the nun found out where she lived, with whom and for how long. Maybe, thought Nancy, being here will have settled Agatha's mind to rest. Now she's achieved what she always wanted. She had imagined a sober building set against the sin of laughter. The nun opened a door. Agatha was sitting by a window at the back of the house, rosary in both hands. The friendly nun smiled.

'I'm sure you'll be wanting a cup of tea?'

'That would be lovely, thank you,' said Nancy.

The nun smiled as she left the room.

'Hi,' said Nancy.

Agatha nodded. Nancy sat down in the chair next to her.

'Sit across from me, Nancy. I can't see you properly without hurting my neck.'

Nancy switched to the chair on the other side of the window. It had to be north facing. The parlour at the farm was too. She could see the sun shining on the ground twenty feet away but none of its warmth reached the room.

'She's very nice,' said Nancy, pointing towards the door.

'Sister Joseph. Talks.' Agatha's face, framed by white and black, looked younger than it had a few weeks ago.

Nancy looked around at the upright chairs and small bookshelf by the door. Because there was no TV the chairs all faced each other, the window or the wall.

'Is this your room?'

'Don't be silly, Nancy.'

Sister Joseph came back and hovered next to them. Nancy smiled at her.

Agatha sighed. 'You need to fetch that little table, over there.'

Nancy carried it and placed it between the chairs.

'A bit closer to me,' said Agatha, 'and mind my toes.'

Nancy rearranged it. Sister Joseph settled the tray and left again. Nancy sat back in her chair.

'You have crumbs on you.' Agatha pointed.

Nancy looked down and brushed the crisp crumbs from her t-shirt. Agatha watched the crumbs fall onto the colourful squares, like an old pub carpet, and shook her head. Nancy felt thankful that her son wasn't here after all, but missed Elian's incessant need to fill quietness with words.

Agatha looked back out of the window and began to finger the beads on her rosary. Nancy tried to remember what the sequence of prayers was, but she didn't know whether Agatha was picking up where she'd left off or was starting again. She seemed to remember Agatha's lips moving when she'd done this before. Maybe she was just fidgeting. Maybe she wasn't even called Agatha any more. Nancy tried to enjoy the calm and looked out across the mountains. It must be odd to have switched to this view after decades of looking out over a farm yard, the view restricted to thirty feet. She saw a couple of black veils in the mid ground. There seemed to be no boundary between the house and the mountain. Maybe they owned the mountain. Maybe –

'Nancy!'

Agatha was pointing to the teapot. Nancy placed the strainer on top of the teacup closest to Agatha and poured. She moved the strainer to her own cup. It looked exactly the same as the one Agatha had used at the farm. She didn't remember seeing it after Agatha left, but then they used tea bags now rather than the thick loose strands. Maybe she'd brought it with her. Maybe all the novices had to bring their own tea strainers. She tried not to giggle.

'Why are you smiling?'

'I'm not used to the quiet. It makes me nervous.'

'And that makes you smile?'

Nancy shrugged. 'How have you been?'

Agatha didn't reply. Nancy wasn't sure if she'd started praying again. She added the milk to the tea and wondered how long it would take to drink all the tea in the pot. It was a family sized one and they were very small cups. She blew on hers.

'You never did have any patience.'

So she couldn't be praying if she kept talking whenever she had something to say. She was just being awkward. Or quiet. Or godly, or something.

'The other nuns seem nice. Well, Sister Joseph does.'

Agatha grunted. 'People pleaser.'

232

Nancy wasn't sure if she meant her or Sister Joseph. Both, probably.

'Hurley's enjoying being at the farm.' Nancy drank her tea and poured another. 'We've been very busy. We went to Portstewart, some standing stones near Belfast and he went to a science museum which he really liked. I helped Donn move the sheep from one field to another and we nearly lost one, but he got it back, so that's fine. We went to see Auntie Beth too, which was nice.'

'No, it wasn't. She just about threw you out, you were so rude.'

Nancy drank her second cup and her mouth filled with bitter tea leaves. She held them in her mouth and then swallowed them down.

'Is that what she said? Have you seen her?'

'Of course I've seen her. She's my sister.'

Nancy didn't pour another cup. She wasn't here to entertain a bored nun. She was here for a reason.

Agatha sipped at her tea until the cup was empty.

'Sisters,' she said again.

Nancy remembered to use the strainer when she filled Agatha's cup. They both looked out of the window and Nancy didn't say anything this time. Clouds passed over, making the ground flicker with shadow. She thought of Hurley and Elian in their den. She imagined that Elian would raid the garage for tools to do it properly, saws to hack off branches and nails to secure them together. He wouldn't make a den that lasted a day or two, it would have to be a permanent reminder that he was there and he did this. She hoped Hurley would get a go at something and not be left to witness Elian's triumph over nature. She should have thought of it. She would be better at getting Hurley involved, and her den wouldn't have involved saws. She'd done that kind of thing all the time as a child, all the time before Bernie –

'Sisters,' Agatha said again, 'should look after each other.'

'I know.'

'But you didn't.'

'I tried.'

'No, Nancy. You were a slave to vanity. You wanted to be adored and, more importantly, you wanted everyone else to know that you were adored. There is only one kind of love worth having, and that isn't from a man.' She held her rosary still now but it seemed to tremble in her hands.

Nancy said, 'Look, every girl, every child wants to be loved. That's why people get together and have children, that's the whole point. People want to be loved. Most people. I didn't know.' Nancy rubbed her face and then sat forward on the chair, resting her arms on her knees. 'I didn't know. I was stupid. She spoke to me, Bernie spoke to me and said she wants to know the truth, but she doesn't. She wants what she believes to be confirmed and I can't. I couldn't stop it. It wasn't my fault that she went mad. I was just a bit of it.'

She waited for Agatha to say something, but she just looked at her beads.

'It was the counsellor she ended up with. She'd trained at this stupid course and encouraged Bernie to remember things that never happened. She had a breakdown, that was all, because of what happened when the car broke down, and the counsellor made everything worse. It wasn't anything I did. She said I could have made people believe her but I couldn't have. She wasn't making any sense, was she? Dad was with her in the car, and look what she ended up saying about him.'

Agatha picked up her cup and sipped it dry.

'The farm's fine,' said Nancy. 'Donn's well.' She picked up her cup.

'No he isn't. He's selling up and he'll never be well again.'

Nancy put the cup down again. 'Is he ill? Is that why he's selling?'

'Not physically ill. Spiritually.' Agatha nodded to herself or an unknown being. There was a burst of laughter from

234

somewhere within the building. Agatha frowned and crossed herself.

Nancy said, 'Why did you say Donn is spiritually sick? Did you really all know about your brother?'

'"Set a guard, O Lord, over my mouth; keep watch over the door of my lips!"'

'You know we've found a body? Bernie thinks it's Ryan. I think it's Ryan. It's all coming out, Agatha.'

'Only God can separate the light from the darkness. Whatever is found has nothing to do with Bernadette. Nancy, people always blame the last straw for being the one that broke the camel's back. But what about the million straws that somebody had already placed there? People cope with all kinds of situations if they know they can rely on somebody.'

Nancy waited for an answer to come. She felt her legs wobble and placed both feet flat on the floor.

'Why is it that you call Donn sick and you can be a nun?'

'I confessed and have been forgiven.' Agatha crossed herself. 'Think on that, Nancy. The only person you need to tell is God and he will forgive you. No-one else needs to know. No-one else would understand what a silly, selfish girl you were in the way He does. It's between you and Him. Here, I have a gift for you.' She put her hand into her pocket and pulled out a string of beads. 'Say your rosary and pray for guidance.'

Nancy took it and poured the beads into one hand. It felt like a centipede. The beads were made from dark wood, like fat, polished apple seeds.

'Think of your mother. Think of Beth. Think of the promise you made to me to look after Donn. Think of everyone but yourself. What you could say to Bernadette can only make her worse. There is nothing you can say that will make her better. She has her own sins to seek forgiveness for.'

'Like what?'

'Most of the commandments.'

Nancy clenched her teeth. 'Not murder though? Not

235

murder, Agatha. You welcomed the devil into your house and fed him.'

She looked at Nancy with pride. 'But, Nancy, that's all I did with him.'

Nancy's hands tightened on the beads.

'I promised to look after Donn, no matter what, and I did. I didn't turn from my duties, like you. You didn't look after your sister, but you can't punish everyone else for that. Be loving, Nancy, confess your sins and forgive us all.'

Agatha's face reminded Nancy of the nameless dog. She stumbled to her feet and banged against the table.

'Give your mother my address will you? I'd like to hear from her.'

Nancy breathed hard before answering. 'She's got it. Shall I give her your phone number?'

'I don't use the phone now. Just my address, Nancy. Something for me to remember her by.'

Nancy closed the door behind her. The hallway was silent again. She turned left and followed the turns past all those closed doors until she reached the front door. She twisted the door handle. It didn't open. Panicked, she twisted it the other way and then, harder, both ways. The tears began to come back and she bit her lip hard and let go.

Her mum saying before she dies. Bernie saying before she dies. Agatha, horrible Agatha, wanting a memento. She realised that her mother was dying, not being dramatic. And then what would happen to Dad? Who would care for him after she'd gone?

She had to get back to Bernie. She swallowed hard and wiped her eyes.

There were two locks. She turned the Yale lock with her left hand and the door knob with her right, and stepped out into the sunshine. She opened her hand to look at the rosary beads. She saw the barn and insects and the rosary beads held tight in Bernie's cold hand.

33

Then

Nancy's last words this morning echoed around my head.

'Behave yourself, Bernadette.'

As if.

I thought about when I'd seen Tommy. It was rarely two days together. There was usually one or two days in between them. So, if I'd seen him yesterday I wouldn't see him today. Dad was coming the day after next and then I wouldn't see Tommy at all. So, he wouldn't be here today, but probably would be tomorrow. And before Dad came, I would look at the missing part of the circle that Dad had mapped out.

Even in England Dad liked to get out into fields, but there weren't many stones near us. He had a metal detector and everything. Some people didn't like him having it. They thought it made him a thief. I thought that if he found something they didn't even know was there, if wasn't really stealing. Anyway I'd seen him find things and he always showed the farmers, who turned up their noses and said, 'If it's not worth money you can have it.' It might be half a belt buckle or a button, but it hadn't been worth money very often. I got a bit bored when I realised there wasn't going to be any real treasure even though he said it was precious. I had even seen it and not noticed. That's when he explained to me about the field, how he thought it was a bigger and more important Giant's Ring, cut into sections by later roads and hedgerows. Mum didn't care what he thought it was. She said it was up to

Donn and Agatha what went on their fields. They hadn't had pylons and they weren't going to have scientists and historians and signposts, and he had no right to tell them otherwise. If anyone turned up they'd know who to blame, and anyway, they all knew that their great grandfather had put the stones there and that was that.

Last summer I had crossed the road with Dad to look in the other fields for large stones in the walls around the field. Dad said that's most likely where they would have put them. It was hard to see though because there were often hedges too, or brambles or gorse that had grown to like the shelter of the wall and clung to it. Now that Nancy was busy I decided I would work harder at this and hand all of my work to Dad when he came over.

Nancy wasn't around. I didn't know if she was with Tommy or Catriona or some other exciting adult, and I didn't care. As I didn't have Nancy, I took Bruce. I stumbled over the cow grill at the bottom of the drive and crossed the road. I wasn't going to go straight in the field. I would keep watch, especially for Nancy who would love to have something to tell Tommy. Bruce followed, his nails clicking on the tarmac. I opened the gate opposite and crouched down to see any dip and rise in the field. Bruce nuzzled at my hand for a stroke. I stroked him twice, then raced Bruce to the middle of the field and looked back towards the road.

I seemed to be higher up here, but the slope was too gradual to mark out with the eye. The long grass didn't help. The sheep would be moved here next once they'd eaten all the grass in Bryn's field and after that it would probably be clearer. If it was there at all. I sat down with Bruce, who immediately flipped over onto his back with two legs in the air. I rubbed his belly as I looked back towards the house, not seeing any of it past the hedges and trees that were thick in front of it.

I made my decision and stood up. Tommy knew about last

time because I used the gate near the barns. If I used the gate on the road he wouldn't see me.

'Come on,' I said. Bruce ran back to the gate and waited for me, even though he could wriggle through. I always left the farm desperate for a dog of my own, a clever and obedient dog who wouldn't snap or bark unless he was supposed to. He sat as I looked at the road, followed me across and waited by the next gate. I wondered about him coming into the field. He would behave, but the sheep might run away like idiots anyway and let someone know we were there.

'Slowly,' I said, and fastened the gate back up. He waited next to me, his eyes on the sheep who all watched us. A couple moved away but the rest looked like they were holding their breath. I walked to the stones and sat down. So did Bruce. The sheep went back to eating, but Bruce didn't fall onto his back. He watched them because they expected him to. I held my hand out to the stones. Dad always did that. I used to think he was working out what kind of stone it was by the temperature, but now I think he just liked touching something so old. It was cool, rough with moss in places.

I stood slowly and looked at the dropped top stone, the uprights pushed out of line. The top stone had dipped but hadn't fallen right down and I crouched down to see how much space was underneath it. There was something there, something black with a slight sheen. I reached out to feel what it was and then got scared and snatched my hand back. We'd seen Tommy here with a black bag. I didn't want to know.

I walked fast, as slowly as I could, to the gate. I slapped my leg for Bruce, but he was already ahead of me. I fumbled the nylon but was finally the other side and hooking it back. I glanced at the sheep. I could see a figure standing by the shed gate, next to the cows. The figure lifted an arm and saluted me. I'd been caught.

I walked back to the front garden, slipping again on the

239

grill, and hid in the rhododendrons with Bruce until I was called in for dinner.

'I'm not well,' I told Mum, holding my stomach. 'Can I just go to bed?'

She placed her hand on my forehead. 'Are you sure you don't want to eat a little bit?'

I saw Nancy behind her, smiling. 'No thanks.'

'OK, I'll come up and see you soon.'

I lay down and tried and tried and tried to sleep but I could only see one thing when I closed my eyes.

I was woken by Nancy poking me in the back. I raised my head.

'What?'

'Tommy wants to see you.'

I sat up. 'What do you mean? Why?'

'You know why.'

I buried my head back in the pillow.

I would talk to Mum in the morning. I would get her to ask Dad to come early. Whatever happened I would keep away from Tommy.

I didn't get back to sleep until I'd heard everyone go to bed. I thought about sneaking out of the room and getting into Mum's bed, but couldn't bear to open the door into the darkness, let alone step out into it.

34

Now

Nancy looked for Bernie when she got back, but couldn't find her. She'd seen the kids out the front with Elian. Adrian was cleaning out the car with a handheld vacuum.

'Where's Bernie?' she shouted above the hum. He shrugged.

She wasn't there. Not downstairs or upstairs. Nancy thought of the hay loft and went past the barns, through the yard still heaped with junk. They hadn't even moved that much of it.

She saw the gate was open. The gate Tommy had leaned on. Bernie had gone to see Tommy. Somehow she knew.

Nancy hadn't put on boots for the search and could feel the mud seeping into her socks as she half ran past the silo. She persuaded herself she was wrong, that Bernie wouldn't go alone, and looked for her in the fields on the way and paused on the bridge to look over the hedges. There was no sign of her. She carried on to Tommy's farm.

She heard the dogs barking and followed the sound. Bernie was shouting somewhere outside, but it sounded like the dogs were inside. Nancy stopped. She saw Bernie standing in a barn and, sitting on a bale, Tommy. He was smiling.

'We've found the body!' Bernie said, her hands open. 'You can't deny a body.'

They both turned as they heard Nancy running towards them.

'Bernie, what are you doing?' she said.

Bernie's eyes were wide and her lashes were clumped with dried tears.

'I'm so sick of waiting, Nancy. I need to know.'

'Need to know what?' asked Tommy, looking at Nancy. Her stomach turned over.

Bernie said, 'I need to know that you killed Ryan. I need to know why. I need to know that what I remember is true, the stones, the barn, the gun.'

'You do know, Bernie,' said Nancy, touching her shoulder.

Bernie moved away. 'I know it's true but I need to hear someone else say it.' She turned to Tommy. 'Just say it! It's not about the police or justice or anything like that, it's just for me.'

'Yeah, Nancy,' said Tommy, 'why don't you just say it?'

'She's told me enough,' said Bernie.

'But not everything.' Tommy crossed his legs. He was so calm, so confident. The anger bubbled up from Nancy's stomach.

'Not everything,' Nancy said. 'She's right, though, isn't she? It was all down to you.'

'So,' Tommy gestured to Bernie, 'go ahead. Tell her everything you know.'

Nancy turned to Bernie, 'Did he tell you anything? Did he tell you that he kissed me? I was twelve. And did he do anything else?' She looked at Tommy. 'Did you?'

He looked confused. His eyes flicked to the farmhouse.

'So, he may be very cool about being a freedom fighter and all that shit, but a paedophile?'

Tommy stood and his smiled faded. 'Hey, hold on.'

Bernie smiled. 'Quite a reaction there, Tommy. There wasn't a flicker when I called you a murderer.'

'It was nothing like that,' he said.

Nancy tilted her head to one side. 'Not in the eighties, maybe. But now? It's seen quite differently now, isn't it Bernie?'

She nodded.

'Just fucking wait there,' he said.

'Paedophile.' Nancy tapped her fingers against her lips. 'That's something that could destroy a family man. That's something that could destroy any kind of reputation.'

'It wasn't anything like that. It wasn't anything to give a name like that to.'

'So, you took a twelve year old girl out in a car under the pretence of giving her driving lessons for what reason, then?'

He looked towards the house again.

'You have a daughter, don't you, Tommy? These things affect everyone, these labels that never wash off. Your daughter will always be that pervert's daughter and your son will have to move away. It's not fair, but that's how it goes.'

His hands flexed in front of him.

'Only it's so easy now to tell people things. We could have a website up and running in a day letting everyone know about you and your – preferences.' Nancy turned to Bernie. 'Have you got your phone on you? We could take a picture for it.'

Bernie patted down her pockets. 'We'll have to come back.'

'What the fuck do you want from me?' he asked Nancy. 'She wants fairytales, but what do you get out of this?'

'Oh, I don't know.' She looked at him. 'Don't buy the farm?'

He snorted.

'I'm quite happy to feature on this website, you know. I don't need to prove anything. I live abroad, it's going to be a local whirlwind. All those instances in the past that people covered up or turned away from. All those glances you thought went unnoticed. They'll snowball.'

Bernie nodded. 'Doesn't take much.'

Tommy walked up to Nancy and spat at her feet. 'You'll pay.' Up close, his thinning hair and drawn cheeks made him look less frightening. He looked old.

She managed not to cry or cringe or run. 'You haven't aged well, Tommy.'

243

He walked from the barn and towards the house.

'Do you think we should go before the dogs come?' said Bernie.

'Yes. Or the shotgun.'

They walked quickly to the gate and then ran down the road. Pausing at the bridge they looked behind them. There was nothing but the sound of distant barking. They smiled at each other and caught their breath.

'That was probably a bit stupid,' said Bernie.

'Probably. What the hell were you thinking trying to get him to talk? Men like him don't last long if they can't keep their mouths shut.'

'What about you? Paedophile? He wasn't expecting that!' Bernie began to laugh and then stopped. 'He didn't –'

'No, he didn't. It was three kisses.'

Bernie shuddered.

'I know.'

They started to walk back. Nancy thought of the places she and Bernie had played and shivered – the hay loft, the dilapidated stables, the field next to the sheep dip, the lanes with their blind corners. She thought she even remembered daring Bernie to jump as hard as she could on the metal disc which covered the well. A well so deep they had never been allowed to even look down it. Bernie wouldn't have done it though. Then again, Nancy had been able to persuade her to do quite a lot.

She realised she didn't want the farm at all. She wanted to be at the farm with Bernie. She wanted to be a child again and play in the hay loft and stroke cows and make plans with Bernie. Everything she thought she'd felt about the farm was really about them.

'I still need to know,' said Bernie.

Nancy sighed. 'What's if it's not what you need to hear? When it's said, I can't take it back.'

Bernie stopped. 'I'll live.'

'When did you last hear from Mum?'

'Not for a while.'

'Is she sick? Is she –'

Bernie looked at Nancy. 'She hasn't said anything. But I've wondered. Adrian says she doesn't look good. I've tried to ask and she puts me off. I thought she might have said something to you.'

Nancy carried on walking. 'Maybe Florence knows.'

'Maybe.'

Nancy sat at the kitchen window after dinner. Bernie kept looking at her. Waiting. Saying nothing.

35

Then

Tommy wants to see me. It ran through my head as I ate my breakfast, brushed my teeth and hung close to Mum.

Nancy didn't disappear. She kept looking at me and saying things like, 'Want to go out the front, Bern? Want to look at the sheep, Bern?'

'Go on,' said Mum, 'why are you hanging around here?'

'I still don't feel well,' I said.

'You'll feel better for a bit of fresh air.'

I followed Nancy through the hall and the kitchen, and took as long as I could pulling my wellies on. She smiled at me and that made me nervous. Donn was out so Bruce wasn't there. I called him anyway. We walked through the yard and she pointed at the small pile of drying peat.

'Donn's cutting more turf.'

'Oh.'

'Where shall we go? The hay barn?'

I shook my head. I wasn't going to walk past those dark windows and sticking doors. I wasn't going to walk anywhere near where Tommy might be hiding.

'He's not there, you know. He's gone to Dublin today.' She looked as if she was telling the truth.

'I just don't want to. It's not raining.'

'How about –'

I took a couple of steps back to the house, 'Look, you're

going to take me to him. I don't care what you say. You're on his side.'

'He's not even here, you idiot!' She laughed.

'Don't laugh at me. You just fancy him. You're the idiot.'

She blushed scarlet and turned away. I walked to the archway at the side of the house and then stopped. She was kicking at the gravel. Like she was actually upset by what I'd said. I watched her walk away, not looking back at me. I didn't want to go back in the house or follow her. I wished I could just sit where I was and have no-one notice, waiting until Dad arrived and it was safe again. The back door opened and I saw Sister Agatha come out. I ran after Nancy.

She was back in the rhododendrons with the bows and the arrows that never flew, snapping them into pieces. I sat down on a lump of tyre and grass and watched her. She sneered at me.

'I don't fancy him.'

'Yeah, right.'

She snapped the final arrow and threw all the pieces into the mass of twigs under one of the bushes. She picked a long piece of grass and began to shred it with her fingernail.

'Want to look for some cartridges?' I said.

She shrugged, and we wandered out into the trees. I found one, not live, and she found two. I walked down to the gate and stood on the bottom fence strut. She straddled the fence and sat on the top one. I leaned my arms over and balanced with my legs out so all my weight was on my armpits. That really hurt quite quickly and I stood up again.

Nancy looked posed as she pulled out her hairband. She'd been brushing again, her long hair shiny.

'What does he talk about with you?'

'Grown-up things.'

'What, like, "Nancy you're so lovely"?'

'Like politics, actually.'

I could hear a tractor further up the road and watched

for it, but it must have pulled into a field. I felt watched. I scanned the trees, the fields across the road, but there was nothing moving.

'How would you feel,' Nancy said, 'if where you lived was full of soldiers, pointing their guns at you? Not being able to drive without being stopped and searched all the time, like a criminal.'

I laughed. 'You have been driving as a criminal. You don't have a licence.'

She sneered. 'You're so childish. Remember how you felt in the village. Not being able to do your shopping without having to look at machine guns.'

I shivered.

'We're part of the occupation.' Nancy, straight backed and solemn, sounded like him.

'I'm not part of anything.' I jumped backwards and began to walk away.

'Tommy says he'll let you look at the stones, but not in the daytime because he doesn't want anyone seeing you there.'

'They're not his stones. What's it got to do with him?'

'Donn wants to keep them a secret. Tommy understands that, which is more than you do. So he'll let you see them tonight.'

'No, thanks. I saw them.'

Nancy ran to catch me up. 'He wants you to be the only person that knows their true history. He chose you, Bern.' Her eyes sparkled. 'You need to prove that you have the right blood.'

That word reminded me of the smell in Cassie's room, the smell of warm copper coins, the smell of meat before it was cooked.

'I hate him. No way am I going to look at anything with him.'

'Dad would love to know though, wouldn't he? He loves stones and history. If there is a story and you could tell him, imagine what he'd say.'

248

I folded my arms. 'So Tommy would tell me a secret that I was allowed to tell Dad? Not very secret after all.'

Nancy frowned and grabbed my left arm. 'You'd have to swear Dad to not tell, like I'm swearing you, Bern.'

'I haven't sworn. I'm going to tell Mum.' I whipped my arm from her hand and ran to the house. Mum was in the kitchen, making a pot of tea. Florence wasn't with her, for once.

'Look at your wellies! You didn't come through the house, did you? Agatha will kill you.'

I didn't look at my wellies. 'Mum, the other night, when Tommy came and Catriona was here, what was in his car?'

'Oh, Bernie, you don't want to know that,' she said. She stroked my head, 'Forget about it.'

'I do want to know, really.' I shook her arm. 'Please.'

She bent down and spoke quietly. 'He'd shot a dog that was worrying his sheep and thought Donn might know whose dog it was. OK? Don't tell the others.'

My hand fell away.

'He lost two. It's important. They're not pets, Bernie, it's his job.'

I looked at the door to Cassie's room. It might have been an animal I heard. It might have been anything.

'What do you think of Tommy?' I asked.

She shook her head and poured some boiled water into the tea pot, swirled it and emptied it. She put the loose tea in and filled it up again. When she looked back I was still waiting.

'Your dad is coming tomorrow,' she said, trying to smile. 'It will be nice to see him, won't it?'

I nodded and went out to the lobby to take my wellies off. Nancy was waiting for me. She'd been listening.

'He'll be waiting for you after midnight.'

'I'm not going out in the dark with him on my own.'

'I'll come with you, silly,' she said, her eyes sliding to the door. 'We can take Bruce as well. It will be the best adventure yet.'

I hesitated. 'I'll think about it.'

'Come on Bern, let's go back outside. I want to go to the hay loft before Dad gets here. We never have any time once he's got his list of places to go.'

I nodded. She opened the back door as Donn came into the yard with Bruce. Donn went inside and Bruce came with us. I caught a glimpse of Mum standing at the kitchen window, watching.

Nancy said nothing else about Tommy for the rest of the afternoon and I started to relax. It was like before, bad singing, stories about Sandra and her hair, looking out for rats and stroking Bruce.

After all, I could just say no.

36

Now

Each time she woke, panicked and breathless, she remembered images from the last nightmare.

Pursued by the devil through rhododendrons with flowers that burst open at enormous speed and smelled of apples.

Hurley standing in the road, listening to her call his name over and over.

Trembling at the top of the stairs, knowing something was coming and she wouldn't see it until it was there.

Bernie whispering, 'Knots undo themselves when I'm not looking.'

Agatha, by the fire, knitting thick black tights with four straight needles, then pulling each one from the loop of stitches and stabbing them into her chest.

Bernie and Tommy, white eyed, turned to stone and crumbling.

'I don't want to remember,' she murmured to herself. Elian grumbled.

She unwrapped the sheet from round her arm, untucked the blankets from round her legs and watched the breeze slip past the edges of the curtains. The windows were as closed as they got, but the rain smattered against the glass so loudly that she wondered if they had been opened and forgotten. She was hot and cold, as if she had a fever. She knew what she had to say but she couldn't admit it to Bernie. She tried to keep awake but each time was dragged under again.

Bernie, mouth a foot wide, eating the post as it came though the letter box – letters, parcels, guns.

37

Then

I never could say no to Nancy for long.

The dark was total when we first went out, but after a while I could make out the lines of the hedge against the sky, the white gravel against the dark grass. I looked back to the house, and slapped my hand on my thigh again.

'Stop it!' hissed Nancy.

'I want Bruce to come with us.'

'He must be asleep.'

We followed the drive under the trees and I couldn't see her very well. I wanted to hold her hand but didn't dare. I listened out for the rooks above but heard nothing above me, only in the bushes either side of the drive. I shuddered.

My bare feet were cold inside my plimsolls, my arms so covered in goose bumps that they were tender against my jumper. The rosary beads were hard against my chest. We came out from under the trees and I stopped at the gate, my arms crossed over.

'I don't want to go.'

'Don't be silly, Bernie, he's waiting.'

'I don't like him. This is crazy.'

'I had no idea you were such a baby, Bernadette.' She carefully crossed the cattle grid and waited on the other side. Her hands glowed white against her black cardigan, her hair brushed to one side made her face look alien, lop-sided.

I looked behind me again. I didn't want to walk back under the trees on my own. I could see only glimpses of the house through the leaves. I heard a bark to my left.

'See?' she said. 'Bruce is already there.'

I balanced on the cow grid and made it across without slipping over. We walked around to the road gate and Nancy opened it. The stones seemed to glow too, although they were a dull grey in the daytime. Bruce was sitting beside them and he stood up and wagged his tail. The gate clanged as Nancy closed it.

Tommy walked around the stones towards us.

'Hello, gorgeous.'

He wasn't talking to me. I looked up the field towards the puffs of sheep while he kissed her on the cheek and then, after looking at me, on the lips.

'Hands up,' he told me.

I put them shoulder high. I watched him pull a handgun from the back of his trousers and hand it to Nancy. It hung heavily in her hand.

'You have to point it,' he said. 'It's no good there.'

'Please don't, Nancy,' I said. 'This isn't funny.'

I saw a frown cross her face as she thought of saying no, and then she did it. She pointed at my face. She didn't look at me though, just slightly to my left. Her hand was shaking a little.

'Now click it like I showed you.'

Nancy looked at him and then at the gun. Slowly she moved her grip until her thumb caught the safety catch. I shook my head and lowered my hands.

'Nancy?' I whispered.

Tommy looked from Nancy to me and back again.

'Good girl.' He took the gun from her and her hands fell to her sides. 'You can leave us to it.'

'No!' I looked at Nancy, 'You promised!'

'I promised I'd come with you.' She didn't look at me, but bent down to stroke Bruce.

'Take the dog, too,' he said.

I didn't believe she'd go. She was still scared of the dark. There was no way she'd walk back to the house without me.

'Come on, Bruce,' she said, and walked to the gate. He left me too.

'Nancy!'

She didn't turn, not even a little. Tommy grabbed my arm and squeezed it.

He whispered with hardly more noise than a breath. 'Shut up.'

I watched her go with the dog and looked up at the blue eyes Nancy had fallen in love with. He was smiling, in a way. He kept quite still and I heard her scrabble over the cattle grid and each step on the gravel until there weren't any more. I hoped that Bruce would come back for me. When she went inside he'd come back. I listened for his quick feet coming back down the gravel but there was no sound at all.

'I have a problem,' said Tommy.

He was talking quietly but each word vibrated in my head. He let go of me but I wasn't running. I could barely get any air in and out and wrapped my arms around my chest as if to hold my lungs together.

'I'm on a mission. The blacks are fighting for their rights, the French are rioting in Paris. I'm part of a revolution where violence is the only way to bring about justice.'

'No, it isn't.' I felt I had been holding my breath and it had all left me at once.

'Yes, it is. Who would have listened to the suffragettes if the suffragists hadn't bombed libraries? They fought their war and then the politicians came in, revoked violence and everyone was so relieved they gave women the vote. Before the ballot, the bullet. But, for that to happen,' he leaned in towards me, 'you have to really frighten people. And we've got most of them frightened and when they're frightened it gets really nasty. House searches, roadblocks, hunger strikers, stop and search, rubber bullets, plastic bullets, shoot to kill and no-one is safe. An eleven year old boy gets shot in the back of the head with a plastic bullet just last April. How old are you again?'

I kept my lips together.

'No answer, blue eyes?' he pointed to the stones, to the gap underneath. 'Have a look down there.'

He pushed me forward and I stumbled onto my hands and knees. I looked down. The blanket that I'd seen on the floor in the kitchen next to the green bag. I could see his hair. I closed my eyes so I couldn't see anything else. I thought he'd got away. I wasn't going to get away either. I sank back onto my calves.

'I told you what happened to tell tales.' He laughed. 'He had blue eyes too, didn't he?'

He pulled me up by my right arm and I staggered to my feet. I heard him unclick the gun.

'Come on,' he said.

I looked at the gate and took a tiny step backwards. He grabbed my arm again. This time we didn't stand still. He marched me up the field, through the sheep, past my mother's window. He opened the gate at the top of the field and pulled me through it. I gasped, tripped and found my feet somehow on the mud. He didn't loosen his grip. Outside the barn with the Tardis blue door he stopped and turned to face the scrubby square of metal and tyres. He let go now and looked up and down from one gate by the yard to the other by the silo. He gestured with the gun.

'Welcome to Skull Lane.' He pushed me down to my knees and held the gun to the back of my neck. 'Is there anything else you want to know? Because after tonight you don't get

256

to say anything at all. You don't ask anything, you don't talk about anything. Got it?'

I heard a click on the gun again and nodded.

'Look in front of you.'

All I could see were bits of tractor and spikes of metal.

'That's where the people who talk go, under the soil and the rubbish. Out of sight, out of mind. There's plenty of space for a wee thing like you. But I want you to think about who's really responsible for this. Your da, the Englishman who never gets his hands dirty, who turns a blind eye, who doesn't care about people dying, only stones and fame. Your da who showed you the stones and encouraged you to go where you shouldn't. Your da who is never here. You've been warned too many times now and this is it. Get in the barn.'

I stumbled to my feet and tugged at the door of the barn, my barn, and waited.

'Inside and kneel down.'

I knelt next to the spiders and couldn't feel the beads against my chest anymore. I thought they'd gone, fallen somewhere. I moved a hand to check.

'The second you move, you're dead.'

My hand froze.

'It might not be me, it could be anyone. We are all watching you, Bernadette.'

I heard the gun click again and closed my eyes, but all I heard were his footsteps and the bang of a door. I stayed as still as I could, my knees pressing into stones, but somehow my hands clasped themselves together in front of my chest as if they were tied. I didn't know if he was coming back. I opened my eyes. The sky seemed brighter. I wondered if the angels were coming to get me. I couldn't see him, but that didn't mean he wasn't there. I wasn't going to turn, I wasn't going to move. I listened for the sound of Tommy coming to find me. I listened for the spiders and beetles.

Blue eyes.

He knew I wasn't one of them. They wouldn't miss me as much as Nancy or even stupid little Florence.

Everything began to hurt now, my arm, my legs, my knees. I let myself cry for my knees. I quickly pulled the beads from around my neck and held them in front of me.

I waited.

38

Now

She was woken by a dog barking. First she thought it was Bruce and then she thought it was Tommy coming to kill them all. It was dark but she had to do it now, with the nightmares fresh in her mind. She pulled a jumper over her pyjamas.

She crept into Bernie's room and saw her asleep on her side, next to the fireplace. She shook her gently but Bernie was awake straight away, as if she'd been waiting. She'd always been waiting. They felt their way downstairs. Neither said so, but they knew that if anyone else got up the spell would be broken, the words gone.

Nancy's feet ached on the cold floor. She opened the door to the best room and Bernie followed her inside. They sat in the paired armchairs by the fire and Nancy talked.

Bernie shook a little, her hands clasped tight.

'I took you to Tommy knowing he was going to scare you. He said that, but I swear I didn't know how. I didn't know he was going to give me the gun and tell me to point it at you. I left you and went back to bed. In the morning I got really scared when you weren't there. We looked for you all over and I knew you might be in the stable but I didn't want to say that we'd been in there before, so I said nothing until it was nearly dark.'

Bernie leaned towards her. 'That's not true. Only the truth, Nancy.'

259

Nancy nodded and started again. 'I did know about the gun.' She paused but Bernie said nothing. 'I didn't want to find you because you'd tell them what I did. But then it was dark and I thought he might really have hurt you, even though he said he'd only scare you. And then I pretended I heard something and opened the door and you were lying there with the rosary beads in your hands and you hadn't slept at all and only talked about angels, so I didn't mention Tommy and I didn't tell them what I did. And I'm sorry.'

'What else did I say?'

'You said, "Tell them what happened, Nancy. Tell them who did it."'

'And why didn't you say? Why did you do any of it? I don't understand.'

Nancy closed her eyes and then forced them open. 'He gave me the gun one other time. He said, with all I'd seen, I could be one of them or their enemy. He said if I was one of them I had to learn how to shoot. He told me to aim at the blanket. He said it was full of clothes, just to give me the idea. And I did, twice. And I remember smiling because it was exciting and I was trusted and then I realised that the noise hadn't been a thud against the ground. And the blood poured out through the hole in the blanket and he pulled it back a little and I saw hair. I didn't know, I swear I didn't, but it was me.'

Bernie's eyes were glistening. That was all Nancy could see.

'All this time I thought it was Tommy,' said Bernie. 'And then, after talking to Tommy, I thought that you must know it was Donn. And it was you. Did Donn know?'

'Maybe. I never told him. I never told anyone. I nearly persuaded myself that I'd imagined the blood, that it was just a trick. Just blankets. But I couldn't forget what I'd done to you. I will never forgive myself.'

Nancy had nothing else to say. She waited for Bernie to

scream or shout but she just sat calmly with her head resting on the back of the chair. Eventually she spoke.

'Why did you keep quiet?'

'I was ashamed. I pointed a gun at you.'

'Why did you do it?'

'Fear. I was scared. I'd held the gun. I'd fired it. Fingerprints, guns, blood. It was all I could think about. It was all too much. I couldn't say anything. All of those people there, they were witnesses.'

'Other people?'

'You know those other men we'd see coming out of the barns?'

'I remember shiny shoes.'

'He was there. It was like Tommy was showing me off to him, a performing monkey. He's the one who gave me the gun, like it was a prize.'

'Did he threaten you?'

'No. he said nothing at all. I knew I'd go to prison or he'd come and shoot us all without anyone saying it.' Nancy looked at her hands. 'And I left you with Tommy. That was worst of all. I couldn't live with anyone knowing that. I couldn't even admit it to you and just hoped, that with everything else, you'd forget. Basically I wanted us all to forget. Especially me.'

She looked up to see Bernie close her eyes.

'Are you all right?' asked Nancy.

Bernie voice sounded thick, 'I think so.'

Nancy waited.

'I'm very cold,' said Bernie.

'Let's light a fire in the parlour.'

The sky was still black to the west, but in the parlour she could see the glow of day rising cold over the corrugated roofs.

'Jesus,' she said.

Bernie made her jump. 'Jesus what?'

261

'I don't know. Jesus whatever's going to come next.'

Bernie glanced at her. 'You look terrible.'

'I feel terrible.' She felt that she'd welcome some purging vomiting session, that it may clear the dreams from her. She felt a sneeze build in the back of her nose. She managed to keep it down.

'You really don't look well,' said Bernie.

'I'm tired, that's all. I didn't sleep well.'

Bernie had rings under her eyes too.

'I've missed you,' Nancy whispered. Bernie squeezed her hand and let go.

Bernie had the fire ready to light. Nancy sat in Agatha's chair. It was just like one of Agatha's fires, a little wigwam of kindling over barley twists of newspaper, the peat on the hearth ready.

Nancy couldn't remember seeing a paper since she'd arrived.

'Where did you find the newspaper?'

'Cassie's room.'

Nancy shivered.

Bernie reached up onto the mantelpiece for the long matches. She lit all the paper twists with one match. Agatha never approved of using more than one.

Nancy said, 'Isn't it weird how the little things stick? Stupid little things like the glacé cherries in that cupboard.'

'Shall I see if they're still there?' Bernie opened the cupboard and pulled out a plastic tub. 'Still here. Expired . . . 1990.' She put the tub back and closed the door. The kindling had taken enough for her to put some of the peat bricks on.

Nancy thought about Elian. 'Do you feel guilty about using peat?'

'No. This is what it was always used for, a little at a time. Not trailer loads so people could have bigger pansies.'

Nancy smiled. That's what she'd said. They must have both heard someone else say it. Bernie sat in Donn's chair and closed her eyes. Nancy felt another sneeze building and couldn't stop it.

'Bless you.' Bernie smiled but kept her eyes closed. 'You'll be in bed for a couple of days with that cold. Good old summer colds. I'm sure we never got them as children and we were always out in the rain then.'

'Not as bad as the chilblains though.'

'God, no, they're the worst.'

Nancy smiled and waited for Bernie to open her eyes. The longer she kept them closed, the more she thought, this is it. This is the start of the breakdown. She'll never come to terms with it now. She should have been quicker, planned better. She would have to tell Adrian, warn the girls that Mummy wasn't feeling well. Should she have let her light a fire? She began to edge herself from her chair. Bernie opened her eyes.

'Where are you going?'

'Tea.'

Nancy made two mugs while keeping an eye on her. The rainclouds were so heavy it looked as if morning hadn't progressed any further than when she'd got up, but it was seven o'clock now. She set the mugs in front of the fire. Bernie still had her eyes open.

'How do you feel?'

'Quite warm now.'

'No, about – what I said. You seem too calm.'

'I said I needed to know. Now it makes sense. You were scared for your life too. Maybe I'd have done the same. I needed to know why and now I know.'

They were both quiet then.

'It wasn't you that killed him, though,' Bernie said after a while. 'It was your hand, but not your fault.'

'I know.'

'If he was wrapped up he was probably dead already.'

'I tried to believe that. I don't think there would have been blood if that was true, but it kept me going for a while. It

263

didn't feel much different, in any case. I just got really good at not thinking about it.'

Nancy gave Bernie her mug and they drank the tea. There were footsteps on the stairs and Nancy could see Bernie adjust herself.

'So, you're OK?' Nancy said.

Bernie nodded, 'I will be.' She turned to greet the girls.

Nancy watched her carefully all day. She noted what she said and what she omitted, how she explained the end of operations to the girls, and how she reworked it for Adrian. In both forms it was a victory. She had defeated evil, silence and apathy with good, shouting and action. It didn't feel so final to Nancy, more a hole that had been placed where the question was. Bernie could fill it again and again. Nancy kept quiet.

At dinner Bernie announced they were leaving.

'Tomorrow?' echoed Adrian. 'Do we have a booking?'

'We can sort one. We can be flexible, catch a cancellation.'

'But we're booked for the day after. I don't understand the rush. I'd rather have a booking set before we get the kids in the car, really.'

'We'll be fine,' said Bernie, flapping one hand toward him.

Nancy looked away. There was something lighter about her as if she may drift off, untethered, a flickering sky lantern across the sea. Adrian didn't seem to notice any difference. The children probably did but would hide and deny it if asked. And Elian? He was looking at her, waiting for Nancy to catch his eye.

'I was thinking of taking Hurley to Italy for a few days,' he said. 'We have a couple of weeks left and things seem to be breaking up here. There are places I'd like to go, like to show him.'

Nancy nodded.

'What do you think?' he asked.

She wasn't sure what he was asking. Was she included in this or just required to give another nod? She put a hand to her forehead.

'I don't feel well.'

'Have a lie down,' he said. 'We can talk about it later.'

She stood up, steadying herself on the table. There was a movement outside in the shadows. She had seen Donn in the yard a couple of times during the day but he hadn't come inside. She wasn't sure if he had been inside at all since they started to move the scrap, other than to phone her mother. Maybe he'd been staying in one of the barns. Maybe at Tommy's. He never even looked towards the house and she felt that they'd moved in and evicted him. He must be just waiting for them to leave.

One time she saw him and ran outside to catch him, but he'd gone. The next time she looked out his car had gone. Whenever Bernie caught her eye she tried to smile, but she felt responsible. They'd ruined his life. He had nowhere to run home to.

She sneezed again. 'I think I will just lie down for a bit.'

Nancy went upstairs and got into bed. The light through the curtains could have been from any time of day, diffused through gallons of raindrops and her lashes.

When she woke Elian was asleep. She was hungry now and tried to walk down the stairs in the dark but ran back to the light switch and turned in the landing one, and then the hall one and then the parlour.

Donn was sitting by the cold fireplace.

'Sorry,' she said, 'did I wake you?'

He shook his head. He had a blanket bunched up on his lap, his feet in their heavily darned socks crossed in front. She sat in Agatha's chair.

'Are you OK?'

He snorted and then there was a high pitched sigh. Her throat seized. She couldn't cope with him crying. There was no sign on his face that he would. He stared into the fireplace.

'Shall I light a fire? It's chilly.'

He shook his head. She waited for him to offer something else but he just looked at the ashes.

'We'll clear it up before we go.'

He looked at her.

'The fireplace.'

There was another sigh, like a whimper. This might be the last time she saw him, the last chance to ask anything. The blanket on Donn's lap stirred and the head of a border collie puppy emerged from the folds.

'Shh, back to sleep, Bran,' he said, stroking between its ears.

He was staying. Maybe Tommy didn't want the farm any more, maybe the hold was broken. Maybe there was a price on Donn's head and the rest of them.

Nancy said, 'I'm glad he's got a name. Will Agatha come back, now you're staying?'

'I am selling.'

Nancy was shocked. 'Who to?'

'Do you really want to know?'

Nancy paused. She didn't want to have to lie to Bernie, but she didn't want to imagine Tommy owning her farm. It would always be her farm.

'Maybe not,' she said. 'Did you know, Donn?'

She meant about her, about Ryan, but didn't want to say. He didn't answer.

Nancy thought about getting something from the fridge and then decided she wasn't hungry anymore. She pushed herself up from the chair. At the door she turned to ask if he wanted the light off again.

'It's someone else buying the farm,' said Donn. 'Not Tommy.'

Nancy didn't believe him. 'Thanks.'

'It was only ever supposed to be guns,' he said.

Nancy switched the light off.

'At least they told me they were guns,' he said.

'I understand. We can only know what people want us to know.'

39

Then

I woke up filthy and cold in Florence's bed. I couldn't remember getting there. All I remembered was being quiet and still and not being killed. I heard a car start up the driveway. I dragged myself out of bed and peeped over the window sill.

Dad's car, our car, rattled up the driveway with Bruce at his side. The engine shuddered as if it was trying to turn itself back on even when he'd got out of the car. I ran downstairs to see him hug Mum, then Florence and then it was my turn. Nancy wasn't there. I cried all through tea as Dad apologised for the car breaking down, for missing the boat.

Mum and Sister Agatha kept offering me food and blankets but no-one asked what had happened. Dad kept looking at me as if he was wondering but he said nothing either.

Mum put me to bed even before Florence. I left Nancy's bed and got into Florence's again. I didn't think I'd sleep but I did, badly. I woke up to the sun, but I wasn't sure whether it was morning or evening. Florence was asleep, her arms thrown over her head, and I could hear Nancy downstairs. I got up, pulled my jumper over my pyjamas, and went to Mum's room to find Dad. The door was almost closed and I pushed it partly and then fully open. I watched them standing at the window. Dad had his arm round Mum and they were looking out of the side window.

'Poor thing,' Mum said, and rested her head on Dad's shoulder.

268

'Donn will sort it out,' he said. 'I'll ask him to do it before the girls get up.'

My stomach turned.

'What is it?' I asked.

They both turned, spinning away from each other.

Mum smiled awkwardly. 'How did you sleep? You must have been tired.'

'What is it?' My breath was coming fast. I felt dizzy.

'Nothing, Bernadette. Go and join Nancy for breakfast.'

I gulped, 'It's a body, isn't it? There's a body!'

I ran towards them and tried to push Dad out of the way. He held my sides, lifted me up and put me on the bed.

'The rooks have hurt a sheep, Bernie. It's not nice, we don't want you to see it.'

'A lamb?' It wasn't a man, a person. It was a lamb. I burst into tears.

'It was probably sick or injured,' he said. He put his arm around me and I heard him whisper to Mum. She stood by the window and he sat on the bed next to me. When I'd calmed down to sniffing and rubbed my eyes on the jumper sleeve, he made me look at him.

'Bernie, Mum's told me that you've been sick, but I was wondering if you'd like to go on a really long trip today.'

'What for? Where are you going?'

'There's an important ring dyke that I've never visited, the Ring of Gullion. And,' he tipped my face up, 'I think you need a bit of time away from here and a nice long sleep in the car. What do you think?'

I felt tired and sick, but I wasn't going to let him leave without me. He was the only person who could keep Tommy away. Tommy knew everything, when he was here and when he wasn't.

'Take me with you,' I said. Mum caught my eye with her finger on her lips.

*

It took three goes to get the car started, choke out and foot on the accelerator. He let me release the hand brake as we left the drive without Bruce. He must have been with Donn, I thought, and then I remembered the sheep and tried not to cry again. I carefully followed where we were on the map in case Dad asked which way, but my eyes felt too heavy and I closed them just for a bit. I dreamed of darkness and knowing something was there, was following me, was catching up and woke with a gasp.

'Are you OK?' asked Dad.

I looked down at the map. 'Where are we?' Then I noticed the scream from the engine. 'Why is it making that noise?'

'It's, um, I don't know.'

Dad was frowning and shifted down a gear. The noise got quieter.

'Dad, do the people here with guns have a good reason?'

He raised his eyebrows. 'Does anyone with a good reason need a gun?'

I sighed. He glanced at me.

'Sorry. No, I don't think so. They do have reasons, on both sides, but I don't see how killing people can ever be a good reason for anything. The more people get killed, the more people will be killed in the future. Both sides benefit from the deaths. They make people angry, and angry people will hold guns too. So they get bigger and more powerful and more righteous and no-one can say anything to stop them. They just say, well, my brother, my dad, my wife was murdered and I have to.'

We turned a corner and began to climb a steep hill. The engine screamed and shuddered again.

'Oh, Christ.'

I imagined what Sister Agatha would do if she heard that. He grated the stick down to first gear. The scream came back and then there was a bang. The engine went quiet and grey smoke poured from the engine. There was another louder bang.

270

Dad talked quickly and lightly, 'Let's get out of the car, OK? Take the map!'

I scrambled out, the smoke burning my eyes and throat, and stood with Dad a few feet behind the boot.

'Will it explode?' I grabbed for his hand.

He frowned. 'I'm not sure.' He looked at me. 'We're a bit stuck, even if it doesn't, Bernie.'

'Where are we?'

'South Armagh. We were only a couple of miles away from the dyke, it's a real shame.'

We watched the car smoking for a little while.

He said, 'I think it would have started burning if it was going to.'

Dad took the map and let go of my hand. We sat on the verge and he flicked through the pages to find us. He put his finger on a road.

I said, 'There's was a farmhouse before we turned the corner. I saw it over the fields. We could ask for help.'

Dad smiled sadly and shook his head. 'This isn't the kind of place where you can walk up to someone's house without being invited.'

'But we need a phone.'

'Trust me, Bernie, it's complicated. We'll have to walk to a village and find a phone box. Maybe there'll be a garage and they can sort the car out too.'

I could tell he was hiding something.

'And I'll buy you something to eat while it all gets sorted. It'll be OK, right, Bernadette?'

I nodded. He stood up and pulled me up.

'Just a bit of a walk, nothing to worry about.' He didn't look as if there was nothing to worry about.

We walked back up the hill, more quickly past the car which was still smoking. At the top he looked back at it.

'I hope that hand brake holds. I should have left it in gear, probably.'

I could tell he was thinking of going back, so I pulled his hand and we walked down the other side of the hill.

'Can I see the map?'

He handed it to me with his finger pointing to where we were. The village looked quite close on the map but I was used to car pace, marking off roads and places at speed. The road was all hills and after half an hour we hadn't passed another road to cross off.

'At least the weather's nice,' Dad said.

At the top of the next hill we could still see the smoke showing where we'd stopped.

'It's going to take hours to get there.' I handed the map back to him.

'Can you hear a car?'

I listened and shook my head. 'Someone might give us a lift.'

Dad looked around. 'If someone stops just leave that decision to me. Don't say anything, promise me.'

I nodded.

He started to walk faster, dragging me a little. We were at the bottom of another hill now and there was a signpost just ahead.

'This is good,' said Dad, 'we're on the right track.'

Now I speeded up too. It would tell us how far and then I'd know how long it would take. Three miles an hour I could walk, Dad said, but I didn't know if that counted hills.

'If you want to have a rest, we can,' said Dad. 'You can tell me what's been happening. Whatever's upset you, you can tell me. I'll try to answer all your questions.'

I focussed on the signpost. I just wanted to know and then I could think about telling him, about how to tell him. We were nearly there, nearly there. I could nearly read it. Behind us there was a massive explosion and we turned together. There was much more smoke than before, black now and billowing.

'We can't go back, Dad.'

'What do you mean?'

I waited for him to look at me and took a deep breath, 'Tommy killed Uncle Ryan. Please don't take me back to the farm. We have to go home. Everyone knows it's true, Dad, even Mum, and they're scared of him and he said he'll kill you and me and –'

'Oh, Bernie,' he stroked my hair, 'you've been really ill. You must have had some horrible nightmares. It was a sheep that died, I told you. Honestly.'

'Dad, listen!'

'Hold on.'

He stared up, following the smoke. We both heard the engine this time as the army truck raced up to us and screeched to a halt across the road. Four soldiers jumped out, guns pointing at us.

'Get down on the ground! Get the fuck down!'

40

Now

'An hour and half to check-in,' Adrian shouted. 'Can we make it?'

'Yes, book it!' Bernie shooed the children upstairs, 'Ten minutes and we're gone. Anything that gets left is your responsibility. We're not coming back for it. Go!'

The girls squealed and ran past Nancy. She heard them arguing over whose bag was whose.

Elian was already in the bedroom with the cases zipped up on the bed.

'You're very prepared,' said Nancy. 'Eager to leave?'

'I'm just eager to see something else.' He looked at her sideways. 'I do understand why you had to come. But, really, it's a god-forsaken place. If you're not emotionally attached to it, I suppose.'

'I suppose.' She was trying to be placatory, but couldn't. 'No, it's a fabulous place. I just went about it all wrong. We should have had a car, we should have done more. I messed up and tried to recreate a childhood holiday with an adult. But I've come to decision about Hurley.'

'You have? Do I have a say?'

'Yes, but so does he. I say no drugs. He doesn't learn like other children, so what? He's not hopeless, he's just different. He doesn't need to be doped up. I am going to fight for him, not the version that makes his teacher's life easier.'

Elian nodded.

'What do you say?'

Elian fiddled with the locks on the cases. 'Life is easier if you play by the rules.' He looked up. 'But we'll ask him. After the holiday.' He put the cases on the floor. 'I'll see if he's done.'

Nancy carried down the two wheeled cases to the hallway. Bernie went past her with a laundry bag.

'Is that what you brought your stuff in?'

'Most of it. It's easier to fling it in the roof box. Want a go?'

'I'm OK. I'm just going to take a few photos. I meant to take loads and never got around to it. How long until the off?'

Bernie checked her watch. 'Fifteen minutes, but if anyone else asks it's five.'

'I'll be quick.'

Nancy went past the car and round the side of the house. She wanted a picture of the blue door before it disintegrated or the sun ate the last colour from it. There was a tangle of metal in front of it but that was fine. It was part of it now. She took her phone from her pocket and pressed the camera app. While she was focussing, framing it just right, the battery beeped and died. She realised that she'd been hearing beeps all morning, but not quite pinning them to her phone. She'd have no chance to charge it now. She stared at the door and fixed it in her mind. That would do.

She picked her way back to the gate. The car was surrounded.

'Did you pack the charger, Elian?'

'Yep.'

Bernie was ordering people into certain seats for political reasons.

'Not next to each other. You'll fight.'

Adrian was locking the roof box.

Nancy looked up at the house. Of course it was brilliantly

sunny today. The house didn't look worn and unloved as it did on their arrival, it looked experienced. It looked beautiful. Her throat tightened and she swallowed.

'One minute!'

Nancy ran back upstairs and fetched the box with the shells. She gave it to Bernie.

'Don't forget this.'

'Police car!' shouted Erin, pointing. 'Everyone act normal!'

Nancy stood next to Bernie and they watched the car drive down the road around the farm, past the far entrance.

'Did you call them?' whispered Nancy.

'They may find something. Worth a go.'

Nancy looked back to the house as Donn appeared in the doorway. She wondered if he thought the police had been coming up this drive.

'It's a puppy!' shouted Maeve.

'Don't you dare undo that seatbelt!' shouted Bernie.

Nancy walked up to him. She felt that she should say something but had no idea what.

'I'll write,' she said.

He half nodded, half shrugged.

Bernie was in the driver's seat. The engine started.

'Come on, Nancy, we have to go!'

She waved at Donn and climbed into the middle between Erin and Maeve. They pulled down the gravel driveway and Nancy had to look back. She never usually looked back.

Bernie pulled out onto the road.

'Did you get your photos?'

'No. My phone died.'

'I took loads,' said Maeve. 'Here.'

She handed Nancy her DSi and helped her click to the gallery.

'Thanks,' said Nancy. Her throat tightened again.

'I did too,' said Erin, 'but mine broke.'

'Yes, OK, Erin,' said Bernie. 'No need to bring it up again.'

Nancy could hear Elian talking to Hurley in the rear two seats.

'Wow, a ferry trip. I've never done this, only a little rowing boat. It'll be fun.' He raised his voice, 'Will there be WiFi on the ferry?'

Bernie said, 'There's WiFi everywhere except the middle of nowhere.'

Elian paused. 'Is that a yes?'

'Who knows?'

Nancy caught Bernie's eye in the rear view mirror.

Bernie said, 'I have some barley twists and aniseed balls for the journey.'

'Sounds exciting,' said Elian, dubiously.

'It's a tradition,' said Nancy, trying to keep the smile out of her voice.

July 1982

Before

I swore I would never get on another boat. No more brandy balls and aniseed twists inched out of paper bags. Each glimpse of the scratchy tartan blanket that had covered me, now folded under Mum's arm, made me feel like retching.

I stood between Mum and Nancy, waiting to be allowed off the boat, pushing my books back into my bag where they didn't seem to fit anymore. I could smell the sandwich crusts in the picnic bag, cups dyed by the dregs of orange squash and crisp crumbs from the picnic somewhere between Liverpool and Ireland. I heard the lorries start up in the belly of the boat.

'I am never, ever going back on a boat,' I announced.

'It will be fine next time,' Mum said. 'It was very unusual.' She didn't sound that sure. She'd been sick twice and had to hold Florence while she was sick too.

'I've never heard the plates flying around in the kitchens before,' said Mum. 'And for all the crew to be sick like that . . .' She put her hand over her mouth.

I closed my eyes and could feel the sway skywards and seawards, could smell the sick seeping outside the stainless steel toilets. Nancy poked me. I opened them quickly and edged forwards into the space in front.

Auntie Beth picked us up from the terminal with her bump sticking out in front of her. Mum kept up the conversation past three roundabouts and onto a fast road before falling asleep. I could see Florence splayed across her in the front seat.

'Eithne. Eithne!' Auntie Beth tutted and stopped talking.

We drove away from the port on the good, hard ground, through the slabs of grey pebble-dashed villages under a greyer pebble-dashed sky. It was cold but I inched the window open to let the smell of food out.

Auntie Beth shouted, 'Close that window, Bernadette!'

It hadn't been this bad before, Mum was right, but we made this trip every year and it had never been pleasant. This holiday had been the first to get a reaction from my friends at school. Maybe it was the first time that I'd said Northern Ireland, instead of just Ireland. Maybe we were all learning what the difference was. I knew people died there, I'd seen the masked men firing guns over coffins. I didn't think that I'd get blown up though. Drowning in the Irish Sea seemed a much more realistic possibility.

I didn't feel so bad now, and wasn't sleepy. I did rest my head on the suitcase on the seat between us, but it was just to look out of the window. The lights of the cars on the other side of the road swept over us and turned red as we left them behind. There were houses lit up by the road and distant points of light in the fields and hills above them. The stars were there. I couldn't see many now with all the lights, but I knew when we got there I would see all of the stars in the universe. Not like at home, too many street lamps and house lights and car beams. Not like here where, for days, you would only see the people who lived in the same house.

Auntie Beth cleared her throat, 'I hope youse two are going to be helping your Mammy out. You're old enough now to not be running wild and worrying her.'

I sat up and looked at Mum. 'I don't worry her.'

'All children are a worry.' Auntie Beth looked at me in the rear view mirror. 'Some more than others.'

I looked at Nancy. She moved her head from side to side and twisted her finger around. The laugh burst into my throat. I tried to turn it into a cough.

'You'll wake your ma!'

'Sorry,' I managed to say, and rested my head again.

The car turned gently, and then more sharply. The lights became occasional and shockingly bright. I waited until I saw the sign for the bar, lifted my head to see the phone box, and put my nose to the window.

Our road. Our home from home. Down the dip and up the rise, right and bumping over the cow grill, then Bruce jumping up at the window and barking. He weaved in front of the car and I held my breath, but there he was on the other side, safe. Mum was awake now, yawning and sitting Florence upright.

Auntie Beth pulled up on the left in front of the light blasted windows and we tumbled out of the car, fighting over Bruce. He remembered me best because I stroked him and fed him Sugar Puffs. Dogs don't forget things like that. I walked up the steps, but he nudged at my hand again and again. I didn't forget you either, I thought. I kissed his greasy furry head.

'Come and help with the cases, girls,' said Auntie Beth, holding only her own stomach.

I rubbed my face against Bruce's neck and took a bag inside.

'Auntie Agatha has a quick sandwich for you before bed.' Auntie Beth guarded the outside door. 'In you go.'

In the kitchen Sister Agatha and Uncle Donn were sitting in the armchairs by the fire. They looked towards the open door as if they weren't particularly glad to see me. Then Donn smiled and Sister Agatha went to wet the tea. On the way she firmly closed the door to Cassie's room and turned the key in the lock.